PRAISE FOR

The Diva Runs Out of Thyme

"[A] tricky whodunit laced with delectable food . . . [and] stuffed with suspects—and a reminder that nobody's Thanksgiving is perfect."
—*Richmond Times-Dispatch*

"[A] fun romp into the world of food, murder, and mayhem."
—*Armchair Interviews*

"Filled with humor, delicious recipes, and holiday decorating tips, *The Diva Runs Out of Thyme* is . . . a must-read to prepare for the holiday season."
—*The Romance Readers Connection*

Berkley Prime Crime titles by Krista Davis

THE DIVA RUNS OUT OF THYME
THE DIVA TAKES THE CAKE

The Diva
Takes the Cake

KRISTA DAVIS

BERKLEY PRIME CRIME, NEW YORK

THE BERKLEY PUBLISHING GROUP
Published by the Penguin Group
Penguin Group (USA) Inc.
375 Hudson Street, New York, New York 10014, USA
Penguin Group (Canada), 90 Eglinton Avenue East, Suite 700, Toronto, Ontario M4P 2Y3, Canada
(a division of Pearson Penguin Canada Inc.)
Penguin Books Ltd., 80 Strand, London WC2R 0RL, England
Penguin Group Ireland, 25 St. Stephen's Green, Dublin 2, Ireland (a division of Penguin Books Ltd.)
Penguin Group (Australia), 250 Camberwell Road, Camberwell, Victoria 3124, Australia
(a division of Pearson Australia Group Pty. Ltd.)
Penguin Books India Pvt. Ltd., 11 Community Centre, Panchsheel Park, New Delhi—110 017, India
Penguin Group (NZ), 67 Apollo Drive, Rosedale, North Shore 0632, New Zealand
(a division of Pearson New Zealand Ltd.)
Penguin Books (South Africa) (Pty.) Ltd., 24 Sturdee Avenue, Rosebank, Johannesburg 2196,
South Africa

Penguin Books Ltd., Registered Offices: 80 Strand, London WC2R 0RL, England

This is a work of fiction. Names, characters, places, and incidents either are the product of the author's imagination or are used fictitiously, and any resemblance to actual persons, living or dead, business establishments, events, or locales is entirely coincidental. The publisher does not have any control over and does not assume any responsibility for author or third-party websites or their content.

PUBLISHER'S NOTE: The recipes contained in this book are to be followed exactly as written. The publisher is not responsible for your specific health or allergy needs that may require medical supervision. The publisher is not responsible for any adverse reactions to the recipes contained in this book.

THE DIVA TAKES THE CAKE

A Berkley Prime Crime Book / published by arrangement with the author

PRINTING HISTORY
Berkley Prime Crime mass-market edition / June 2009

Copyright © 2009 by Cristina Ryplansky.
Cover illustration by Teresa Fasolino.
Cover design by Diana Kolsky.
Interior text design by Laura K. Corless.

ISBN: 978-0-425-22840-1

BERKLEY® PRIME CRIME
Berkley Prime Crime Books are published by The Berkley Publishing Group,
a division of Penguin Group (USA) Inc.,
375 Hudson Street, New York, New York 10014.
BERKLEY® PRIME CRIME and the PRIME CRIME logo are trademarks of Penguin Group (USA) Inc.

PRINTED IN THE UNITED STATES OF AMERICA

10 9 8 7 6 5 4 3 2 1

For Elizabeth NINA Strickland
Susan REID Smith Erba
and Amy NORWOOD Wheeler

ACKNOWLEDGMENTS

As always, I'm grateful to my mom, Marianne; and Janet Bolin, Daryl Wood Gerber, Betsy Strickland, and Susan Strickland, my invaluable first readers who cheerfully and patiently keep me on the right track. Many thanks to my editor, Sandra Harding, who is a constant delight and whose editorial advice is always dead on, and to my agent, the charming Jacky Sach.

Thanks to Captain Scott Ogden of the Alexandria Police Department and Felicia Donovan, fellow author and law enforcement expert, for providing information about police procedures. Any errors are my own.

Special thanks to Rachel Ann Hollis for patiently mixing drinks until she arrived at the delicious Wedded Blitz Martini. Also to Terry and Harry Hoover for their helpful knowledge about the syndication of newspaper columns. Laurie Petty at dazzlingice.com was wonderful to share her expertise on ice bars, for which I'm very thankful.

And last, but not least, much gratitude to the unsung heroine, Teresa Fasolino, the artist who always provides such beautiful covers for the Domestic Diva Mysteries.

GUEST LIST

Hannah

Paul and Inga Bauer
Sophie Bauer Winston (maid of honor)
   and Wolf Fleishman
~~George and Lacy Bauef~~
Jen Bauer (flower girl)
~~Uncle Fred and Aunt Molly~~
Phoebe Ferguson (bridesmaid)
   and Joel Yancey
Mars Winston
   and Natasha Smith
Wanda Smith
Bernie Frei
Humphrey Brown
Tucker Hensley V
Mordecai Artemus

Craig

Kevin Pointer ~~(best man)~~
Robert Beacham (best man)
Stan Beacham
Darby Beacham

ONE

From "The Good Life":

Dear Sophie,

My fiancé's former girlfriend showed up at our engagement party uninvited and released four dozen white mice. I'm worried sick about what she might do at our wedding. How do we stop her?

—No More Mice in Morristown

Dear No More Mice,

Choose a venue with a security department, like a hotel. Alert your vendors and wedding planner and plant some teenage relatives at strategic entrances to be on the lookout for the big rat.

—Sophie

As I trudged along the brick sidewalk carrying shopping bags of gifts for the bridal party, I realized a woman was standing across the street from my house studying it. Although I'd lived in a historic house in Old Town Alexandria for years, I'd never gotten used to the strangers parading through the ancient streets admiring the quaint buildings.

Pausing to catch my breath, I tried to see my home with fresh eyes. In a nod to my sister's wedding colors, the begonias, ranunculus, and Wave petunias spilling liberally from the window boxes were a happy mix of soft pinks and a color we were calling cherry, since the groom had an aversion to fuchsia.

Hand-trimming the boxwoods had been a chore, but they presented a neat border along the red brick. Additional pots of pink flowers graced the front stoop. Pressured by my mother, who had been inspired by a TV episode featuring the local domestic diva, Natasha, I'd made a living wreath for the front door out of variegated ivy. If I didn't forget to water it, it might last through the wedding.

A gracious oval plaque of bronze next to the front door designated my home as a historic building. It was more than a hundred years old, the floors canted and creaked, and odd things happened that I couldn't quite explain, but I adored the place. I continued walking, flicking my gaze from the woman to my house.

"Excuse me?" The woman approached me. Attractive and close to my age, in her early forties, I guessed. Her dress revealed far too much bosom for early morning in Old Town and her high heels were a mistake on the uneven sidewalks. Clearly a tourist.

She smiled at me and held out a sheet of paper that appeared to have been taken off the Internet. In a New Jersey twang she said, "I can't seem to find this address."

My hands full of bags, I tilted my head to look at the

paper. Her fuchsia fingernail in a long, squared-off manicure pointed to—my address!

I jerked involuntarily. On the upper corner of the paper
was a picture of my sister, Hannah, and her fiancé, Craig.
The middle section listed every wedding event we had
planned—the dessert party for out-of-town guests, a walking tour of Old Town, the rehearsal dinner, the ceremony,
the reception, and brunch the following day. Times,
addresses, and even directions to each venue were also
included.

"You're here for the wedding?" I mumbled. Even though
I'd been tapped as the unpaid wedding planner, worked on
it for months, and had taken time off from my event-
planning business this week, the stranger's presence was a
wake-up call. The guests had begun to arrive.

"I'm an old friend of the groom and was hoping I could
catch up with him for a visit." She shuffled papers. "But this
address is different."

She showed me another wedding page from the Internet. It featured a different picture of Hannah and Craig,
and whoever had entered the information had mistyped my
house number.

I'd never thought about Craig having friends. Truth be
told, I'd disliked Hannah's fiancé from the moment we met.
Recently I'd mellowed a little. I even felt sorry for him when
I realized that none of his relatives had been invited to the big
event. But this real, live, breathing, and apparently nice woman
made Craig seem more like a regular guy.

A diamond set in a circle of gold hung on a chain in the
hollow of her neck and glittered in the sun. It was just big
enough to make me wonder if it was real.

I felt shabby in my oversized white shirt and jeans that
had fit once, but must surely have shrunk from being washed
too many times. "I'm Sophie Winston," I offered, "sister of
the bride. If you want to give me your name and number, I

can pass them along to Craig. He's not here yet, but they're scheduled to arrive soon."

She wrinkled her nose. "I'd like to surprise him. Which house is yours?"

I nodded in the direction of my front walk.

"Oh, the pretty house."

Well! Who wouldn't like this woman?

"I'll stop by later, then. Thanks for your help."

She strode away, or tried to, since she wobbled on her high heels with every step and her thighs pushed against the too-tight skirt of her dress.

"Who's the tramp?"

I turned to find my across-the-street neighbor and best friend, Nina Reid Norwood, lowering her sunglasses for a better look.

"One of Craig's friends."

"Reeaaally." She drawled it out in a deep North Carolina accent. It was pretty funny since Nina's own deep V-necked T-shirt showed ample cleavage.

She snorted. "And he always acts so conservative. Everything ready for the big onslaught of family?"

"Almost." I checked my watch. "Oh no. Time to put the pork on the grill."

"Sophie, you won't be eating dinner for a long time yet."

"It's pulled pork, has to slow-cook on the grill for hours. And I have to roll your grill over to my yard for the ribs. Why don't you come early? You can help me get ready for the party tonight."

"Yeah, like I'm such a domestic diva."

Grinning because Nina was actually an anti-diva, I rushed up the walk to my house, unlocked the front door, and deposited the bags on the kitchen counter. I washed my hands, pulled two Boston butt roasts from the refrigerator, rubbed the raw meat with a grainy mixture of paprika, brown sugar, salt, and pepper, and wrapped each piece in aluminum foil.

But something wasn't right. Where was Mochie? Not quite a year old, my rambunctious Ocicat with the M on his forehead always met me at the door. Though he was a purebred Ocicat, his fur bore the American Shorthair pattern instead of the trademark spots. But his lively personality was all his own, and there was no way he wouldn't be interested in huge hunks of raw meat.

"Mochie?" Carrying the meat on a tray, I walked through the sunroom, calling his name. No sign of him. Where was that little devil?

I let myself out the side door and hurried around to the brick patio. In anticipation of parties and a house full of guests, I'd worked like a demented gardener to achieve a garden in full bloom for the wedding. My sunroom had taken on a jungle theme in the spring when I coaxed the plants into blooming early. With the help of my favorite nursery and the cooperation of the weather, pots of hibiscus and mandevilla bloomed like it was mid-July instead of the first week in June.

Hastily, I dampened mesquite and started the grill. But I couldn't concentrate until I knew Mochie was all right. Leaving the pork on an outdoor table, I jogged into the house and called Mochie. I ran up to the second floor, which contained my bedroom and two others. From the landing, I could hear faint mewing.

On the third floor, the plaintive mew grew stronger. When I opened the closet door in the bedroom, Mochie marched out and wound around my ankles. I picked him up and held him close. He purred and head-butted my chin.

How could I have shut him in the closet? I'd been a bit crazed the last few days getting things ready for my houseguests, but I couldn't remember being on the third floor this morning. And I did recall feeding Mochie when I snarfed a chocolate-iced Krispy Kreme doughnut for breakfast, rationalizing that I had to eat it before my mother arrived and told me to lose weight. I gazed around, but nothing seemed out of place.

Years ago, in an attempt to enlarge the house, someone had finished the attic. As a result, the ceilings were a decent height, slanting downward only at the outer edges of the room, although the windows sat flush on the floor, not at eye level where one would expect them. Fortunately, they were large windows in the colonial fashion and their odd location gave the room a fun, slightly off-kilter appearance.

Yesterday I'd turned down the bed and left a pot of coral begonias on the dresser for a splash of color. Hannah would be staying in the third floor room while Craig and my parents occupied the guest rooms on the second floor.

Carrying Mochie, I peeked into the teeny attic room next door. The daybed where my niece would sleep was made up as I'd left it. Faux diamond hair clips to fasten her crown of tiny roses sparkled on the round table next to a basket of purple petunias. They were a departure from Hannah's pink, but Jen loved purple. Her fancy dress for the wedding hung in a dress bag on the back of the door.

Still totally confused about Mochie and his closet escapade, I set him on the floor. He bounded downstairs and headed straight to the kitchen and his food. I returned to the grill wondering how he'd managed to get stuck in the closet, but with the party tonight and the wedding the day after tomorrow, I didn't have time to figure it out.

The woody aroma of mesquite already perfumed the backyard. I plopped the huge roasts, wrapped in foil, onto the grill, turned down the heat, and closed the cover, making sure the vents were open so the mesquite smoke could escape.

No sooner had I returned to the house than the kitchen door slammed.

"The wedding is off!" my sister, Hannah, proclaimed as she wrenched her engagement ring from her finger and threw it onto my kitchen table.

TWO

Dear Sophie,

My fiancé's family is coming from out of town and staying at a local hotel. His sister said she's looking forward to the treats in her gift basket. I've never met some of these people. Am I expected to buy them gifts?

—Clueless in Clinchport

Dear Clueless,

It's not obligatory, but it is a nice gesture to prepare goodies for out-of-town guests. They can be prepared well in advance. Use baskets or a container that ties in with your wedding theme. Include a list of wedding events with times and locations as well as relevant maps and phone numbers. Local food specialties are always popular. If your budget permits, personalize treats, like M&Ms with your names on them (http://www.mymms.com) or water bottles bearing special wedding labels (http://www. my ownlabels.com).

—Sophie

The pink three-carat princess-cut rock set in yellow gold that Craig had given Hannah with great pomp at Christmas landed squarely amid boxes of exquisite Belgian truffles I'd been wrapping as favors. Mochie immediately leaped to the table, hunted down the ring, and pawed at it.

I held my breath. I would have been thrilled if Hannah called off the wedding. Her fiancé, Dr. Craig Beacham, creeped me out. But I knew better than to butt into my sister's life. Hannah needed to make her own decisions—no matter how much I disliked Craig. "What happened?"

"He's been married before."

My hope deflated as fast as a released balloon. "Hannah, you're forty years old. Don't you think most people our age carry some baggage?" I steered clear of pointing out that this would be Hannah's third trip down the aisle.

"I don't care about the women in his past. But I don't think he was ever going to tell me. And that's outrageous. How can I marry someone who keeps secrets from me? What will I find out next? That he has a family? Two little kids in Tulsa?"

She had a point. And a good one at that. Secrets would make for a difficult marriage. Unfortunately I could relate all too well. Detective Wolf Fleishman, whom I'd been out with a few times, had yet to tell me the details of what had happened in his marriage. Or more specifically, what had happened to his wife, who some said had been murdered.

Her mouth drawn in anger, Hannah leaned against the kitchen counter. "He's afraid she might show up and make a scene at the wedding. Can you imagine? That's the reason he had to come clean. He thinks we need security at the wedding."

"Security? Who is this woman? Some kind of commando?"

"And what's worse—he's blaming it all on me." Hannah tossed her long blond hair in a gesture I knew well. She was angry and defensive. Craig would have a tough time easing back into her good graces. "He neglects to mention a former wife, and now the consequences are my fault."

She'd lost me. "It's your fault that his first wife is unstable and might make a scene?" Maybe Craig had made the whole thing up. I found it hard to believe that an ex-wife would be so jealous about Craig, the comb-over wonder. Then again, that woman had been looking for him a couple of hours ago. Some people obviously liked him. Unless . . . surely she wasn't the ex-wife?

"He said she never would have found out if I hadn't posted online about the wedding."

The two wives would never have known about each other. That sounded like the Craig I despised.

Just then Hannah let out a high-pitched squeal that caused Mochie to jump like a Halloween cat. "He's outside the kitchen door, looking in." Now, to be fair, Craig's presence wasn't exactly surprising since he and Hannah had planned to drive up from Berrysville together.

"Get rid of him."

"Hannah!" She disappeared so fast that all I caught was a flash of golden blond hair. Swell. There were few things I disliked as much as being alone with Craig. Grumbling to myself, I opened the door.

Craig strode in. "Hannah!" He whirled around and loomed over me. "Where is she?"

"She doesn't want to see you right now."

His pristine polo shirt revealed well-muscled arms. "You must be very pleased by all this."

I wasn't exactly brokenhearted, but mindful of my promise to myself to accept Craig and not butt into Hannah's life, I merely said, "I never like to see my sister upset."

For a few seconds I had the feeling he wasn't sure if I was friend or foe.

"Well then, we have something in common after all." He headed for the door. "I'll be back in a couple of hours."

The door clicked shut behind him, and I wondered if he knew my sister better than I thought. In two hours, Hannah would have cooled down.

I walked into the foyer and yelled up the stairwell, "He's gone!"

Hannah's voice came from behind, spooking me. She must have been in the dining room.

"So I heard. He doesn't know anyone in Old Town. Where could he go?"

She couldn't be serious. Old Town was located just outside Washington, D.C. There were hundreds of places to go.

Hannah fingered the skirt of her pale peach dress. She wore teeny pearl earrings and shoes reminiscent of ballet slippers. My vibrant, lively sister had become a faded mouse.

I ushered her across the narrow foyer and into the kitchen. Handing her ribbons in soft pink and the brighter cherry color, I said, "Tie up the favor boxes while we talk. Mom and Dad will be here soon, I need to pack cookies to add to the out-of-town-guest baskets and deliver them, the whole family's coming for dinner, and I have to set up the dining room for the dessert party." She could complain all she wanted as long as she worked.

Hannah sank into a chair at the kitchen table and held the ribbons without enthusiasm. "Everyone's on their way and now there might not even be a wedding. What a nightmare. Why did he do this to me?"

I put on a kettle for soothing tea, every fiber in my body itching to scream, *He's awful. Be glad you're rid of him.*

But I knew better. If I said that, Hannah would hate me by dinnertime, when she'd have gotten over the blow of Craig's deception.

Instead, I asked, "How about a piece of Chocolate Hazelnut Torte? I made it for the dessert party tonight, but no one would mind if we stole a piece. After all, this is an emergency."

"Chocolate? Are you insane? I have to fit into my wedding dress in two days."

I stared at her.

Hannah burst into wry laughter. "My life has been focused on this wedding for so long, it's second nature to think of it." She sat up straight. "But this *is* an emergency. Bring on the cake."

I cut a hefty piece for each of us and placed the slices on pink earthenware dessert plates I'd bought for the dessert party Natasha and I were hosting.

"Did you confirm with all the vendors?"

For pity's sake, I was an event planner. I couldn't control Craig or his ex-wife, but the wedding should go smoothly. I ticked them off on my fingers as I talked. "Yesterday, I confirmed with the caterer, florist, rental house, ice sculptor, musicians, Carlyle House, and minister. All systems go."

The kitchen door swung open, and Hannah leaped to her feet but relaxed when she saw my neighbor, Nina.

"I thought you were here. Craig pulled out in a big hurry, spinning his tires. What's going on?" Nina extended her arms for a hug from Hannah.

I cut another slice of cake and poured vanilla spice tea while Hannah filled in Nina about the evil ex-wife. They pushed the cute favor packages together to make room for plates and mugs.

While Hannah unburdened herself, I fetched boxes of gift baskets from the den and deposited them at their feet.

The bags were almost finished—all except for the butterscotch cookies Hannah wanted to include. I'd baked the soft, chewy cookies in advance and stashed them in the freezer. While they started on their cake, I brought the container of cookies to the table. Although they'd been stored in the freezer, they didn't actually freeze. And I had discovered that like the brownies I was forever sticking in the freezer so I wouldn't eat more, they were almost as good nearly frozen.

I stashed two cookies in each small pink bag, which I passed to Nina until all the bags were full. Nina ignored them as long as she could. "I don't do bows."

"No bows necessary. I took a curling ribbon from a silver roll and another from a cherry roll and tied them around the top of the cookie bag. Using a kitchen knife, I pulled along the ribbons to make them curl.

"You try." I pushed the ribbon toward her.

"I didn't do this kind of thing for my own wedding." She leveled a gaze at Hannah. "Are you sure this is necessary?"

Hannah stared into her tea like she hoped she would find answers in the cup. "Craig is unlike any man I've ever known. He's so precise and organized. Very private and subdued. You know, like not wanting fuchsia as a wedding color. He's not into flashy stuff."

Not much of a reason to marry the man, as far as I was concerned.

"He almost clings to me." She dropped a package of the cookies into a gift basket and tied a beautiful bow with translucent hot pink, *excuse me, cherry* ribbon shot through with silver thread. "I've never felt so needed by a man, even if he does have an ex-wife."

I half expected violins to start playing and did all I could to maintain a straight face. Nina's eyes grew large and she clapped a hand over her mouth. "Oh, Hannah, honey. The ex-wife is already here!"

THREE

Dear Natasha,

All my girlfriends are getting married next year, as am I. One of them selected bridesmaids' dresses identical to mine, and now she's considering the same reception site. I want to be married on July 13 because it's my parents' anniversary. I'm afraid she'll steal the date if I announce it. How do I keep my date quiet?

—Tying the Knot in Tyrone

Dear Tying,

You don't! As soon as you book the reception site and church, send Save the Date announcements. They have become a must so your guests can plan ahead. Use good quality card stock, handwrite them with a calligraphy pen, and add a simple ribbon or go all out with rhinestones or glitter stamps.

—Natasha

I stood up, waltzed behind my sister, and waved my hands at Nina, signaling her to knock it off. "You're going to scare Hannah. We don't know if that woman was Craig's ex-wife."

Hannah didn't miss a beat. She twisted in her chair and demanded, "You knew about this and didn't say anything?"

I tried to be the voice of reason. "She claimed to be a friend of Craig's. Don't you think she'd have told me if she was his ex?"

Nina licked chocolate icing off the back of her fork. "Not if she planned to disrupt the wedding."

"She's already being disruptive," whined Hannah. "Why did he keep her a secret? My first two husbands were slime, but at least I knew about their previous wives and girlfriends. Do you keep secrets from your husband, Nina?"

"Absolutely. But he's not allowed to have any. I warned him before we were married, and I suggest you do the same—I will snoop. When he takes a shower, I go through his wallet. When he goes for a walk, I go through his brief-case. I always check his pockets, and he knows I review our credit card bills with a skeptical eye. My first husband never met a woman he didn't like, and I'm not going through that again."

I plopped back into my chair and savored the moist torte quietly, glad that I'd never had issues of trust in my marriage to Mars, short for Marshall. Instead of putting effort into the marriage, we'd thrown ourselves into our jobs until it seemed like we only passed in the night and shared the same coffeemaker. We eventually went our separate ways and managed to remain friends, but I had mixed feelings about the fact that he'd set up housekeeping on my block with Natasha, the local domestic diva who had her own TV show. For the most part, though Natasha and I sometimes clashed, Mars and I got along fine.

"What did she look like?" asked Hannah.

"A little flashy. Brunette hair, stilettos, and a honker of a diamond around her neck."

I suppressed a grin. Nina had studied the woman rather carefully. Was she worried about someone tracking down her husband? A forensic pathologist, he traveled constantly and could easily have another wife stashed somewhere.

"Not like me at all? Physically, I mean?"

"Quite the opposite." Nina appraised Hannah. "I see what you mean. Men are often attracted to the same type."

Hannah swallowed her last bite of cake. "What do I do now?"

I bit my lip to keep from telling her *my* opinion. But I couldn't resist scolding her a little. "Those wedding Web sites are scary. I had no idea they provided so much information. If Craig's ex-wife wants to make a fuss, she not only has dates and addresses, but directions, too."

"I didn't know I had to hide anything." Hannah adjusted a big bow. "Everyone uses those wedding sites now. They're so convenient. No one had to call me and ask about hotels. They just clicked on the link and made reservations. Besides, if Craig had been up front with me, we wouldn't be in this mess."

The phone interrupted our conversation, and I rose to answer it.

Natasha spoke testily over the line. "Your dear dog Daisy has been howling since I got home ten minutes ago. I have guests arriving soon and the party tonight, and I don't have time to walk her. Come over here and pick her up now!"

I could hear my poor little hound mix yowling in the background. I hung up, grabbed Daisy's leash, and told Nina and Hannah where I was going.

Neither Mars nor I could bear to give up sweet Daisy

when we divorced, so we shared custody. Now that Mars and Natasha lived in the massive house at the end of the block, transfers had become quick and easy. Technically, this was Mars's week to have Daisy, but I thought I'd better rescue her from Natasha.

I strolled along our street, enjoying the gentle air of early summer. A white clematis bloomed amid ivy on my neighbor's house but, like several houses on our block, the owners were away. Mars's mother and a host of my older neighbors had embarked on a three-week trip that included cruising in Egypt and Greece.

I crossed the street to Natasha and Mars's home.

A curving stairway with a wrought-iron railing led up to the front door. Carefully trimmed topiary flanked the base of the steps, and periwinkle petunias cascaded from boxes hanging on the railing.

The doorbell played the wedding march when I pressed it. You'd have thought it was *her* sister getting married.

Although we could barely squeeze in all the wedding events, Natasha had insisted that she absolutely had to throw a party for Hannah and Craig. My mother and Hannah, huge fans of Natasha's, compromised by suggesting she share hosting duties with me at the dessert party. I balked, of course, since I knew Natasha's personality so well, but I had to concede that she'd always been nice to Hannah and seemed to like her a lot.

Natasha and I grew up together in the small town of Berrysville, Virginia. We competed at everything as children—everything except the beauty pageants that made Natasha think she was a queen. Now that we were adults, one would expect the rivalry to be over, but Natasha went after the things she wanted. The truth was that she did *not* steal Mars from me, but no one believed me about that. And when I bought out Mars's share of our house and Natasha realized she wouldn't be living there, she had the nerve to buy a house on my block. It was on the other side of the street, and on the opposite corner, but it wasn't quite far enough away for comfort.

She flung open the door, her dark hair perfect, an impeccable silk outfit hanging on her slender figure like it would on a mannequin.

I flicked away a bit of chocolate cake on my own shirt but only succeeded in smudging it into a brown blotch.

"Daisy is downstairs and she won't come up." Natasha led me across gleaming hardwood floors and an Oriental carpet to an open door at the top of stairs.

"Daisy!" I called.

Paws thudded against the wood stairs. Daisy's tail wagged, and she wriggled with excitement. I grabbed her in a big dog hug when she emerged.

"Thank goodness. I couldn't stand that howling another minute. Could you try not to pet her inside? You'll leave dog hair all over my clean floor." Natasha pressed a careful hand against her brow. "I know it's Mars's week to have Daisy, but I just can't have her here with company and the wedding and all. You'll have to take her."

I'd rather keep her all the time, but I didn't want to be unfair to Mars, and if I let on that I was happy to have Daisy, Natasha would want her back. Keeping my tone low-key, I muttered, "No problem."

"About the wedding. Did you talk Hannah out of those hideous pinks? They're so juvenile. And they simply don't match my decor. I can't possibly decorate for the dessert party if she uses pinks. I assume that's why you used those unfortunate colors in your window boxes. They're not becoming against the brick."

"You know it's too late to change the color scheme, Natasha. And I thought we agreed the party would be at my house."

"But I didn't have a pergola then. It's perfect for a garden party."

I sucked in a deep breath. "The invitations state *my*

address." Fortunately, Daisy tugged me to the door. They say an owner's emotions run down the leash, and I wondered if she'd picked up on my impatience with Natasha.

"Oh, all right. She's shedding. Wait outside on the stoop, please."

We stepped out like we were unworthy.

Natasha reappeared with a heart-shaped topiary in a black pot. Two feet tall and nearly as wide, ivy wound upward to form a heart, and Natasha had tucked in yellowish orchids with burnt-orange markings. A sheer chocolate-colored ribbon with wired gold edges coiled delicately around the heart shape. She must have started the topiary months ago. It didn't suit Hannah's colors, but it touched me that Natasha had bothered to do anything so extravagant and I told her so.

She beamed. "I'll be along shortly to arrange the table-scape."

I thanked her again and walked carefully down the stairs. Her gorgeous topiary weighed a ton, and I wished I could hang on to the railing so I wouldn't fall if Daisy pulled at her leash. She seemed to sense that she ought to be on her best behavior until we reached the bottom. But when I hit the last step, Daisy propelled me to the gate on the south side of Natasha's house.

"C'mon, Daisy." I pulled at the leash, but she maintained her ground and scratched at the gate.

Afraid she would mar the white paint and wondering what she wanted, I set the topiary down, opened the gate, and peered into the shady passage that led to the backyard.

Nothing seemed amiss. Daisy had probably seen a squirrel through the window and expected it to be there waiting for her to chase it.

I grabbed her collar to turn her around, but she lunged, breaking my grip, and raced to the backyard. Natasha would have a fit if she saw her. Daisy wasn't permitted in Natasha's fancy garden. I closed the gate and jogged after her, calling, "Daisy!" in a loud whisper. But when I rounded the corner of the house I stopped short.

Daisy whined and nuzzled the feet of the woman who had been looking for Craig. Her limp body hung from Natasha's brand-new pergola.

FOUR

Dear Natasha,

My cousin's fiancé showed up at their wedding in white patent leather shoes and a powder blue tuxedo. I'd like to think that my darling has better taste, but just to be sure, how can I approach this subject without offending him?

—Disco Is Dead in Denton

Dear Disco,

Go with your sweetheart and his groomsmen to select what they will wear. <u>Never</u> leave the groomsmen's attire up to them. They must try on their tuxedos and they must show them to you. You don't want to learn on the morning of the wedding that someone's trousers don't fit.

And don't overlook their feet. Men won't think twice about

*wearing filthy, frayed running shoes, but you will remember
every time you look at your wedding photos.*

—Natasha

Was she alive? I raced to the pergola and grabbed the
woman's legs. They buckled at the knees when I tried to
lift her to release tension.

"Natasha!" I screamed. "Call 911!"

Did she hear me? I needed help. I was way too short to
do anything useful for the woman.

Mars's old pal Bernie lived in the apartment over the
garage in back near the alley. I glanced in that direction
but suspected I would have better luck on the street. I ran
back through the narrow passage and out to the road in the
hope that someone tall would be around.

The only person I saw was Craig. At least he was tall.

"Craig! Help! Come quickly."

He frowned at me but must have heard the panic in my
voice, because he didn't hesitate to run along the street toward me.

In the meantime, I hurried up the stairs to Natasha's
front door again, rang the doorbell, and stumbled my way
back down.

Craig reached me at the same time Natasha answered
the door.

I shouted up to her, "Call 911."

"Sophie! Don't leave my centerpiece on the ground.
Honestly."

"Just call 911."

Craig dutifully followed me to the pergola, where Daisy
was still sniffing the woman's feet. Craig's eyes opened
wide, but he didn't stop, not for a second.

But even he wasn't tall enough. A small table lay on its

side a few feet from her legs. I righted it and carried it over
to him. He stepped up on it and tried to loosen the noose,
but I feared it was too late. He whipped a folding hunting
knife out of his pocket and began the laborious task of
sawing into the rope.

As I watched helplessly, it dawned on me that she might
have stood on the table and kicked it away, and now I'd
disturbed the evidence.

"Is she . . . dead?" I asked, my voice shaking. I reached
up to hold her hand. It didn't feel cold.

Fortunately, Old Town wasn't big and I could already
hear the sirens of emergency vehicles on the way.

Craig didn't stop hacking at the rope. "I can't just leave
her like this."

Natasha emerged from the back side of her house onto a
deck, her hands pressed against her cheeks in horror.

The sirens, now excruciatingly loud, came to a halt. I
jogged out to the street to show them where to go. Neighbors appeared on their front lawns, among them Hannah
and Nina, who saw me and sprinted my way.

I led the rescue squad and a young cop to the pergola.
Just as we rounded the corner, the woman's body dropped to
the brick patio with a thud.

Daisy moved in to inspect her face, and Craig jumped
off the table. I weaved through the rescue people, grabbed
Daisy's leash, and pulled her away. Nina and Hannah crept
up and peered over the shoulders of the emergency medical technicians.

Natasha joined us and asked, "Who is she?"

Nina's eyes met mine. She gestured toward Craig, who
had collapsed into a garden chair, and said, "His ex-wife."

Hannah shrieked. But even her shrill scream didn't appear to impact Craig. He slumped in the chair, his eyes
glazed and fixed on one spot.

Hannah rushed to his side and threw her arms around
his shoulders. I guessed all was forgiven.

The cop pulled a pad from his pocket and asked, "What's her name?"

Hannah stroked Craig's arm and repeated the question.

He raised his head. His blank eyes strayed like he couldn't quite grasp it all. Finally, he muttered, "Emily."

"Emily Beacham," said Hannah.

Craig blinked hard and turned his head slowly to look at Hannah, as though he'd just realized she was there.

"I'm so sorry." Tears brimmed in Hannah's eyes. "This is all my fault."

The young cop swiveled toward her, holding his pen midair. His incredulous expression changed to one of hunger, like a hunter who had spotted elusive prey.

Good heavens, the kid thought Hannah was confessing. I leaped toward her, shouting, "No!"

The young cop's brow furrowed. "Who are you?"

A deep, masculine voice answered. "Sophie Winston." Detective Wolf Fleishman's generous lips pulled tight. Sun glinted off the silvery hair on his temples as he strode toward the pergola with the confidence of a homicide detective who'd been around long enough to know his stuff.

The mere sight of him brought on conflicting reactions within me. Mostly I felt relief that he was here to take over, but that relief must have diminished the adrenaline flow because my knees buckled as shock set in. I tugged Daisy over to a chair and sank into it. The shaking in my hands jiggled her leash.

The young cop straightened up and tucked his shirt into his uniform trousers, even though it wasn't necessary. The hand holding a pen came to rest on the gun in his holster.

Hannah choked out, "I'm so sorry."

"Hush!" Didn't she realize that her words would be misinterpreted? The woman had quite possibly killed herself, but now that I had moved the table, that wouldn't be immediately obvious. Hannah whimpered and wrapped her arms around Craig's neck.

Wolf exchanged a few quiet words with the young cop and an emergency technician before turning to us. His expression grim, he asked Craig, "Am I correct in understanding that the deceased is your ex-wife?"

Craig didn't lift his eyes to Wolf, but he bobbed his head in assent as though he'd been drained of energy.

"Who found the body?" asked Wolf.

"That would be me." I raised my hand a bit and wiggled my fingers at him.

"Naturally. You," Wolf pointed at Craig, "and Sophie stay here. Everyone else go home."

No one moved.

"Now!" he growled.

The crowd filtered out through the small passage to the street. Nina didn't leave. She narrowed her eyes to mere slits as she observed Wolf and Craig.

"Hannah," I hissed, "go with Nina."

Hannah's face worked into a determined expression that meant she'd made up her mind and wouldn't listen. She shook her head.

Wolf motioned to me. Holding Daisy's leash, I walked beside him deeper into Natasha's walled garden. Roses, yellow lilies, and bold purple Dutch irises bloomed in beds along the fence. He slung his arm around my shoulders and if there hadn't been a dead woman nearby, it might have been romantic.

I hadn't seen much of Wolf lately. We'd both been busy, and though we kept trying to set up dates, it simply hadn't happened. It didn't help matters that my job kept me busy at night and on weekends. But Wolf planned to attend the dessert party at my place tonight and had promised to be my date for the wedding. For once I wouldn't be seated next to my ex-husband, and I wouldn't hear my parents' friends whispering about my unmarried state.

Wishing we could have met under different circumstances, I stood in front of him, taking in his broad shoulders and strong jawline. Wolf carried a few extra pounds, but they looked good on him. He puffed out a deep breath and stared at me like he couldn't believe I found the body.

I explained what happened. "I moved the table. I'm sorry. She must have stood on it and kicked it over because it was on its side and then we were so desperate to get her down that I gave it to Craig to stand on before I realized that it was important."

"What do you know about this woman?"

"Nothing. She walked up this way earlier today, looking for Craig. I didn't even know she existed until this morning. Apparently Craig thought she had some emotional issues and was afraid she would make a scene at the wedding."

Natasha screamed, and for a second I thought maybe Emily had been revived. But she pointed at Wolf and me, her face screwed into anger.

Wolf bit back a smile. "I think she's upset with Daisy."

I looked down to see Daisy squatting among Natasha's gorgeous blooms. I shrugged at Natasha. I couldn't stop Daisy now.

"What about Hannah?" he asked. "Had she met Emily before?"

"She didn't even know Craig had been married before."

"His family in town yet?"

"They're not coming. It's kind of sad," I said, "they've been estranged for a long time."

"Wolf!" An officer called him back to the body.

He rested a hand on my arm. "You okay?"

I still trembled, but I nodded anyway.

"I'll see you tonight then, if the party's still on."

I returned to Hannah and Craig, who hadn't moved.

"Hannah," I said gently, "I think you should come with me." I wasn't leaving my little sister behind to get herself into trouble.

I wished I hadn't been stupid enough to move the table. The cops might not find suicide as obvious as I did. They would look to Craig first as a potential murderer, but as his fiancée, Hannah would be a close second. My sister might be a computer wiz, but sometimes she didn't have much common sense. She would defend Craig, not considering the peril her words might create for herself.

I grabbed her arm. "Come on. You know Wolf doesn't bite. Craig will be fine. I'm sure he'll come over shortly."

Hannah shook me off. "No, I'm not leaving my husband when he needs me."

Her husband? They weren't even married yet. The tragedy of a stranger's death had wiped out her doubts and anger about Craig. Amazing.

"Go on, Sophie." Natasha waved at me to leave. "Hannah and Craig can come up to the kitchen with me and wait for Wolf."

Backing away, I said, "Hannah, don't say a word. Not one word."

Daisy and I hurried through the service alley and burst through the gate, alarming a cluster of cops who were encouraging gawkers to move on. Yellow police tape already circled Natasha's property, and Nina waited for me on the other side.

"Hannah won't come."

"Don't worry, she's a sharp cookie."

"Not when it comes to love." Hannah had already married two losers, and, in my opinion, Craig would be number three.

A woman in the crowd tangled with a policeman, arguing incoherently, her arms waving as she tried to pass him. Salt-and-pepper hair escaped an untidy ponytail and gray wisps frizzled around her face. Her multiple bracelets jangled, adding to the confusion, and her low-slung jeans would have been better suited to a teenager and needed to be two sizes larger.

But something about the blue eye shadow and neon orange lipstick struck a chord with me.

FIVE

Dear Sophie,

My Nana makes the most delicious cake in the world and has offered to bake my wedding cake as a gift. I don't want to sound like a spoiled child, but while her cakes taste wonderful, they don't look as professional as I'd like. Okay, they're downright homely. Finances are tight for her, so she thinks a cake will be less expensive but much appreciated as a gift. I don't want to hurt Nana's feelings. Any suggestions?

—Wedding Cake Blues in Bloxom

Dear Wedding Cake,

Tell Nana you'd rather have her attend as an honored guest. Look for a bakery willing to make custom cakes based on family recipes, and ask Nana to compile her favorite recipes as a gift so you can carry on cherished family traditions. In fifteen years, when you prepare a holiday meal, you won't remember who gave you place settings of silver or china, but you'll always think of Nana when you reach for her recipes.

—Sophie

"Mrs. Smith?" I said.

"Sophie," she begged, "tell them who I am."

Nina and I made our way to her. I grasped Wanda Smith's hand gently. "Natasha is fine. Relax, she's okay."

Nina turned to me, her face incredulous.

I couldn't help grinning. Few mothers and daughters differed as much as Wanda Smith and Natasha. Wanda had scrabbled to provide for her daughter after Natasha's father walked out on them. She'd waitressed at The Dixie Diner, the local watering hole in our hometown, for as long as I could remember. I gave Wanda a lot of credit for managing on her own. Natasha's participation in beauty pageants must have cost a small fortune.

Nina held out her hand. "Mrs. Smith, I'm Nina Reid Norwood, your daughter's neighbor a few houses down."

Although she appeared distracted and bewildered, Wanda shook Nina's hand.

"Come with us. Everything will be all right," I assured her. "You can call Natasha from my house."

Wanda followed us across the street, where my parents and niece were stepping out of a Buick.

Frowning, Dad demanded, "What's going on?"

My ten-year-old niece, Jen, launched herself at me for a hug. "Can I pleeeese stay with you after the wedding?" She looked up at me with innocent blue eyes, her silky auburn hair gleaming as only a child's can. Whispering, she pleaded, "They're driving me nuts!"

My brother and his wife had left the week before on a

sabbatical in the Sahara. Hannah had made a fuss about them missing the wedding, but our brother pointed out that he'd done the wedding thing for her twice already and neither of those marriages took.

Jen, an only child whose parents were certain they couldn't have produced anything but gifted offspring, would be spending the summer in the country with my parents.

"We'll try," I whispered back.

Wanda threw herself at my father and leaned her head against his chest. "Paul, thank goodness you're here." Dad stiffened as though a snake had crawled up his leg. Mom rushed to his aid and delicately pried Wanda away, patting her reassuringly.

I coaxed them into the kitchen, except for Jen, whom I sent upstairs to see her wedding finery so she would be out of hearing range. Nina fetched a bottle of rum from the den while I put on the kettle and explained what had happened.

My mother cupped a hand over her mouth, her eyes enormous.

Dad, always practical, said, "Let me get this straight. Craig didn't tell your sister he'd been married before. And now his ex-wife is dead."

I poured boiling water over organic English Breakfast tea in a strainer on a Spode teapot and set it on the table. I added a sugar bowl, a creamer of milk, and coordinating mugs.

Mom, in her tidy aqua blouse, pearls, and white skirt watched me, motionless and apparently deep in thought. Even Mochie couldn't distract her as he wound against her legs.

I set miniature fruit tarts, their glossy glaze shining over strawberries, raspberries, and blueberries, on a white serving platter, scattered chocolate-dipped strawberries among them, and set the platter on the kitchen table. I added forks, paper napkins in Hannah's paler pink color, and more of the cheery pink dessert plates.

Nina brought the rum and poured some into Wanda's mug. Wanda reached out a deeply tanned, gnarled hand with blood-red nails and a ring on each finger, including her thumb. She tapped Nina's wrist so that more rum spilled into her mug. With a wink at Nina, she said, "I've had a shock, dear."

Mom finally came around. "She was so upset about Craig marrying someone else that she killed herself."

It was hard for me to imagine that anyone could love Craig that much. Then again, Hannah had fallen for him and appeared determined to stick by him.

Dad ran steady hands through his hair. "I suppose Hannah is Craig's alibi?"

"No one needs an alibi, Dad." At least I hoped no one would.

Nina glanced at me. "They had a spat and Craig took off in the car. Hannah was here in the kitchen with Sophie and me."

"Do you think he was gone long enough to . . . to . . ." I didn't want to come right out and say it.

Nina sat down and helped herself to a chocolate-covered strawberry. "I'm afraid so."

"Now, girls." Mom's brow furrowed. "Don't jump to conclusions. Maybe Craig met his ex-wife and told her he loves Hannah and she was distraught."

Wanda rose and wandered around the kitchen. "I feel something here. Was the dead woman in your kitchen? I'm getting vibes."

Mom closed her eyes, and Dad looked at me with dread. I knew what they were thinking. Mars's Aunt Faye had left us the house, and his mother was convinced that she could converse with Faye's spirit in the kitchen. None of the rest of us had ever heard Faye. We'd chosen to keep Mars's mother's quirk a secret from Natasha, so I wasn't about to spill the beans to her mother.

Wanda peered at the photograph of Aunt Faye that hung

on the stone wall surrounding the fireplace. "So this is the house my Natasha wanted so much. There are definitely spirits here."

The picture of Aunt Faye swung to a slant, and Wanda stepped back in alarm. "Did you see that?"

Dad coughed. "It's a draft."

"No, I feel it." She shifted her shoulders uneasily and looked out the window. "I can't see Natasha's house from here. She must be devastated. You know how delicate she is."

I knew what a drama queen her daughter was.

But my mother, who adored Natasha, said, "Poor Natasha. How odd that the woman would have chosen her yard."

Handing Wanda the phone, I suggested she let Natasha know she'd arrived.

Mom blurted, "We'll have to call off the wedding."

"You can't do that when Natasha put so much effort into the wedding cake," protested Wanda.

Everyone seemed to be on different tracks of thought. A stranger had died and touched all of our lives. We should have been worried about her and why she'd chosen to take her life, but we couldn't help thinking about how her death impacted us individually.

A face with hair so blond it verged on white peered through the window in the kitchen door. Humphrey— painfully slender, almost delicate, and shy as a sparrow. Pale Humphrey had grown up with Natasha and me. Although I'd been oblivious, he claimed he'd had a crush on me during our school years which had somehow lasted through the decades. I'd managed to put him off by telling him I was involved with Wolf. It was a major exaggeration, but kinder than telling him I found him as exciting as elementary school paste. But that hadn't stopped him from hanging around in the hope I would change my mind.

Reluctantly, I opened the door. After a polite exchange

with my parents and Wanda about his mother and her health, which was fine, thank you, he pulled me aside and whispered, "I need to speak with you privately."

I balked.

"Sophie," he insisted, "this is of vital importance."

Against my better judgment I let him tug me outside. We walked around to the grill, and I took the opportunity to see how my meat was progressing.

"I was just picking up a body . . ."

Goose bumps crawled along my arms at the thought. All in a day's work for Humphrey, since he was a local mortician.

". . . and everyone was talking about Craig's ex-wife. I thought I'd heard wrong. I couldn't believe that something so terrible could happen to Hannah right before her wedding."

I concentrated on the meat, which was coming along nicely. The musky aroma of mesquite still wafted in the air above the grill.

"Hannah's in big trouble, Sophie."

I finally bothered to look at him.

"Craig's ex-wife didn't kill herself. She was murdered."

SIX

Dear Natasha,

I booked the most gorgeous place for my wedding, but they have a strict maximum on the number of guests. I have to whittle down the guest list, but I know some people won't be able to come. Do I act like an airline and send more invitations than we have seats and hope some people won't make it?

—Overbooking in Orange

Dear Overbooking,

You don't want empty seats on your fabulous day. I always create an A list and a B list. Send invitations to the A list first. As regrets arrive, move to the B list and send those invitations. That way, you never have to go over your maximum, but you'll be sure to have a full house.

—Natasha

My hand slipped and hit the edge of the hot grill. I jumped back and blew on the red welt that sprang up on the back of my finger.

"That can't be. She kicked over the table."

Humphrey took a deep breath. "The marks on her neck run from front to back, like someone strangled her from behind. If she'd died from hanging herself, the marks would run sort of upward."

I steadied myself by holding on to a nearby chair. "Somebody killed her and then strung her up? How horrible. Why would anyone do that?" Even though I didn't know Emily Beacham, I felt like someone had kicked the strength out of my legs. She seemed nice. Why would anyone kill her so brutally? I collapsed into the chair as the horrific implications became clear.

Craig was the only one of us who knew Emily. We hadn't even known of his previous marriage until shortly before her death. What a lucky break Hannah hadn't married him. If he'd killed his first wife, he might not hesitate to murder the second. "You have to tell Hannah as soon as she comes home."

In spite of the warm June weather, I felt chills. The horror of Emily's murder might have saved Hannah. I took Humphrey's milky-white hand and raced for the kitchen door. I'd promised not to butt in. I'd been determined not to interfere. But this was different. I had to save Hannah from Craig.

I towed Humphrey back into the kitchen. Wanda and Nina had left, and Mom and Dad were discussing whether to call off the wedding. It would be best if they heard the bad news from Humphrey, whom they would see as a more neutral source of information. At my prodding, he shared what he'd learned.

"Dear Lord!" Dad fell into a chair.

Mom rested a calming hand on his shoulder. "He's not going to hurt Hannah."

Dad stared at her in astonishment. "He managed to kill his ex-wife in broad daylight, Inga!"

Always one to think the best of people, Mom said, "That can't be. Craig . . ." She faltered and fell silent.

But Dad wasn't through. "I knew there was something wrong with that boy. Why can't Hannah ever find a nice man?"

Mom persisted, her face taut. "Let's not be hasty. Even if she was murdered, that doesn't mean Craig killed her." She brushed an imaginary errant hair out of her face and said, "The three of us and Humphrey will keep our ears to the ground tonight. Wolf will be here, thank goodness, and we'll tell him anything we learn. And now I believe I'll make sandwiches. Panini, Humphrey?"

I'd only recently come to realize what snoops my parents were. They had no qualms about eavesdropping. I figured I came to it naturally with snooping genes on both sides of the family.

If it had been up to me, I would have canceled the wedding so fast that Craig's comb-over would have flapped in the resulting breeze. Instead, my mother was making sandwiches, proving that I wasn't the only member of the family who could eat no matter what happened.

Mom looked at the boxes loaded with gift baskets that still cluttered the kitchen floor. "You'd better deliver these, Sophie. Even if we cancel the wedding, guests ought to get some small token for their efforts." I figured she was right, so Dad helped me load them into my hybrid SUV and I left my parents and Humphrey behind to break the news to Jen and deal with the mayhem of Craig's ex-wife's dramatic death.

Life went on as normal a few blocks away on King Street, in the heart of Old Town. I pulled into a loading zone in front of the hotel, and a bellman appeared as if by magic. When I explained about the gifts, he acted like he'd done it a million times before.

I handed him a copy of the list of names and went inside to speak with the manager again. Just to be on the safe side. Two men and a woman waited at the front desk. The woman smiled at me. The shorter of the two men, small and wiry with a wizened face, spoke slowly, drawing out his words in a crackling voice. "Beacham. We checked in last night. Beacham, Beacham, Beacham. How many times do I have to tell you?"

The clerk drew back. "I'm sorry, sir. I cannot just hand you a key card. Security regulations require that you show me identification."

Craig's last name was Beacham. "Excuse me," I said, "are you here for the wedding?"

They looked at me like I had butted into their private business.

"Yes." The wiry guy drew the word out slowly. "Are you the bride?"

The thought of marrying Craig made me queasy. "I'm the sister of the bride." I leaned toward the desk clerk. "The Bauer-Beacham wedding. We have a block of rooms reserved at a special price."

"The sistah of the bride?" The chestnut-haired woman gushed in a nasal New Jersey accent. "Can you believe this?" She pushed the shorter man's shoulder. "And you're so adorable. Is your sister as adorable as you, honey? I'm Dawby, Craig's cousin."

I would never have pegged her as a relative of Craig's. Wearing a summer suit that screamed high fashion, she was loud and bubbly. She probably hated her prominent nose, but it suited her expressive face and wide mouth.

"Dobby?"

She nodded. "Dawwwwby."

The taller man wore a suit that must have been hand-tailored. It fit him perfectly, in spite of his considerable height, and imparted a distinctly European elegance.

"Darby," he said, "give somebody else a chance. I'm Craig's Uncle Stan." His voice came from a place low in his belly, deep and husky. "And this is his father, Robert."

His dad? Dear Lord, they'd decided to put aside whatever quarrel they had with Craig, and now they'd arrived just in time to hear that a former family member had been murdered.

"It's . . . wonderful that you decided to come." Either they'd made the trip for nothing, or my mother would have a cow when she found out we had to add three guests to an already full guest list. I tried to remember the maximum capacity at Carlyle House.

"Does Craig know you're here?"

Darby grinned, revealing perfect teeth that had surely been whitened. "We thought we'd surprise him."

The last person who'd said that hadn't fared well. "He'll be surprised, all right."

I gave them my address and directions to my house. "It's an easy walk." They would encounter the cops on my street, but somehow that didn't seem like the right thing to say. Craig should be the one to break the bad news to them.

"We're having a dessert party tonight. Nothing fancy, just a come-as-you-are-when-you-arrive-in-town kind of thing. Oh, but you're family now. You should definitely come for dinner beforehand."

Uncle Stan jumped at my offer. "We'll be there."

The desk clerk handed Robert a key card, and as they walked toward the elevator, I wondered how many family holidays we'd be spending together.

After a quick chat with the manager, I tipped the bellman for distributing our gift baskets and headed home, brimming with the news of Craig's relatives but determined to keep it quiet so I wouldn't ruin the surprise for Craig.

Driving by rote, I slowed for a light. My mind still on Craig, it took a minute before I recognized the guy driving the car in the lane next to mine.

I took a hard look.

He flashed a wicked grin at me.

If we hadn't had trouble before, it had just arrived.

SEVEN

Blond, blue-eyed, the bane of women everywhere, there simply was no doubt about it. Hannah's second husband, Tucker, had rolled into town.

Tucker Bradford Hensley V, to be very precise. Lady's man, gambler, sought by mothers on three continents. Money rolled off him like sweat, yet he had no apparent means of support. He broke hearts everywhere he went. He had most certainly broken Hannah's.

If I hadn't been on Duke Street in the middle of congestion, I'd have taken off like a drag racer to escape him. He drove a red convertible, and I could see women in other cars admiring him. I wasn't an expert on cars, but it looked like a vintage Alfa Romeo, the sexy car Dustin Hoffman drove in *The Graduate*.

I gunned my engine and contemplated getting away from him so he couldn't follow me home. But sanity took over and I realized how futile that would be.

I squinted at him with suspicion. Tucker wasn't on the guest list, and I felt certain his sudden appearance in Old Town couldn't be a coincidence. Surely he hadn't come to interfere with Hannah's wedding. Why would he want her back after all these years? Good grief. I wasn't sure which would be worse, Tucker, who couldn't keep his trousers zipped, or Craig, the killer. Wait, what was I thinking? Craig made Tucker look like a gem.

The light changed and so did my mind. I drove steadily but slow enough for Tucker to follow me. Hannah probably wouldn't fall for him again, but if he could drive a wedge between her and Craig, that might be a good thing. Despite Tucker's shallow nature and many shortcomings, he was harmless enough. We'd had some good times when they were married.

Just to amuse Tucker, I made a few sudden turns and wound through Old Town a bit. If he thought I wanted to lose him, he'd be more likely to follow.

He bit like a hungry dog offered a sausage.

Back near my house I had to park on a side street because police cars still crowded my street. I waited for him on the sidewalk and neatly sidestepped the hug and kiss he aimed at me. "I never thought I'd see *you* again."

"There are no coincidences, Sophie. Who said that? Someone wiser than I."

Maybe he was right. He had appeared just when I needed someone to make Hannah reconsider her decision to marry Craig.

"How is my darling Hannah?"

How to answer that? *She's engaged to a murderer who killed his ex-wife just this morning.* No, that didn't seem right. Tucker was so darned cocky and full of himself that I hated to bloat his head any more. But I needed to plant the idea that Hannah could still be interested in him.

"She's pretty busy. Her wedding is the day after tomorrow."

"Who's the lucky dog?"

"A doctor." I bit my lip to keep from grinning. The Tucker I remembered would be desperate to win Hannah away from someone who might pose a challenge. "He's tall and athletic and adores Hannah."

"Good hair?" he asked.

No point in lying about something he'd figure out the second he saw Craig. "No, you still win in the hair category."

We reached the front stoop. "I know she'll be excited to see you." *Dismayed* would have been more truthful.

We walked inside and I led the way through the arch to the kitchen. Mom tied the last ribbon on the favors and tucked the little package into a box with the others.

"Look who I found," I said.

Tucker held his arms wide like a showman. "You know how I love a wedding."

My father remained seated and grumbled, "You've certainly had enough of them."

My perky mother, who would sooner eat dirt than be rude to anyone, said, "I need an aspirin." Her shoulders sagged and for the first time in my life, I saw her place her elbows on the table.

But Tucker was on top of his game. The second he saw Jen, he said, "Excuse me ma'am, I'm looking for a little girl . . ." Tucker pretended to gasp. "Can it be? No, I'm looking for a child, about this high." He bent over to indicate a one-foot-high kid.

Jen ran to him and threw her arms around his neck. It must have been gratifying to know that one person still liked him. He swung her around in a circle, and she giggled like most women did when Tucker fawned over them. It wasn't fair of him to work his charm on anyone as young as Jen. She hadn't built up immunity yet.

When he set her down, Tucker, never one to believe that people didn't adore him, clapped Dad on the back and asked about his golf game. I fetched the aspirin for Mom. She swallowed them with a sip of tea and said, "I wish you had told me you were going to cancel the wedding."

Tucker latched onto the conversation immediately. "Cancel? The wedding? Trouble in paradise already?" He didn't seem too troubled by the news, though, as he helped himself to a fruit tart.

There was no way to avoid it. He'd hear about it sooner or later. But while I wondered how to tell him without Jen hearing, Jen said, "Craig's ex-wife was murdered."

"The groom's ex?" Tucker's pretty-boy face crumpled with worry. "I'm the bride's ex. Hope no one does me in."

"Many would like to." Dad said it with a straight face, but Tucker guffawed.

"My winsome Hannah has seen the light now?" he asked.

Mom sighed and ignored him. "Why did you cancel Carlyle House? Did you run into Hannah?"

"I didn't cancel anything."

She frowned at me. "They called here upset about the last-minute cancellation. I tried to explain, but they were quite put out. Rightly so. Fortunately, they were able to book someone else."

I figured it could only be Hannah who'd canceled the wedding venue.

Mom rubbed her temples. "I hate to think how many people have already made the trip here for the wedding."

"I suppose we should still go ahead with the party tonight," I said.

"Party?" Tucker perked up. "Will you be my date?" he asked Jen.

Mom looked like she wanted to toss him out. "If Craig isn't up to it, everyone will understand. We'll have to entertain them to try to make up for their trouble. And we'll do the tour of Old Town tomorrow as planned."

Tucker consulted his watch. "What time shall I return for dinner?"

"Six." I hadn't invited him to dinner, but I figured the sooner he came between Hannah and Craig, the better.

He snatched another fruit tart. "For the road." Jen held his hand as we walked him to the front door.

He blew kisses to Jen, and as he left, I spied Humphrey watching Craig and Hannah leaving Natasha's house, as cheerful as if nothing had happened.

EIGHT

Dear Natasha,

My mother stopped speaking to my sister for a week because she didn't get thank-you notes out fast enough. How do I avoid getting behind?

—Writing Fast in Wrightsville Beach

Dear Writing Fast,

I don't know why this poses a problem for brides. Before the wedding, spend a fun afternoon crafting thank-you notes. Use your wedding colors and embellish card stock to reflect the theme of your wedding. Then handwrite a lovely note on the day each gift arrives. You'll never fall behind. Some guests will bring gifts to the wedding, but one afternoon after the honeymoon is all it takes to catch up.

—Natasha

Craig laughed at something Hannah said. Hardly the bereaved ex-husband.

I sidled up to Humphrey. "You have to tell her."

But at that moment, Phoebe, Hannah's college roommate and dear friend, arrived with her boyfriend. Lively Phoebe inspired fun everywhere she went. Petite and perky with hair the color of gleaming copper, she edited scientific books for a publisher in New Jersey. I was thrilled to see her because Hannah would need her closest friend when she heard about the murder.

Phoebe's boyfriend, whom Hannah introduced as Joel, barely spoke and hung back the way strangers do. He had an open, agreeable face, but his crew cut did nothing to enhance his looks. Although he was portly, I suspected substantial muscle lurked underneath.

I coaxed everyone into the kitchen, where Joel stroked Mochie, who lapped up the attention. While Phoebe and Hannah chattered, it dawned on me that Hannah wasn't acting like someone who had canceled her wedding. She was playing the happy bride to the hilt.

I studied Craig with suspicion. Tall and strong, he could have lifted Emily. He wasn't unattractive, in spite of the flap of hair he combed over his balding head, but now that I knew what he was capable of, dread swelled in me just from looking at him. Poor Emily. Would she have caused such a scene that he was driven to kill her? Or would she have exposed him for the dangerous man he was?

He must have felt my scrutiny because he turned his gaze to me. Level and cold, he didn't flinch.

"Hannah," I said brightly, "can we borrow you for just a moment?" To the others I said, "Boring wedding detail."

I motioned for her to follow me to the living room. Humphrey tagged along, and I thought we maneuvered that fairly well.

Hannah gushed over the growing mound of gifts.

Whispering, I said, "I'm glad you canceled Carlyle House. I know that wasn't an easy decision."

"Oh, that." She said it flatly, like it was a subject she'd hoped to avoid.

I waited for her to continue, but she ignored me in an annoying sisterly way and picked up a boxed gift to inspect.

"Well, did you cancel the wedding or not?" I asked.

She sang her response in one high note. "Not."

I began to feel like strangling someone myself. She'd canceled Carlyle House but not the wedding? In a hushed voice, I said, "Tell her, Humphrey."

He whispered the bad news, and Hannah lifted a hand to her mouth exactly as our mother had earlier. Unlike Mom, she squinted at me and said, "It's not what you're thinking."

I didn't argue. Just raised my eyebrows and waited.

"It could have been someone else." Her chest heaved as she took a deep breath. "He wouldn't kill anyone. He wouldn't. The fact that you're jealous doesn't make my fiancé a killer."

"Jealous? Of Craig?" I said it too loud.

"Face it, Sophie, Wolf won't even take you out. And you lost Mars to Natasha. Do you really think I'm going to listen to your advice on love or marriage?"

I intended to shoot a clever remark back at her, but just then I saw a flash of green in the dining room. Tiptoeing as softly as I could across the old hardwood floor, I caught Craig returning to the kitchen, his kelly green shirt unmistakable.

When I turned back to the living room, Humphrey hugged Hannah. I should have done the sisterly thing and joined their little hugfest, but at the moment I wanted to shake some sense into her.

"Did you tell Mom and Dad?" Her mouth twisted into a pout.

I couldn't believe she even asked. "This isn't like you lost the keys to the car, Hannah."

She blasted me with a steamed expression before stalking toward the kitchen.

Humphrey looked like he might be sick. "She's in denial. We can't let her go through with the wedding."

Dad ambled down the stairs. "We ought to put up the tables and chairs in the backyard. Maybe I can convince some of these strong young men to give me a hand."

Humphrey volunteered immediately. While Dad and Humphrey arranged tables in the backyard and Mom looked through my refrigerator, I walked to Nina's house to pick up her grill, something I should have done days earlier.

Nina opened the door before I could knock. Words spilled out of her mouth in a torrent, and she paid no attention to a little blur that shot past us into the living room.

"Everyone is talking about Craig's wife. She got into town last night and stayed at that B&B with the pretty gate out front."

We walked through her house to the back door, followed by the brown blur, who appeared determined to sneak up behind us. I paused and looked over my shoulder at a nervous dachshund who sniffed my ankles.

I stooped to pet her, but she ran away from me and barked from a safe distance.

"Abused, I'm afraid," said Nina. "I'm trying to prove to her that no one will hurt her anymore. Her name's Hermione." We stepped outside and Hermione whimpered behind the screen door, brave now that I was ten feet away.

"The cops have been swarming the B&B and the owner is none too happy about that. Apparently Emily paid cash for her room for two nights. Now why would she do that if she planned to kill herself?"

"She didn't. Someone murdered her."

Nina's eyes flicked wide. "I have *got* to get better sources of information."

I told her what Humphrey had learned.

She stopped in front of an enormous stainless steel grill. "Might have been two people, huh? I mean, it took some strength to string her up like that."

Nina was too considerate to come right out and say it, but I knew what she meant. What if Hannah had helped Craig murder Emily and then they staged the fight? No. That couldn't be what had happened because I knew my sister. She might lose touch with common sense when it came to Craig, but even her addled love for him wouldn't cause her to do something against her core principles.

But the cops didn't know that.

I wished I could roll back time. I felt certain Emily didn't deserve her terrible death, and I wished Hannah could return to being the feted bride instead of a murder suspect.

Why had Emily come in the first place? "How many nights did she pay for?" I asked.

"Two." Nina inhaled sharply. "I see what you mean. If she came yesterday and only paid for two nights, then she didn't intend to stay for the wedding."

"So much for Craig's claim that she meant to ruin the wedding. But then why did she come?"

NINE

Dear Natasha,

I found the wedding dress of my dreams. But my fiancé's sister, who is getting married one month before us, has bought two wedding dresses! Everyone will compare our weddings. What's up with the extra dress?

—Dressed Up in Duck Springs

Dear Dressed Up,

A chic bride wears two haute couture wedding dresses on the day all eyes are on her. A demure, traditional gown for the ceremony and a slinkier dress for dining and dancing at the reception. Those who go all out with a post reception party may wish to change into a third high fashion dress for dancing.

—Natasha

I lifted the lid of the grill. Three huge burner compartments gleamed. "Have you ever used this?"

Nina hesitated. "There are people who believe I've used it."

I couldn't help chuckling. Nina loved to eat but hated cooking.

"The barbecue joint over on King Street is terrific," she whined. "I couldn't make anything that delicious if I tried. Actually, you're doing me a big favor by using it. My story will be much more believable if the grill gets a little charring on it."

We rolled it through her service alley and out to the sidewalk. The thing weighed a ton, so we would have to be very careful getting it over the curb. I focused on the wheels, ready to help the first set over the hump.

"Can I give you a hand with that?" Craig called from across the street. He and Hannah dashed over. He planted his feet firmly and scooted the whole thing off the curb. Before I knew it, Hannah had stopped oncoming traffic and Craig was lifting the grill over the curb in front of my house.

Meanwhile, Humphrey joined us on the sidewalk. "I must return to work. But I look forward to dining with you this evening."

I feared he was leaning in for a peck on the cheek, so I rotated and called out to Hannah. Now was as good a time as any to find out what was really going on with her wedding. "Wait a sec, Hannah."

Craig rolled the grill through my gate and disappeared into the backyard, but Hannah crossed the street and joined us.

As sweetly as I could, I said, "See you tonight," to Humphrey. He walked away, looking dejected and making me feel terrible.

I didn't have time to dwell on it, though. Addressing Hannah, I asked, "If you canceled Carlyle House, where will the wedding take place?"

Hannah tossed her hair dramatically. "Natasha booked a better venue. They squeezed us in as a favor to her. I only wish we'd made the change sooner because we could have invited so many more guests."

Even though I was stunned, I managed to choke out, "And where is this better place?"

"It's a big hotel, very modern. They can set up an after-dinner ice lounge for dancing the night away."

"Ice lounge?" She rendered me speechless. Hadn't we sat at my kitchen table and planned it all? I distinctly recalled her saying she wanted a garden wedding, refined but not stuffy. And Craig had been adamant about a small wedding. When we found that Carlyle House had a limited capacity, that solved everything.

"I saw a picture on the Internet. It's all blue with dim lights and acrylic chairs and everything in it, the tables and the bar and the vases, are all made of ice."

"I know what an ice lounge is," I said, a wee bit of frostiness creeping into my tone, "but that will cost you a small fortune. Did you or did you not sit in my kitchen and tell me that you had a firm budget?"

Hannah placed her fists on her hips. "You see? There you go, trying to spoil my wedding. This is exactly the reason I've asked Natasha to help you. She doesn't hate Craig like you do, she's not jealous that I'm getting married, and she's much more in tune with modern weddings."

As though the devil had been summoned by mere mention of her name, Natasha strode toward us, every last hair in place, carrying the heart topiary I'd forgotten about. "Hannah, come on, we have so much to do. These things never should have been left for the last minute."

That barb hit home and I could feel my ears flushing. Nothing had been left undone, and I resented the implication.

"Phoebe's coming with us," said Hannah. "Wonder what the guys will do to keep busy? Uh, Soph, could you change the flowers on your house to tans and chocolates? Before tonight's party, if possible."

My sister had officially lost her mind. As if I had the time or inclination. Tans and chocolates? Did flowers even come in those colors?

Natasha handed me the topiary. "Try not to lose it this time. If we return early, I'll come over and help you wash your windows."

My windows glistened. "I had them done last week."

Natasha squinted at my house. "I wouldn't use that service again."

I hadn't noticed all the brown and black cloths hanging over her arm. She peeled them off one by one with detailed instructions about which ones went over the other ones and where ribbons and bows ought to be placed. She loaded them over my forearms and finally said, "You'll never get this right, but I don't have time now that I have to pick up the pieces of the wedding and make it happen. Well, try your best. Maybe your mother can help. She has good taste."

What nerve. I never should have left Hannah with Natasha, even for a few minutes. I knew exactly who had fueled the bridemania in my sister.

As Natasha and Hannah strode away, Nina couldn't contain herself and shrieked with laughter. "Change the plants on your house? Maybe she'd like you to dig up your backyard, too."

Although my immediate instinct was to pack up my toys and walk away, instead I closed my eyes and counted to ten. Slowly. I opened them again and took several deep breaths. I couldn't let everyone down, even if Hannah had turned to the dark side. We would have the party tonight and it would be fabulous. And pink. Very, very pink.

"Well," said Nina, "the good news is that it appears the wedding is Natasha's problem now. Except for that pesky detail of the groom being a killer."

"Maybe Wolf will arrest Craig before the wedding.

That would prevent the marriage, or at least delay it." But as I spoke the words, I knew the truth. We would have to stop Hannah from making the biggest mistake of her life. And considering the mistakes she'd made with her first two husbands, that was asking a lot.

I might have vowed to butt out, but this was entirely different. Eventually Hannah would change from a Bridezilla to my good-natured sister again. She couldn't be reasoned with now, though. I needed proof to make her see Craig for what he really was.

Nina returned to her house, and I carried the topiary home feeling like I'd been demoted. I had been. But that was okay. If I didn't have to worry about the wedding, I would have more time to bring Hannah to her senses. But how?

I spied Phoebe's boyfriend, Joel, hanging out in front of my house studying the historical plaque. Maybe I could get Craig out of the house long enough to do a little snooping. I strolled toward Joel. "I hear you've been abandoned." When he smiled, I could see why Phoebe was attracted to him.

His gentle eyes regarded me politely. "Let me help you with that." He took the topiary in his arms. "Oof. Heavier than I thought." I held the door for him and pointed him toward the dining room.

"This is a great house," he said. "I'm a bit of a history buff and I'm really looking forward to the tour of Old Town tomorrow. That was a terrific idea."

A history buff? This would be easier than I'd expected. "Why don't you and Craig walk down to the Bayou Room for a beer? You can get a feel for Old Town, maybe stop in at Gadsby's Tavern and have a look around the museum."

Excitement lit Joel's face. "Are you sure you don't need us to help around here?"

"Of course not. You're a guest. You should be out enjoying yourself. Go on, and take the groom-to-be with you."

"That's not a bad idea. I'd like to get to know Craig better. We only met once before."

From the window over the kitchen sink, I watched Craig and Joel walk away to be sure Craig wouldn't turn around for something. To be on the safe side, I stared at the clock and waited four minutes before tearing up the stairs, Mochie and Daisy scampering along at my side.

I'd put Craig in a guest room on the second floor. Decorated by Faye, it was decidedly unmasculine. A canopy bed took up too much space, but I'd kept it because it bestowed a colonial grace that Mars's mother particularly liked.

Craig had left his suitcase next to the rocking chair by the window that overlooked the backyard. Generic gray Samsonite, it could have been purchased anywhere. I pulled it toward me and the chair tilted forward. Kneeling, I laid the bag on the floor and hit the latches on the front. They were locked.

I sat back on my heels and stared at it. Who locked a suitcase for a trip by car? I tried again with no luck.

Where would a man keep a suitcase key? In his wallet. And he'd surely taken it with him.

I rose and peeked in the closet, where I found an inexpensive gray hanging bag, the kind they give you when you buy a suit. I unzipped it and felt around inside. It didn't contain much. A navy suit and the tuxedo he'd bought for the wedding.

Even though it was a long shot, I checked the pockets of the suit. Nothing. Not even a stick of gum. I pressed the fabric of the tuxedo between my hands. Nothing in the trouser pockets.

But when I pried at the lining of the tuxedo jacket for an inside pocket, I felt a little key.

Eureka! I pulled it out, but when I saw what hung on it, chills ran through me.

TEN

From *"The Live with Natasha Show"*:

Weddings are the biggest event in our lives. You can sew and craft incredible things to make your wedding special. But this is the one time you ought to hire a professional, too. Don't leave it up to your sister to run the show. No matter how good her intentions, a wedding can be a disaster in the hands of an amateur.

On the end of a delicate chain hung a sparkling diamond set in a ring of yellow gold. I staggered backward a step, my breath coming hard. It looked suspiciously like the one Emily wore when I'd met her that morning.

Lots of people owned diamond necklaces, I rationalized. I had no reason to believe that this particular one had circled Emily's neck earlier in the day. I tried to remember if she wore it when I found her, but I had paid no attention to her neck other than to realize that a rope had cut her life short.

But if Craig had killed Emily and taken her necklace,

wouldn't he hide it in the locked suitcase? The diamond gleamed at me evilly. I was cramming it back into the inner breast pocket of the tuxedo when I heard shuffling at the door.

I whipped around, the damning key still in my hand.

Mom watched from the doorway. "What are you doing?"

Why hadn't I prepared some clever lie? "Just . . . making sure he has everything he needs."

"Sophie! You're snooping."

"Mom, he killed Emily."

"We don't know that for sure. What's in your hand?"

Debating whether to mention the necklace, I opened my fingers and showed her the key in my palm. "I think it will open his suitcase."

She raised her chin, and I expected a well-deserved scolding. "You'd better hurry before he comes back."

I fell to my knees by the suitcase, inserted the key into the lock, and twisted. The latch clicked open. I repeated the procedure on the other side.

Lifting carefully, I raised the top.

"Gracious, but he's neat."

I had to agree with Mom. I was a tidy suitcase packer, but I'd never seen anything like this. It appeared that he'd packed outfits together. A yellow polo shirt folded over navy shorts on the right. On the left, a white sweatshirt folded over exercise shorts, and a pair of white socks peeked out.

"If you touch it, he'll know. You'll never get it back the way he has it."

Mom was right. Holding my fingers as straight as possible, I felt around the edges of the suitcase but found nothing. I pressed against the clothing and perceived lumps, but they could have been anything from a blow-dryer to shampoo or shoes.

"Inga? Sophie?" Dad's voice called from a distance.

"I bet he's back. Close the suitcase, Sophie. I'll stall him as long as I can." Mom hurried out while I slammed the suitcase shut and locked it.

I could hear voices downstairs. As fast as possible, I slipped the key into the tuxedo pocket where I'd found it and zipped up the garment bag.

And then I stared, for what seemed an eternity, at the closet door. Had it been open? Closed? Partially open? Rats. I had to start noticing details. No time to waver. I shut it. A man who packed such a neat suitcase would surely close the door.

The suitcase! I'd forgotten to stand it up near the rocker. Even though I tiptoed, it seemed like I hit every squeaky floorboard. Sweat broke out on my upper lip. I righted the suitcase and shoved it near the rocking chair.

I leaped around the bed and out the door. Panting, I edged toward the top of the stairs so I could see who had arrived.

Old friends of my parents and distant relatives crowded my foyer. With a huge sigh of relief, I joined them and saved Jen from a woman who couldn't stop pinching her cheek. Claiming I needed Jen's assistance, I steered her into the kitchen. I could hear Mom and Dad starting to give a tour of my house.

Meanwhile, Jen helped me toss fresh shrimp, still in the shells, into a boiling mixture of water, vinegar, and Old Bay Seasoning to steam. The spicy aroma reminded me of summertime at the beach.

The shrimp turned bright pink, making me sorry that Natasha wasn't there to see a pink food being served. I transferred them to a colander and shook it to get rid of the excess water. Jen poured our favorite shrimp cocktail sauce into a bowl and set it in the middle of a larger bowl of ice. Working fast, we piled the steaming shrimp on top of the ice in a decorative pattern. By the time the tour came through the kitchen, the shrimp were on the table, along with a crab dip I'd made in advance, a pesto torte, marinated mozzarella, and a sliced loaf of rosemary bread.

Midafternoon seemed a bit early for cocktails, and after the long drive, everyone preferred the raspberry iced tea I'd made the day before. Talk turned to the murder, and I thought I'd better remove my impressionable niece. "Jen," I said to the munchkin who held a shrimp in each hand, "would you mind helping me set up the dining room and the tables outside?"

She helped me carry linens, round bowls of crackled glass, and rustic curved hurricanes with white pillar candles to the backyard. In minutes, cheerful pink gingham tablecloths transformed the utilitarian tables.

While Jen played with Daisy, I cut lush rose and white peonies, their heads so full that three filled a bowl. Next I snipped stargazer lilies. Hannah loved the fragrant flowers so much that she'd planned her wedding around them. We'd based the cherry and pink colors of the wedding on their vivid pink centers, and I had planted them by the dozens for this day. For contrast, I added a few vibrant purple-blue delphiniums and solid white lilies as well. After I added clusters of tiny pink roses, my tall tin French market buckets spilled with blooms and I headed for the potting shed.

Located in a back corner of my yard, the little square building looked like it came straight from Williamsburg. Mars and his friend Bernie had installed a moon and star weathervane on top of the cupola. I opened the arched double doors. Inside, someone had whitewashed an ancient stone wall years ago. Mars and I theorized it might have been part of a summer kitchen once. The chipping paint complemented shabby chic weathered cabinets. Flecks of green and brown hinted at the colors they'd been before the cream paint that covered them now.

Jen brought round bowls to the rustic work table, and we sorted flowers into vases.

After setting bowls of peonies on the outdoor tables, we retreated to the house with the now shamefully incorrect pink blooms in a collection of mismatched silver, glass, and crystal vases.

Ignoring the cloths Natasha had given me, Jen and I spread a pink jacquard tablecloth over my banquet-sized table. I set Natasha's gigantic heart topiary in the middle. I had planned to use a peony-filled sterling silver trophy of my grandfather's there, but reluctantly relinquished that honor to the topiary and found a place for the trophy in the living room.

The knocker sounded on the front door, and I hurried to the foyer in time to see Jen open it for Tucker.

"Now that you're grown up, you probably don't like Gummi Bears anymore." He pulled a package from his pocket, and Jen pounced on them.

While I arranged cups and saucers on either side of a vintage silver samovar, Jen told Tucker all about her new dress for the wedding. She continued chattering and placed tiny glass vases of delicate pink roses among the cups.

Meanwhile, I clustered an assortment of liquors on a brass tray for those who wanted to spike their after-dinner coffees.

Tucker was about to help himself to Grand Marnier when Joel ambled by. He cried, "Joel!" and embraced Phoebe's boyfriend, clapping him on the back like a long-lost friend. "I heard about your father. I'm really sorry."

It was the first sincere thing I'd ever heard him say. "How could you two possibly know each other?" I asked.

Tucker's arm hung around Joel's shoulders. "I was married to your sister, dimwit. How do you think Joel and Phoebe met?"

Flashing Tucker a dirty look, I fetched a couple of footed cake stands and positioned one on each side of the heart topiary, then added three empty Christmas cookie tins of different heights, all slightly shorter than the cake stands.

They didn't match in size, but that would provide additional interest.

"This guy's father got me out of more than one jam in Atlantic City," Tucker said. "Sold me three or four engagement rings, too."

"Three or four?" said Jen.

"They didn't all work out, sweetheart."

"Where's Craig?" I asked. The first meeting between Craig and Tucker might be interesting.

"We split up when we left the bar." Joel took sunglasses off the top of his head and shoved them into his pocket. "I wanted to go over to the apothecary where George Washington shopped. Have you been there? It's so cool."

I tuned him out and concentrated on the table. To disguise the cookie tins, I draped them with white napkins and added smaller pinkish ones shot through with metallic thread for a punch of color. When I brought out the dessert goodies later on, the upside-down tins would provide large stable surfaces to hold the plates.

Moving a tall crystal vase of long-stemmed pink and white lilies, I arranged it on the bombe-style commode in the foyer as Joel disappeared to the half bath at the end of the hall.

"His father was a great guy," Tucker said sadly.

"What happened?"

Whispering, he said, "They owned a snazzy jewelry store. High roller kind of stuff. A bit of bad luck resulted in Joel's family losing the store. The stress of it all caused his father to have a heart attack that killed him. A real tragedy for everyone."

After a last look at the dining room, Jen and I high-fived and returned to the kitchen, where the guests seemed to be in shock. I wasn't quite sure if they were more stunned by Tucker's presence or the news of Emily's murder.

Tucker very kindly introduced Joel to everyone, and the two of them disappeared to the sunroom while I started dinner. I rubbed the ribs with a mixture of cayenne pepper, paprika, white pepper, brown sugar, kosher salt, and powdered garlic and onion, then moved the now reddish bronze ribs onto a tray to carry out to the grill. The three chickens I planned to roast needed nothing but a quick wash, removal of the gizzards, and salt spread on the skin for a nice crunch.

The front door banged open. Seconds later Hannah and Phoebe burst into the kitchen, and everyone spoke at once. Amid hugs and kisses, Hannah slid a long dress bag onto one of the chairs by the fireplace.

I busied myself making Wedded Blitz Martinis, the signature drink we had concocted for the wedding—in the now offensive wedding color of pink. As the bride, Hannah tasted the first one and approved. She'd just taken a second swig when Tucker waltzed into the kitchen and gushed, "Darling!"

When Hannah spewed martini, I felt a twinge of guilt for not warning her about his presence. But Tucker played his role to the hilt, scolding her for not giving him another chance and clinging to her as she tried to talk to guests.

Hannah begged off to change clothes, but instead she towed Phoebe and me to the foyer. Stepping back so we were out of view of the kitchen, Hannah clutched the sides of her face and said, "He wants me back! What do I do now?"

ELEVEN

From *"Ask Natasha"*:

Dear Natasha,

My daughter and her bridesmaids are thrilled with the idea of black bridesmaids' dresses. Call me old-fashioned, but I think it's ghastly. I was raised to know that one doesn't wear black to a wedding. Help!

—Mortified Mom in Morristown

Dear Mortified Mom,

I agree with you. One doesn't <u>wear</u> white after Labor Day, and one doesn't wear white, cream, or black to a wedding. Besides, black is yesterday's color. The new trends are light blue and brown, and silvery gray, which looks so rich in silk.

—Natasha

"Oh no, you don't." Phoebe shook a finger at Hannah. "We went through the same thing when Junior Wiggins wanted you back our senior year. How is it that you always forget the misery they put you through?"

Ordinarily I'd have agreed with Phoebe, but she was messing with my plan to drive a wedge between Hannah and Craig. "I'd forgotten how good-looking Tucker is," I said innocently.

"Seeing him brings back so many memories." Hannah pouted and nibbled at a fingernail.

"Let's look at this rationally," said Phoebe, lifting her palms as though weighing her thoughts. "On the one hand, we have a doctor—loyal, considerate, and doting. On the other hand, we have a cheating, lying, unreliable, gambling scoundrel."

This wasn't working out at all. "But the doctor may have killed his first wife," I pointed out.

"Knock it off, Sophie," Hannah moaned. "We've been through all that. I feel horrible about what happened, but Natasha says I didn't ask for Emily to come here, and it's not my fault that someone killed her. Too many people have paid for hotels and travel and put off other things to come to the wedding. It's just . . . I didn't expect such a strong current of emotion on seeing Tucker again." Hannah scooped her hair up with one hand and held it off her neck. "I'm okay now. Everything is clear. Tucker just surprised me and threw me off."

I wasn't exactly sure what was clear, but Jen found us and handed Hannah the dress bag she'd left in the kitchen.

"A going-away dress?" I asked.

Copping an attitude, Hannah said, "If you must know, it's another wedding dress. You could have told me everyone is wearing two dresses these days, sometimes three."

"Hannah, you're not having a four day Hindu wedding."

"You're so behind the times. Everyone is doing this."

Hannah made a decent living as a computer systems

analyst, but she and Craig meant to buy a house and had set a precise budget for their wedding. She had already lost the entire deposit at Carlyle House. A second dress? The bag bulged. Were there two more dresses in there?

She smiled and said cheerfully, "Have you forgotten that I'm marrying a doctor? He's more than happy to pay for extras."

I threw my hands in the air. If I could nail him, she wouldn't need one dress, much less three.

Hannah ran up the stairs with Phoebe, and I trudged up behind them to change clothes for dinner. After a quick shower, I stepped into a gauzy periwinkle and avocado skirt and matching sleeveless top. But when I looked for earrings, I found that one of the drawers in my nightstand hung open as though someone had been going through it. The contents, nothing exotic—lotion, a flashlight, books, and the remote for the TV—had been rooted through. I closed the drawer and put on festive dangling earrings, and, since I was finally going to see Wolf, I spent a few minutes applying eyeliner, mascara, and lipstick, and spritzed exotic Opium on my neck. But all the while I wondered what someone needed from my drawer.

I returned to the kitchen, grabbed three cans of cheap beer from the fridge, and enlisted help in carrying everything out to the grill. Shortly thereafter, Craig joined us, a drink in his hand and jollier than I had ever seen him. Then the guests began to arrive, including washed-out Humphrey, who hovered near me as I manned the grill.

I dashed inside to mix more Wedded Blitz Martinis and was passing through the foyer when Mars, my ex-husband, barged through the front door without knocking. Ordinarily I'd have protested, but he appeared upset. He carried a box of desserts.

I took it from him. "Do these need to be refrigerated?"

He looked at the box as though he'd never seen it before and shrugged. "Who the heck is Kevin?"

"Kevin?" I'd expected Mars to be worried about the corpse in his backyard and wondered if the two things were connected. "You think this Kevin murdered Emily?"

His face went through a series of confused contortions. "Murder? I thought she killed herself."

I brought him up to speed.

"Good golly, don't tell Natasha. She's a wreck over this. She already contacted somebody to tear down the pergola because it's now tainted."

Mom appeared from the kitchen and held out her arms. "Mars." She cupped her hands around his face. "You're as handsome as ever."

Even if he was my ex, I had to admit Mars was attractive in a polished good-old-boy way. A political advisor, he had better TV appeal than some of his clients. And he could turn on the charm.

"Inga, if I didn't know better, I'd think you were Sophie's sister."

She actually giggled. Besides his looks, he could dish out baloney as well as any politician. He roughhoused with Daisy, and the two of them went off in search of Dad.

Mom sighed.

"Don't start," I said through clenched teeth.

She eyed me oh-so-innocently. Our mothers couldn't imagine a world in which Mars and I weren't together. "Thank you for wearing makeup. Though you could have worn something that shows a little cleavage. Honestly, Sophie, it wouldn't hurt you to wear something sexy. No wonder Natasha managed to steal Mars."

Ignoring her, I stashed Natasha's box of desserts in the kitchen.

The knocker on the door sounded, and Mom opened it.

When I peered into the foyer, Natasha stood possessively close to a man whose muscles bulged so dramatically they looked on the verge of exploding.

Natasha introduced the muscular man as Kevin Pointer.

It took me a moment to realize where I'd heard his name. "You're the best man." I felt guilty for thinking it, but my mind went straight to how helpful he might have been to the killer. With those arms, carrying the body would have been a snap.

Like Mars, he leaned toward preppy attire, but the sleeves on his lemon yellow polo shirt could barely contain his biceps. He wore light khakis and when he shook my mother's hand, it was hard not to miss the tight, round bottom and slender waist.

I'd expected Kevin to show up, though not with Natasha, but I hadn't expected Professor Mordecai Artemus at all. One of the most elusive characters in the neighborhood, he was known to be a recluse. I'd seen him peering from the front windows of his home but had never encountered him outside. He lived across the street in the enormous corner house on the next block. If I strained forward a little, I could see his place from my kitchen window. I'd always admired the long ecru home with a front porch of pillars that rose to create arches. Whimsical dormer windows and intricate ironwork decorated the mansard roof.

Mordecai wasn't on the guest list, but that was now Natasha's problem, I thought with wicked relief. I greeted him politely but received nothing more than a head bob in acknowledgment. Unruly hair fluffed around the base of his head, but the top was completely bald. His shirt, a faded jumble of blocks that probably hadn't been attractive when new a few decades ago, clung to his chunky physique. And then something squirmed on his shirt.

I drew back before I realized that he held a Pomeranian.

"Isn't she adorable?" Natasha squealed.

She was. Right down to her gold-painted claws.

"I never go anywhere without my Emmaline." Mordecai made a kissing noise at the dog's head, and Natasha led him to the sunroom.

Mom seized me to rave over Wanda, who had clearly been the recipient of a Natasha makeover. The gray had vanished from Wanda's tresses, leaving her with ebony hair pinned up in a French twist. Makeup softened the edges of her weary face, and she wore slender eggplant trousers with a matching top that my mother would have approved as man-catching clothing. Bold silver earrings gleamed against her skin.

I was closing the door when I realized that Wolf paced the sidewalk in front of my house. I motioned for him to come in but he didn't seem to notice, so I dashed outside. "What are you doing out here?"

He tugged at his collar. "I've been uninvited. Natasha has informed me that my presence would disturb the guests of honor."

I was stunned. "It's my house and my party and you're my date. Forget about Natasha."

He looked doubtful. "Maybe it's better this way, given the circumstances."

I could feel my ears heating up. How dare Natasha un-invite *my* date? "Please come in. I'll protect you."

He glanced toward the house, and I followed his line of sight. Natasha loomed in my doorway like a vulture.

"Thanks, Soph, but I'd rather avoid a scene. Besides, there's been a development . . ."

"I know Emily was murdered. I heard about the marks on her neck." I made upward motions with my fingers.

"Where'd you hear that?"

I wasn't about to betray Humphrey. "Word gets around," I said lightly. "Hey, was Emily wearing a diamond neck-lace?"

His right eyebrow rose. "I don't think so."

I could hardly contain my excitement. "Craig must have ripped it off her neck when he killed her. He has it in his pocket upstairs. Is that enough evidence to arrest him?"

"You're certain it's the same necklace?"

Darned cop. "No. I only saw her for a few minutes. But I bet it's hers. Rats. Is there anything I can do?"

Wolf appraised me. "I can't talk about the case. But if Hannah were my sister, I'd do my best to postpone the wedding. And I believe I'd ask around to find out where the victim stayed last night."

"At that B&B with the fancy gate."

Wolf tried to hide his amusement. "You always amaze me. Follow that lead." He looked into my eyes in a way that made my pulse quicken before he walked away in the direction of Mars's house.

He'd thrown me a bone, but I couldn't abandon everyone and run to the B&B. I'd have to go first thing in the morning. Boiling mad at Natasha, I barreled through the gate to the garden, ready to have it out with her. But no sooner had I spotted her than I heard a crackling voice utter, "Well, well, if it isn't the groom."

TWELVE

Dear Sophie,

I'm having an open bar at my reception, wines specially chosen for each course at dinner, and champagne with dessert. My uncle can't drink alcohol, and my mother thinks we should offer punch. I think that's too childish and old-fashioned. I'd rather he drink a soda from the bar.

—Enough Beverages in Belvidere

Dear Enough,

Your uncle won't be the only guest avoiding alcohol. Some guests won't want to drink because they're driving, some for religious reasons, and don't forget that a few of your friends might be pregnant. Offer a special alternative, like half lemonade, half iced tea, or a refreshing fruit spritzer. Serve in wineglasses and they'll be very elegant.

—Sophie

I swiveled around to watch Craig.

He blanched. I'd have said his face froze but he never showed emotion, so it wasn't really any different.

The wiry man with a long face and a bad toupee addressed him in a slow, gravelly voice. "Where is my new daughter-in-law?"

Craig's Adam's apple bobbed. "This is Hannah." He wrapped an arm around her waist and pulled her to him.

Hannah smiled at the little man in genuine pleasure. "You're Craig's father? What a wonderful surprise!" She promptly hugged him and kissed him on the cheek. "I'm so glad you could come for the wedding."

"Ye-e-es." He pulled the word out but didn't have any hint of a southern accent. "And look who else came, Craig. Your Uncle Stan."

It didn't escape me that father and son didn't hug or shake hands. Had he been brought up that way, or was it a remnant of hostility based on whatever drove them apart? At the mention of Uncle Stan's name, I thought I detected an almost imperceptible change in Craig.

Uncle Stan towered over Craig's father. His wavy black hair fell into a precision cut, highlighting aristocratic features. If they were brothers, the only resemblance I could see was the long face. Stan's dark eyes hinted at Italian ancestry.

But Stan didn't hesitate to slap Craig on the back and embrace him. I couldn't tell if Craig was glad to see them or not.

Craig's father laughed unpleasantly, sort of a "heh, heh" donkey bray. "And best of all, look who else came—your cousin Darby."

Craig turned quickly and Darby pointed at him. "You didn't expect to see me, didja?" Punching him in a playful way, she said, "Hello, cuz."

Hannah took over, a good thing since Craig seemed to

be at a loss. She called Mom and Dad, and I focused on the food.

The chicken would be ready shortly, as would the ribs. I returned to the kitchen for the potatoes I had put in the oven and platters on which to serve the meats, and found Natasha talking with Mordecai and Wanda in my kitchen.

"Faye would have liked what you've done with your kitchen, Natasha," said Mordecai.

Her kitchen? What had Natasha told him? She'd never said one nice word about *my* kitchen.

Natasha laid a hand on Mordecai's arm, which still held little Emmaline. "I'm afraid you're confused. This isn't my house. Goodness, no. My kitchen is tastefully refined."

Wanda edged toward Mordecai. "You knew Faye? Do you feel it? The spirit in the kitchen?"

Mordecai leaned away from her. "I am a professor, highly educated and well traveled. I can assure you, madam, that there is no such thing as a spirit."

"Mother doesn't believe in them either, do you, Mother? She likes to joke about them, though."

Mordecai snorted. "Such nonsense. Faye held séances, but I refused to take part in that claptrap. I don't associate with people who believe such ludicrous things."

A witchy expression developed on Wanda's face, and Natasha abruptly changed the subject. "What's for dinner, Sophie? Can I do anything to help?"

I pulled a pan of steaming garlic and thyme roasted potatoes from the oven. "That's the wonderful thing about barbecue, it almost takes care of itself."

Natasha sniffed the air. "Are you grilling salmon on a cedar plank? That's one of my favorites."

"Pulled pork, chicken, and ribs."

"Oh, that kind of barbecue. I don't eat that kind of food."

I brushed off her snooty attitude. "Would you hand me

the bowl in the cabinet above the pantry?" If she was going to insult my kitchen and my barbecue, the least she could do was hand me a bowl that I was too short to reach.

Natasha swung the cabinet door open, and a paper fluttered to Mordecai's feet. Wanda picked it up while Natasha handed me the large bowl.

"Wouldja look at this," Wanda said smugly.

Mordecai's face flushed paprika red. "You set me up."

I leaned over to see what had upset him. Wanda held a photograph of Faye and a much younger Mordecai seated at Faye's dining room table with a woman in flowing robes. All of them held hands.

"Sophie couldn't have known we would talk about this." Wanda flapped the photograph under Mordecai's nose. "This is a message from Faye!"

"Mother! Don't be silly." Natasha rushed them out the door.

After a flurry of trips inside, the buffet was ready and my hungry relatives led the way, helping themselves. In the Bauer family, no one ever had to be coaxed to take a plate and eat.

I relaxed with a martini while a parade of guests loaded plates and sat down to dinner.

Craig's father, Robert, and his Uncle Stan zeroed in on Wanda like bees on honey. Wanda enjoyed the attention, flirting like a young girl. Hannah gabbed with Phoebe and another of her bridesmaids while Craig watched his father, showing as much enthusiasm as a Civil War statue. I didn't know much about his family and wondered whether he was in shock, upset, or just being his usual poker-faced self.

Nina showed up with the dachshund Hermione, who lifted her long nose and sniffed the air, no doubt glad she'd come to the barbecue in spite of all the people to fear. Daisy trotted over and after the requisite snuffling one another in greeting, they raced off toward the back of the walled garden. Poor Emmaline wasn't permitted to play with the other dogs. She squirmed on Professor Mordecai's lap, but he clearly didn't want to let her go.

"Which one is Craig's father?" asked Nina.

"The short one."

"They don't look a thing alike. He still has a decent head of hair." She squinted and lowered her voice. "Or is that a bad toupee?"

"I'm afraid it might be the latter."

"Why is it," she asked, "that men don't understand bald is sexy? The uncle is rather elegant, though, don't you think?"

Nina wasn't the only one who felt that way. Uncle Stan was attracting admiring glances from a number of women.

I filled a plate and sat down where I could keep an eye on Craig. Mars slid into the chair next to me.

I had no idea where Tucker had gone, but he timed his reappearance perfectly. He waltzed in and stopped abruptly. Throwing his hands out dramatically, he cried, "Greetings, all!"

Hannah choked on iced tea, and I admit that I felt a twinge of guilt for bringing Tucker into her life again. He closed in on her right away. "My darling little wife . . ."

For the first time ever, I saw emotion on Craig's face. Clearly horrified, he bent his head toward Hannah, no doubt awaiting an explanation.

Even more interesting than Hannah and Craig, though, was Uncle Stan, who watched Tucker like a hawk. Despite Hannah's protests, Tucker found a chair and insisted on wedging it in next to her. Hannah wore a pained expression, but Tucker acted exactly as I'd hoped, familiarly taking her fork and sampling her dinner.

At the next table over and directly in my line of sight, Natasha flirted shamelessly with Kevin. "What is it with that guy?" asked Mars. "He's grotesquely muscular and a dreadful bore, yet Natasha and her mother act like they think their prince has come." I should have hidden my

amusement, but I had never seen Mars, Mr. Everybody
Loves Me, jealous of another man. I checked out Kevin
again. He certainly wasn't my type.

Humphrey, seated with my parents, was sneaking glances
at me. I flushed, certain my mother had planted ideas in his
head. Darn Natasha for ruining my date with Wolf.

Thankfully, Robert pinged his fork against his glass.
When he had our attention, he raised the glass and said,
"To our children, may they live long and prosper. *Bacio,
bacio!*"

Craig leaned toward Hannah. "He wants us to kiss."

Maybe it was my imagination, but Craig seemed wary
of his dad. I wished I knew more about what had driven
them apart in the first place.

Mars whispered, "Wasn't that toast from *Star Trek*?"

I elbowed him in the ribs as Craig and Hannah kissed to
applause. Tucker even whistled. Not exactly the jealous
suitor I had in mind.

But the happy moment came to an abrupt halt when
Stan asked, "Where is the ring? Why doesn't she have a
ring?"

"It's bad luck not to have an engagement ring. I brought
you up better than that." Robert cuffed Craig's head.

"She has one." Craig lifted Hannah's hand. "Where is
it?"

Hannah gulped. "I took it off earlier and with all that
happened, I guess I just forgot to put it back on." She
smiled at Robert and Stan. "It's the most beautiful ring. He
surprised me with it—"

"I bought it specially for Hannah," interrupted Craig.

Wanda set her glass on the table. "You have to find it.
Losing your ring means you will lose your fiancé."

A hush fell over us.

Darby piped up. "I'm sure she'll find it. I know I can't
wait to see it."

I was relieved that Darby broke the silence. A slow

chatter started again. "The toast you made, wasn't that Italian?" I asked.

"You have a good ear." Robert dug into his potatoes.

"Beacham sounds so English," I mused aloud. I must have said something insulting because Craig's entire family focused on me and not in a happy way.

"It was Piccione in the old country, but at Ellis Island they had different ideas and made us Beachams." Uncle Stan scowled as he explained. I gathered it was still a source of irritation for them and was sorry I'd mentioned it.

On the whole, everyone except Craig appeared to be enjoying themselves. Craig seemed subdued, not unusual given what he'd been through and especially now that Wanda had predicted his demise. I suspected his relatives weren't yet aware of Emily's death but figured it wasn't my place to tell them. I didn't want to be the one who ruined the festive atmosphere, and I barely knew any of them anyway.

Uncle Stan stood to refill his plate and squeezed Craig's shoulder with affection. "In keeping with tradition, Robert and I will pick up the tab for the rehearsal dinner tomorrow."

Craig protested, but Stan interrupted him. "It's the least I can do for the nephew who followed in my footsteps."

Darby had lifted her drink to her mouth and froze as if waiting for something terrible to happen.

Wanda gushed, "You're a doctor?"

Robert looked like he'd heard this one too many times.

"Just like Craig," said Stan. "I feel quite confident in saying that if it weren't for me, Craig would not be a doctor today."

Wanda rose so abruptly that she nearly fell face-first onto the table. She braced herself, patted hair so thoroughly shellacked that a tornado wouldn't have moved it, and took her plate to the buffet table.

I almost laughed aloud at her hurry to meet Stan there.

Everyone appeared to be getting along. As we expected, more friends of Hannah and Craig arrived as we ate. People milled around the table laden with food, some helping themselves to seconds, and that made the latecomers feel they'd arrived right on time. I hadn't had a chance to eat much since that one little doughnut at breakfast, so I pigged out on the pork, so tender it was falling apart, and the juicy chicken, while surreptitiously watching Craig and his family.

Stuffed, I excused myself to start coffee perking and put on tea. It wouldn't be long before people drifted inside in search of dessert. For some reason, Natasha, Wanda, and Mordecai, who clutched his dog, were in my kitchen again. Natasha tried to steer Mordecai out in a big rush, but he said, "I'm glad you left the fireplace in the dining room. A lot of people close them up."

"Mordecai," she said, gritting her teeth, "this isn't my house."

"Didn't Faye leave it to you?"

"She left it to my . . . my . . ."

Natasha wasn't often at a loss for words. I bit my lip to hide a grin.

Her mother jumped to her aid, though. "Faye left the house to Natasha's fiancé, Mars."

Fiancé? That was news to me. My gaze darted to Natasha's hand, but I didn't see a ring. She nearly shoved poor Mordecai and his little dog out the door in her hurry to escape.

Chuckling, I started the coffee in the quiet house and turned when I heard footsteps.

Darby was tiptoeing up the stairs.

THIRTEEN

From "THE GOOD LIFE ONLINE":

No matter how large your wedding, you can personalize it
and add charm by incorporating family heirlooms like
your grandmother's crystal vase or the cake platter used
in your parents' wedding. There's no rule that everything
has to match. Don't be afraid to add your own personal
touches.

—Sophie Winston

Maybe Darby didn't know there was a half bath on the
main floor? I intended to find out and did a little tiptoeing
myself. But thanks to my ever-curious cat Mochie, who
scampered up the stairs ahead of me, his little paws sound-
ing as heavy as Daisy's when they hit the wooden treads, I
lost the element of surprise.

At the top of the stairs, I stopped to listen. Where had
Darby gone? Mochie knew and sprinted straight into the

guest room where I'd inspected Craig's suitcase. I heard snapping, and I swear I saw Darby stand the suitcase upright.

When she saw me, she acted embarrassed and gestured toward the window that overlooked the backyard. "I hope you don't mind. I started out looking for the ladies' room, but this house is so interesting, I couldn't help myself and I took a little tour. How old is it?"

I didn't believe her for a minute. "The original structure was built in 1825."

"What a cute cat," she gushed. "He's very inquisitive, isn't he?"

Pretending to be friendly, I ushered her downstairs. Why would she go through Craig's suitcase? "How long has it been since you saw Craig?"

"Five years, I'm sure. I notice the house doesn't have a garage. Where do you park?"

"On the street."

"That must be inconvenient."

"Sometimes it can be a little aggravating. Like when it's raining and I have to lug groceries inside, but it's one of the minor inconveniences we put up with to live in Old Town."

"You have the most adorable southern accents. I swear you, your sister, and Natasha sound just alike."

When we reached the kitchen, she didn't hang around to chat and she didn't ask about a ladies' room, either. Instead of putting out desserts as I should have, I hurried into the sunroom that overlooked the backyard, but hung back where I wouldn't be so obvious if Darby looked my way.

She returned to the table and said something to Robert. I wished I could have heard what she told him. He didn't laugh or seem surprised.

A few people headed for the house so I hustled to the kitchen, started the coffee perking, and put on the kettle for tea. I cleaned up a bit, tossing crumpled paper napkins into the trash. And that's when I saw them.

Delicate Fairy roses peeked out from behind a wad of napkins. Horror built in me as I retrieved them and stood them in water glasses. If they were in the trash, then—

I ran to the dining room. My peonies and lilies had vanished. And my linens had disappeared, along with my samovar and my grandfather's trophy.

The dining room had been transformed into a black-and-brown wonderland. Natasha's complicated linens dressed the table, complete with gauzy overlays accented with gold sparkles, swags, and bows. Her heart topiary still stood in the middle of the table, but sleek modern risers of glass had replaced my upside-down Christmas tins. Even the buffet sported a black cloth with gold squares around the edge. Two coffeepots, at least I assumed that's what they were, looked like overgrown versions of cheap creamers, shiny and gold. I had a feeling they were supposed to be the latest thing.

I itched to open a window and pitch every last black and brown item out. But people poured into the house, oohing and aahing and helping themselves to the desserts already on the table, on square black plates, no less. I could hardly rip anything out from under them.

I could only smile politely and rush the rest of the desserts onto the table. Furious, I collected the coffeepots to fill them and carried them back to the kitchen. What had Natasha done with my samovar? If I could find it, I would use it, or maybe bonk her over the head with it. I clanked the coffeepots together carelessly. They had probably cost a fortune, but my old samovar had a burner underneath that would keep the coffee warm.

Natasha couldn't have pulled off the switch by herself. She must have had an accomplice who'd hidden all my stuff. I leaned against the kitchen counter, the aroma of

hazelnut coffee swirling near me. Mordecai, Kevin, or—
oh, she wouldn't have! Jen. Even if Jen hadn't innocently
assisted Natasha, she might know where the samovar had
been stashed.

I found her in the sunroom with Kevin and Darby. As I
approached their group, I overheard Kevin say, "I guess you
knew Craig's ex-wife pretty well?"

Darby blinked at him. "Oh, yes. Everybody loved her."

"But you know she's dead, right?"

"Dead?" Darby repeated. "His ex-wife is dead?"

"Oh, gee. I thought you knew. She was m-u-d-e-r-e-d
across the street this morning."

"I think you left out an *r*," Jen corrected him, unper-
turbed.

From the corner of my eye, I saw Craig swivel in our
direction. In a heartbeat, he had a bracing arm around
Darby. "I'm sorry you heard about it this way."

It appeared to me that he meant to steer her away, but
Robert showed up and asked, "Who's dead?"

Craig released Darby. "Jen Ba-ben, would you get Darby
a cup of coffee?"

I gave him credit for getting rid of her so she wouldn't
hear the sordid details. But Jen asked, "Cream and sugar?"

That brought smiles to all the faces.

The second she left, Craig, with an ugly glance in my
direction, said, "My ex-wife, Emily, was murdered this
morning. She was hanged in a backyard across the street."

In his weird slow way, Robert drawled, "Emily?"

"Dad." Craig patiently prodded his memory. "You remember Emily. The woman who made your all-time favorite osso buco."

Robert's eyes widened. "What was she doing here?"

Darby clutched at Craig's arm to steady herself. "She's
really dead? How? What happened?"

I excused myself from the stunned group. They still

needed to break the news to Uncle Stan, and I felt like a terrible outsider, hanging on and watching their shock.

I'd forgotten all about the samovar until I reached the kitchen, where Jen bravely poured cup after cup of coffee from the pot for thirsty guests.

"We need more, Aunt Sophie."

I scooted in to help her and put on another pot. "Do you know where Natasha put my big silver coffee urn?"

"The samovar? Sure. I wondered why it was on the desk chair in the den."

Poor kid. She'd probably inherited the Bauer family snooping gene. "Would you get it for me?"

"I haven't brought Darby her coffee yet."

"I'm not sure she wants it anymore."

No doubt glad to have a task, Jen ran past Darby, who drifted into the kitchen, zombie-like.

I pulled out a chair for her and brought her a glass of ice water. She gripped it with both hands as though she thought she might drop it.

"You must have been close to Emily."

She raised her eyes to me, and I saw something I couldn't quite grasp. No tears yet, but a strange look. "I hadn't seen her in years, but we were once very close. Craig, Emily, and I—we're all from the same neighborhood. Grew up together. Everybody knew everybody else's business. I always thought we'd be friends again, you know?"

It wasn't compassionate of me, but I squatted next to her and asked, "Why would anyone want to kill Emily?"

She locked her eyes on mine in horror. Her voice dropped to barely audible. "You think it was Craig. Of course, you would."

"You know him much better than we do. Do you think he's capable of—"

Darby set the water down and hid her face in her hands. "She adored Craig. Emily's dad was a hard man. You know the kind? Whacks his wife and kids when he comes home drunk? When we got into trouble, Craig used to take the blame for Emily to protect her." Darby's hands slid down over her mouth. "He wouldn't kill her. But then . . ." She stopped herself and blinked at me. "I don't know what to think anymore."

That seemed to end the conversation. Jen skidded into the kitchen carrying the samovar. I thanked her, picked up the coffee carafe, and juggled them both through the cluster of people in my foyer and to the dining room.

I set the samovar on the buffet and poured coffee into it. In sharp contrast to the drama in my kitchen, guests milled about, enjoying themselves. I could hear Hannah laughing somewhere and spotted Wanda making eyes at Uncle Stan, *the other doctor.*

Natasha observed me warily from the living room. If she thought I would make a big stink in front of everyone, she was sorely mistaken. But I'd get even. I had put up with her self-important attitude one time too many, and when an opportunity presented itself, I would pounce. With claws extended.

Hoping to irritate Natasha by not demonstrating my ire, I ignored her and wandered to the sunroom to switch on the tiny lights strung across the glass ceiling. Daisy and Hermione, who still wouldn't let me pet her, followed me out to the backyard. I turned on the battery-operated candles on the tables. In the dark, I couldn't differentiate between them and the flickering of real candles.

A voice behind me whispered, "I'm hiding from Natasha."

I couldn't place the voice and turned to find Kevin, Craig's best man. Maybe I could pump him for information.

"How do you know Craig?" I asked.

"We work out together. Go for a beer or watch a game once in a while."

"Kevin!" There was no mistaking Natasha's trill.

He grabbed my arm. "Save me. Please. I thought it would be fun to stay with a TV star. My mother adores her. But the woman is all over me. Please, just help me hide for ten minutes."

I was headed to the shed to turn on the cute outside light anyway. "Okay, follow me." We hurried across the yard, Natasha still trilling his name. But when I opened the door to the shed, I looked back and a figure in a window of my house stopped me.

The light in Craig's bedroom revealed a man with his back to me. Too short to be Craig. When he moved, I caught the distinct profile of Craig's father, Robert. Was he taking a much-needed private moment with his son? Or snooping like Darby had been?

Natasha's tone had turned to a screech, and Kevin must have panicked. Intent on evading Natasha, he tugged me. We stumbled into the dark shed and he yelped in pain.

FOURTEEN

From *"Ask Natasha"*:

Dear Natasha,

My wife and the wedding planner have arranged every detail from matches and cigars to jewelry and the honeymoon. I would love to surprise my daughter with something special, but they haven't left anything for me to do.

—Left-Out Dad in Lenox Park

Dear Left-Out Dad,

Surprise everyone with a fireworks display. Your daughter and her guests will be thrilled. If it's a daytime wedding, shoot off the fireworks the night before, right after the rehearsal dinner.

—Natasha

I didn't think I'd stepped on his foot. I felt the wall in search of the light switch. When I flicked it, nothing happened. I could barely make out Kevin in the dim light from my house. As I squeezed past him and ran my hand over the work table for a flashlight I usually kept handy, something sharp sliced my finger. I cried out and snatched it back as though I'd been bitten.

"There you are." Natasha's dark shape loomed in the doorway, blocking what little light we had. "Sophie, everyone is looking for you. A hostess never leaves her guests unattended," she scolded. "Oh! Is that Kevin with you?"

Parts of my hand felt wet, and a throbbing pain beat in my finger. I was in no mood to deal with Natasha.

"What are you two doing out here?"

I could hardly tell her we were hiding from her. "Kevin, are you bleeding?" I asked.

"Bleeding?" Natasha seized Kevin and propelled him out of the shed.

Sorry that Kevin had landed in Natasha's clutches again, I followed them. As we drew closer to the lights of my house, I could see a dark stain on Kevin's elbow.

Natasha ushered him into the house and upstairs to my ugly green and black tiled bathroom, leaving me at the kitchen sink to wash blood from my hand. A clean slit soon appeared on my finger, which I found a relief. At least it wasn't two fang marks.

Bernie, who'd been the best man at my wedding to Mars, arrived via the kitchen door and insisted I clean the wound with rubbing alcohol. He wrapped a Band-Aid on my finger and accompanied me to the shed to figure out what happened.

Bernie grew up in England in a variety of households as his mother made her way through enough marriages to rival Elizabeth Taylor. He'd settled, temporarily, in the apartment above Natasha and Mars's garage. He usually sported unruly sandy hair, and though he was well educated and had traveled the world with his globe-trotting mother, he drifted from one job to another, often paying his way by tending bar.

We walked across the lawn, Bernie carrying a flashlight so I could put pressure on my wound to stop the bleeding. He had lived in one of my guest rooms for a couple of months before moving to the apartment, so I knew him well enough to be myself and not pussyfoot around. "Were you home when Emily was killed?"

In his elegant British accent, he said, "Regretfully not. I'm no hero but I might have saved her had I been there. I'm afraid I was at the pub."

"You went in early?"

"Mars didn't tell you about my promotion? I'm the manager now. The place was bought by an ex-pat. An absentee owner, really. I run it. Practically live there."

We stepped into the shed and Bernie trained the flashlight on the workbench. A three-inch knife with a stainless-steel handle gleamed in the light. "Kevin must have knocked it with his elbow."

Bernie picked it up. "Doesn't look like it could inflict that kind of damage."

He tested the blade with his thumb as I cried, "No!"

A thin red line emerged immediately.

"It has a surgical blade. Razor sharp." I muttered what he must have realized by now.

Bernie stuck his thumb in his mouth and mumbled, "It's not like you to leave a knife exposed that way."

"It's not mine." I was scrupulous about putting away knives and scissors that could hurt Mochie or Daisy. "It's not supposed to be there. But Craig is giving knives like that to his groomsmen as gifts."

"Ah, the macho gift. All men are hunters, ergo even those who sit behind desks require an engraved knife with which they could gut an antelope, should the occasion arise." He turned it over. "Oho! Who is KPA?"

"Kevin, the best man." Had Kevin meant to coax me to the shed because he intended to harm me? He barely knew me. "Anyone could have taken the knife out of the box."

"Had Kevin left it here, surely he wouldn't have been stupid enough to cut himself."

"We stumbled around. Maybe he didn't plan on that."

"Stumbled around in the shed in the dark?" Bernie sounded amused.

"Please, it's not like that."

"Sophie! Sophie!"

I recognized Mars's voice. "In the shed."

Mars joined us. "What are you doing in the dark?" He tried the switch on the wall. "The light must have burned out. The outside one is burned out, too. Sophie, don't you ever replace lightbulbs?" He sighed. "I'll come over in the morning and do it for you." Stepping outside, he reached up and the outside light came on. "Look at that, it was just loose."

Bernie showed him the knife.

"Don't touch, it's cursed," I joked. "So far everyone who has come into contact with the stupid thing has been cut."

"Sophie, I swear your mind works overtime on sinister ideas. Emily was hanged, not stabbed." Mars took the knife and flicked it shut. "I'm going to walk Darby back to her hotel."

"She doesn't want to go with Stan and Robert?" I asked.

"The murder shook her up. She liked the woman who died, and she's taking it pretty hard."

The three of us returned to the house, and I went back to my hosting duties. I found Humphrey in the dining room staring at Natasha's heart topiary.

"Must have been a lot of work," I said.

"The ribbon—how does it stay in airborne coils like that?" he asked.

"Thin wires run through both sides. You can position it in any shape you like."

He reached over and squeezed a curl of ribbon. When he released it, the ribbon remained in an ugly clump. "I think this might be what the killer used to strangle Emily."

"Natasha's ribbon?"

"They can't figure out what made the marks on her neck." He ripped a portion of ribbon loose.

I hoped Natasha wasn't watching.

Humphrey pulled the ribbon tight between his hands, twisted it, and tugged on it. "This could make uneven marks of varying size and depth. Where the wires were apart, it might look like two strands but where they're twisted or very close, it would appear as one."

I was in no mood to defend Natasha, but I pointed out that wired ribbon could be bought at any craft store and it wasn't uncommon to find it in grocery stores and drugstores.

He examined the ribbon in his hands. "They found microscopic bits of brown fiber on her neck, Sophie."

FIFTEEN

There must be thousands of chocolate brown wired ribbons within a twenty-mile radius, but it didn't strain the imagination too much to think that the ribbon might have come from the home where Emily had been found.

When we saw Natasha storming toward us, Humphrey hastily stuffed the ribbon into his trouser pocket.

"Someone has tampered with my topiary," she huffed, glaring at me.

One tiny bit of ribbon was missing, and Natasha acted like a major crime had been committed. Never mind that she'd replaced everything I had done in my dining room.

"Why would anyone remove a ribbon? Now it's not balanced." She reached over to adjust it.

Maybe she didn't know about the brown bits on Emily's neck. I'm ashamed to admit that I relished the thought of tweaking her. If she had left my flowers alone or if she had bothered to incorporate them, I might not be inclined to scare her. But I was.

"I expect Wolf took it to compare to the ribbon used to strangle Emily," I said airily. Natasha's perfect makeup couldn't conceal the pallor that swept her face. Underneath her carefully applied foundation, I suspected she might be as pasty as Humphrey.

Her voice quavered when she said, "Strangle?" Before I could say more, she quickly added, "I wasn't even home."

I couldn't help myself. "I'm sure you have a good alibi."

Natasha appeared to stop breathing. She froze, and I don't think her eyelids blinked.

Humphrey glanced at me before grazing Natasha's arm in what appeared to be an aborted attempt to rouse her. He'd reverted to his timid nature, probably shy about touching the great beauty queen from our high school days.

Natasha twitched and brushed her arm, distaste on her face as though a giant fly had landed on her.

"Kevin," she wailed, looking around the room for him. "I believe it's time to go home," she said wearily to no one in particular. "It's been a rather trying day."

What was she up to? Shouldn't she be looking for Mars? Why had he told me where he was going, and why was Natasha hanging on to another man? Natasha planned her life as carefully as she planned a party. Was she preparing to dump Mars?

When Natasha trudged off to find Kevin, I found Humphrey watching me sadly. "At dinner tonight, you and Mars looked like you were still a couple. I feel rather the fool for thinking your relationship was over. I hope I haven't made you uncomfortable by being so forward."

If he'd gotten the mistaken impression that I was still in love with Mars, I was willing to go along with it. "I hope we can be friends, Humphrey."

In a completely uncharacteristic move, he kissed me on the cheek. I couldn't help thinking it felt like the end of something.

⟆⟆⟆

By one in the morning, only a handful of Hannah's best friends remained. They clustered under the tiny roof lights in the sunroom, retelling old stories about each other. Mom and Dad put Jen to bed and retired, leaving me to handle the bulk of the cleanup. Every last crumb of my Chocolate Hazelnut Torte and the Lemon Raspberry Cake had disappeared. But hunks of Natasha's Rhubarb Ricotta Cake remained on her black plates. I put the leftovers into containers.

Phoebe wandered in from the sunroom. "Hannah's a little tipsy at the moment, but in the morning she's going to be upset about losing her engagement ring. I thought she might have left it on the windowsill."

I rinsed the last of the martini glasses. "You know Hannah. She only does dishes if it will get her out of cleaning bathrooms."

"Do you have any idea where it is? Craig is going to kill her."

I almost dropped one of Natasha's plates. "What do you mean?"

"It's a very expensive ring. Joel's family had a jewelry store on the Jersey shore for generations. He practically grew up in diamonds, and he says it's a very pricey ring. One of the benefits of marrying a doctor, I guess."

Mochie watched Phoebe from the kitchen table, his tail wrapped neatly around his paws, Egyptian cat style. I didn't dare tell Phoebe, but I had a hunch that Hannah's expensive ring might have seemed like a fun toy to Mochie.

"I'll check around for it in the morning." Under the furniture, where it probably spun when he smacked it. At the moment, I didn't care how much the ring was worth; all I wanted was to crawl into bed.

Phoebe returned to the sunroom, and I stacked the last dish on top of the others. Bursts of laughter came from the sunroom as I trudged up the stairs to bed. Mochie scampered ahead of me, but Daisy followed slowly, every bit as tired as I was. I drifted off into the deep sleep of the exhausted, but at three thirty in the morning, I woke with a jolt when Daisy let out a little woof.

"Shh. You don't want to wake everyone."

The tip of her tail flapped against the bed. She focused on the door, listening. I did too, and heard the unmistakable creak of ancient floorboards. "It's probably just someone using the bathroom," I told her.

She pricked her ears and I realized that Mochie was listening attentively, too.

To be on the safe side, I dragged myself out of bed to check on Jen. I thought I heard a door shut but wasn't sure. Leaving Mochie and Daisy in my bedroom, I tiptoed upstairs and opened Jen's door a crack. I could see the covers rising and falling. I closed the door and tried the doorknob to Hannah's room. But before I turned it, I had second thoughts. The steps I'd heard could have been Craig sneaking up to Hannah. I coaxed Daisy and Mochie back to bed and drifted off as soon as I snuggled under the blanket.

The next morning, I woke to honeysuckle-scented air wafting through the window. The sun shone and birds twittered, and it was almost impossible to believe that anyone had killed Emily the day before. It all felt like a distant dream that would fade from memory as the day wore on.

The door to my room creaked open, and a ten-year-old pixie bounded through and jumped on the bed. I could hear Daisy racing down the stairs.

"Grandma says it's time for you to get up. I don't want to miss the tour of Old Town."

Jen nuzzled Mochie while I slung on a nubby chenille bathrobe, an old favorite adorned with fluffy white clouds. It fell just below my knees and looked incredibly haus-frauish when I paired it with my fuzzy slippers, but I didn't care. Only family and Craig would be at breakfast, and unless I could prevent it, he would be family soon.

As we walked downstairs, I could hear voices in the kitchen. The aroma of coffee beckoned, and I looked forward to lounging comfortably with a steaming cup of the rich brew before wedding duties called.

I stopped short at the entrance to the kitchen. For a second I was taken back in time. Mars sat in his old spot at our kitchen table in a bathrobe, which if memory served right, he wore over pajama pants and a bare chest. He was eating scrambled eggs with gusto, and I had a sneaking feeling Mom had made his favorite Crabby Eggs.

"What are you doing here?" I asked.

"Sophie!" Mom scolded. "Don't be rude."

Mars swallowed and held half an English muffin in the air. "Let's just say I prefer the company over here."

Mom winked at me as though she thought he meant me. I tried not to laugh. Natasha's mother or Kevin had gotten to him. My money was on Wanda. I poured myself a mug of coffee, and Mom waved one of my many wedding lists at me.

"We need to change the seating plan for the reception. Where do you want to put Craig's relatives?"

Mars grumbled, "Just don't seat Kevin or Wanda at my table."

I slid in next to him and found Daisy nestled by Mars's feet. "I suppose you'd better ask Natasha, since she changes everything I do."

Mars slathered another English muffin with dense Plugrá butter and wild blueberry jam and sank his teeth into it.

I reached for an English muffin, but before I could spread it with butter, Mom, avoiding my eyes, slid the butter dish out of my reach and said, "Mars, you won't believe how stunning Sophie looks in her maid of honor dress."

Two could play that game. "Mars," I said sweetly, "would you pass the butter?"

He moved it in my direction, happily unaware of the little guilt trip Inga Bauer had tried to inflict on her daughter.

Mom poured herself more coffee. "Do you think Craig will want his father or uncle to be groomsmen? We'd have to get their tuxedos today. That uncle is very tall. Do you suppose they'll have his size in stock anywhere?"

"I guess you'd better ask Craig or Hannah." I spread jam on my muffin, anticipating the tangy sweetness of the blueberries. "Are they still in bed? You didn't send Jen to wake them, too?"

Jen poked me in the ribs and pointed to the arched opening to the foyer.

Wearing gray sweatshorts and a T-shirt, Hannah looked like she was ready to burst into tears. "Craig's gone."

SIXTEEN

From *"Ask Natasha"*:

Dear Natasha,

Many of my daughter's wedding guests are traveling a good distance to attend the wedding. They'll be here for the whole weekend, but we have so much going on before the wedding that I won't have time to entertain. I'm worried that they'll feel neglected.

—Proper Mom on Pine Knoll Shores

Dear Proper Mom,

Plan alternatives for guests who aren't in the wedding. Arrange for limos to favorite restaurants and popular destinations. Set up sightseeing tours, beach trips, hiking, shopping, whatever your area has to offer. Always enlist a family member or dear friend to make introductions and ensure an enjoyable excursion for everyone. And make it extra special by crafting gift baskets based on the theme of the excursion.

—Natasha

The flood of tears burst forth. "He's gone," Hannah sobbed. "It's just like Wanda said. I lost my ring and now I've lost Craig."

Mom hurried to her side and walked her to the kitchen table while the rest of us exchanged wide-eyed looks.

"Maybe he went for a run," said Jen.

Mom patted Hannah's shoulder. "I'm sure that's it. Jen's right. Craig loves to run. He's probably out getting some exercise."

I wasn't so sure. I looked at Dad and Mars. Wasn't anyone else thinking he left because he'd murdered Emily?

Hannah sniffed and wiped her nose with the back of her hand in a most unbridelike manner. "I knew something was wrong when we said good night. He kissed me like you kiss somebody you're never going to see again."

Mars reached across the table to her. "Honey, I'm certain he's out running."

Hannah squeezed her eyes shut and wailed, "You don't understand. His luggage is gone."

Dad, Mars, and I leaped to our feet and charged up the stairs to the guest bedroom, with Daisy and Mochie racing along. Neat as a pin, the bed clearly hadn't been slept in. I opened the closet door. The hanging bag and suitcase were gone.

"I have to call Wolf," I said. "He must have known it was a matter of time and took off to evade arrest."

"No!" Hannah spoke from the doorway to the bedroom. "This is your fault, Sophie. Don't you breathe a word of this to your horrible Wolf."

I wasn't getting how this was my fault, but I could understand Hannah's distress and inability to think clearly at the moment.

"I never trusted Craig." Dad sighed. "It always seemed like he was hiding something."

That brought on a new torrent of tears.

"The car," I blurted. "Does anyone know where he parked last night?"

Dad hugged Hannah to him. "He said something about getting a spot across the street from Mars's place when a police car pulled out."

As if we shared thoughts, Mars and I loped down the stairs and out the kitchen door with Daisy running ahead, excited by the commotion. When we reached the sidewalk, Mars slid the fabric belt off his robe and looped it around Daisy's collar as a makeshift leash. We jogged along the sidewalk toward his house, but there was no sign of Craig's Toyota Camry.

"I don't know what we thought we'd find," said Mars. "This stinks. I'd like to punch him in the nose."

Behind him, I could see Natasha striding across the street toward us, her jaw rigid. "How much do you two want to embarrass me? Don't you know what people will think if they see the two of you out here together in your nightclothes?" She paused and made a face like she'd sucked on a lemon. "Sophie," she clucked, "that robe is ready to be cut into dusting cloths."

I pulled it tighter and examined her outfit in a desperate attempt to lash back. But the pale green trousers and matching shell could have come straight from a store window. Even her shoes matched.

"I gave Sophie that bathrobe," said Mars.

A red flush sprang to Natasha's face, and her nostrils flared. "And you, standing out here with your ex-wife, exposing your bare chest to the entire neighborhood."

Mars handed me Daisy's lead and pulled his bathrobe closed. "Calm down, Natasha. This isn't about you. It looks like Craig left Hannah."

Her anger changed to astonishment. "Impossible. He loves Hannah. Craig would never leave her the day before the wedding."

"He left during the night without a word," I said.

"Nonsense," she insisted, "there must be some other explanation."

"There is," I said drolly, "he murdered his ex-wife and strung her up in your pergola and now he's on the run."

Her face stiffened. "Craig would not do that to me."

"I had no idea you were so close."

"You'd best hurry and change, Mars. I see people are beginning to gather for the walk through Old Town."

He allowed her to propel him away, but I heard him mutter, "I live here. I'm not wasting my morning strolling around town like a tourist."

I turned and smacked headlong into Wolf.

Taking an awkward step back, I wondered if I could avoid telling him about Craig's abrupt departure. After all, if Craig had killed Emily, the cops needed to find him. I loved Hannah, but she couldn't see Craig in a true light.

"Missed you at the party last night," I said.

"Did you?" He seemed a little put out with me, as though I'd committed a crime.

"Of course. It would have been more fun with you there." I smiled encouragingly and wrapped my bathrobe tighter. "Any leads on Emily's killer?" Under normal circumstances I'd have invited him in for coffee, but since Hannah wanted to keep Craig's departure secret, that didn't seem wise. Under his scrutiny, I felt shabby and wished I were as put together as Natasha.

"Sophie!" Mom stood in the doorway and motioned for me to return. Hannah and a gaggle of her friends clustered behind Mom.

"I'd better go."

"Uh-huh."

"See you later?" I asked.

"Maybe. I'm not sure."

I walked up to my door wondering what I'd done to offend Wolf.

The second I strode into the foyer, Hannah blurted, "How could you?" and ran up the stairs.

Phoebe and a couple of the other bridesmaids frowned at me and shook their heads.

I followed Mom into the kitchen. "What did I do now?"

She shook aspirin out of the bottle and into her hand. "Craig better not come back or I'll strangle him personally for putting us all through this."

"Why is everyone so mad at me?"

"For talking to Wolf."

"But I didn't spill the beans. And it wasn't easy."

Mom swallowed the aspirin with a glass of water. "I'm going with Hannah and the girls to the salon to have their nails done."

I began to point out that wasn't necessary since there wouldn't be a wedding, but she interrupted me.

"You don't know that. The salon will distract Hannah and make her feel better and they can all commiserate."

"Then I'll go on the walking tour with Dad and Jen and make sure everyone has a good time."

She heaved a great sigh. "Hannah doesn't want us to tell anyone else about Craig being gone. Not yet, anyway. I'm inclined to indulge her on this, at least for a few hours, until she gets used to the idea."

"What about the bridesmaids' luncheon?"

"Given the circumstances, I think that would be unbearable for Hannah. You'd better go change."

I headed for the stairs, but she grabbed my bathrobe. "And Sophie, wear makeup and put on something less frumpy. Mars might be on the tour, and that Wolf of yours is all over the neighborhood working on the murder."

After a super quick shower, I changed into a sleeveless coral top and khaki skirt. I skipped makeup but applied a little lipstick, pulled my hair into a ponytail, and hurried downstairs.

Holding Daisy's leash, Jen grabbed my hand and tugged me out the door. "What took you so long? They're already beginning to walk."

Nina ran out of her house with Hermione and handed Jen the leash. "Jen's puppy-sitting until I get back."

"Cute outfit." I raised an eyebrow at the snazzy tennis togs and short skirt that showed off her slender legs.

"Didn't Jen tell you? I'm playing in a tennis tournament this morning."

Nina dashed back to her house, and we caught up to the rest of our group. Robert and Darby walked with Dad. Natasha was being too friendly with Kevin, and I noted that Mars had managed to avoid the tour.

Jen skipped a few steps ahead to Darby. "Do you think they'll take us to the cemetery?"

Darby stiffened her fingers and walked like Franken-stein, moaning, "Ooooooo."

Our group gathered around a statue in the very spot where soldiers had gathered to join the Confederate army. We walked by buildings where George and Martha Washington and Thomas Jefferson had lived. But when the guide pretended he saw a ghostly face in the window of Gadsby's Tavern, Jen's hand wandered into mine, ice-cold.

"It's just pretend," I whispered.

Darby tried to cheer her up. "Jen, did you know that Phoebe and I have met before? Isn't that funny?"

Jen wasn't interested but I was. "How do you know Phoebe?"

"Oh, you won't believe this. Your sister registered at a branch of the store I work for. So then, Phoebe, she comes in to the china department where I work and she wants to know did anybody get her girlfriend a gravy boat yet? So I look it up on the computer and people have bought almost everything Hannah registered for. I thought to myself—I should be so lucky. So there's a little link to her wedding Web site and I click it and bingo, there's my cousin, Craig, the groom. Who knew?"

"You had no idea he was getting married?"

"Absolutely none. So I called the family and told everybody. My mom probably told Emily's mom. You know how people gossip."

"Darby, it's none of my business, but do you know what drove Craig and his dad apart?"

She paused like she was thinking of a polite way to explain something. "It was a disagreement over a business transaction. You know how stubborn men can be. If everyone had just done what he said, there wouldn't have been a squabble. So, Jen, do you know where Craig and Hannah will live?"

"I think they're going to buy a new house. I haven't been to Craig's house, but Hannah says he lives in the woods. There are lots of birds and raccoons and stuff."

"Sounds adorable. Hey, Jen, whaddya say we peel off from the group and grab an ice cream cone?"

I gladly took the leashes of the two dogs. As they walked across the street, I heard Darby say, "You're so adorable. Do you have a boyfriend? Wait, I bet you have two . . ."

Four portly women holding ice cream cones spied Natasha and ran across the street to fuss over her. When she stopped to sign autographs, I moved in on Kevin and inched him away from the rest of the group. I wanted to question him out of Natasha's earshot—no easy task the way she'd been clinging to him.

Speaking softly, I said, "Craig took off this morning."

Kevin blinked at me with innocent eyes. "What do you mean? Where to?"

"I was hoping you might know. Why would he leave Hannah in the lurch?" I didn't add *if he didn't kill Emily*, but that's what I was thinking.

Kevin grimaced. "I hope it's not his heart."

"A broken heart?" That didn't make sense.

"I mean maybe his heart couldn't take it. Maybe it was too much for him, the wedding and the reunion with his family, and he had to get away so he wouldn't have another heart attack."

"He had a heart attack? When was this?"

"I'm surprised you don't know. That's why he's no longer practicing medicine."

SEVENTEEN

From "THE GOOD LIFE":

Dear Sophie,

I love an open bar, but my fiance's groomsmen could empty a well-stocked bar all by themselves. Aside from turning my wedding into a night of drunken debauchery, I know I'll be thinking they're sucking us dry. How do I control these liquor-crazed heathens?

—Toasting True Love in Towson

Dear Toasting,

Close the bar when it's time for dinner and don't reopen it. Serve wine with dinner, and be sure waiters know to keep the groomsmen's water glasses full and to delay refilling their wineglasses.

—Sophie

"He's not a doctor?" I asked in a low voice so the entire tour group wouldn't hear. "I was there when my dad looked him up on the Internet and found his medical background." It had been sparse, but it confirmed what we knew. He'd attended medical school on the West Coast, interned in South Dakota, and was licensed to practice medicine in West Virginia.

Kevin backed up a step. "This is the suspicious Sophie that Craig warned me about, isn't it?"

I grabbed his arm and didn't let him pull away. "This is my sister's life. If he's not a doctor, you'd better tell me what you know—now."

"Look, Sophie, Craig is my friend and he's very sensitive about this. I better let him tell you the rest." With an eye on Natasha and her admirers, he said, "I'm enjoying the tour, but this is my only chance to escape for a while. You don't know where I am. Okay?" He wound through our little group and ran like a frightened buck until he vanished around the next corner.

Anxiety gnawed at me. What else didn't we know about Craig? Was Hannah aware of all this? I reminded myself that it was over. He'd left, and I hoped he wouldn't return.

I looked around for Jen. She and Darby lagged behind, and I was happy to see Jen licking a chocolate ice cream cone.

Robert stopped and waited for them.

I sidled over and waited with him. "Where's Uncle Stan this morning?"

Darby and Jen caught up to us, Jen reached for Hermione's leash with her free hand, and we all strolled behind the tour group.

Robert's odd voice crackled as he said, "He went to visit a relative. I've been calling Craig all morning but I guess he turned off his phone."

It was Jen, with chocolate lips, who spilled the beans. "He left."

Robert stopped walking. "Whaddya mean?"

There was no getting around it. "He took off during the night."

"No!" whispered Darby. I didn't think she could look more shocked. Her eyebrows lifted and her brown eyes grew huge. And if I wasn't mistaken, a look flashed between Darby and Robert.

"Poor Hannah. I should go to her," said Darby. "I know exactly how she feels."

"You were left at the altar?" I nabbed one of Jen's paper napkins and wiped a drip of chocolate off her shirt.

"My deadbeat husband left me. Never said a word, just didn't come home one day. Now I ask you—is it really too much to expect them to scribble a note on the mirror with your lipstick? How hard would that be?"

We continued on the tour, and I spotted Bernie's pub on a side street. I picked up my pace and caught up to my dad. "Keep an eye on Jen, will you? I'm going to have a word with Bernie." I handed him Daisy's leash, but he seemed more interested in the guide, who was telling a spellbinding story about George Washington. Jen listened at Darby's side, and I figured between Gramps and Darby she'd be okay.

I hurried along Pitt Street, glad I'd worn rubber-soled shoes because the brick sidewalks weren't completely even. I pulled open the heavy front door and found that the "pub" wasn't at all what I remembered. Someone had put serious money into renovations. Brass and glass gleamed against gorgeous dark wood. The bar, a few steps down to my right, reminded me of an upscale men's club. Large leather chairs and sofas clustered around tables. A huge stone fireplace occupied a far wall, and behind the bar, longer than any I could recall seeing, glasses of every imaginable shape and kind glinted under the lights.

I told the host I was looking for Bernie. He led the way through a dining room with French doors that opened onto a private garden that I hadn't noticed from the street. A few steps up, we walked through another dining room, this one with a glass ceiling and wall overlooking the garden.

Lunchtime diners crowded every seat. If the food was half as good as the decor, the place would be a huge success. It was a little hard for me to imagine eternally rumpled Bernie, with the kink in his nose from being broken one too many times, running an elegant restaurant.

At the end of the glassed-in dining room, the host rapped on a door and opened it for me. Bernie, his yellow hair mussed as usual, read the local paper, his bare feet on the desk, reading glasses perched on his nose.

"Sophie!" His feet landed on the floor with a loud *thunk*. Addressing the host, he said, "Could you send us two Irish Breakfast teas and a couple of chocolate mousses." He smiled at me. "I've been wanting your opinion on the mousse."

"When you said you were running the pub, I thought you meant a one-room dive with a fryer in the back."

"So it's a restaurant. And a splendid one, I might add. You'll have to come for dinner sometime. The chef whips up a beef Wellington that you won't believe."

"Have you ever managed a restaurant?"

"The owner's a Brit like me. I suppose we clicked. And I have plenty of help."

A pretty girl in a refined black waitress vest served our tea British style, by pouring steaming water over loose black tea in a silver strainer.

"Your touch, I imagine?"

Bernie laughed. "Worth an extra star, don't you think?"

I sipped the tea. Perfect. Strong flavor, pleasant, no bitterness. I dipped a spoon into the mousse and tried it. Dark chocolate, smooth and dense yet airy and light—I was in heaven. Even if I hadn't been hungry because of a breakfast that had been cut short, I could eat this stuff by the bucket. "It's fabulous," I murmured with my mouth full. Absolutely delicious."

Bernie shoved the newspaper in front of me. "Congrats on the syndication of your column. I imagine Natasha is up the wall about it."

I hadn't mentioned my syndication news to anyone. It wasn't a big deal to anyone but me. The column had been picked up by a few newspapers in Pennsylvania, Delaware, and New Jersey. "How would you know about that?"

"I have my sources." He winked slyly. "Coswell comes in every morning. He brings the paper, and I provide the coffee and a fresh croissant."

Coswell, the editor of the local rag, never seemed to have time to dally. I made a mental note that I could catch up with him at Bernie's pub.

"Smart fellow, Coswell. Keeps his ear to the ground. Likes to hear what everyone's bellyaching about." He tapped the newspaper. "Emily Beacham was the topic today. She was in here the night before she died."

"Why didn't you say something before?"

"Didn't know she was the dead woman until Wolf turned up this morning asking questions. When I saw her in here night before last, I thought she was just some pretty girl Tucker had picked up."

"Tucker? Did they come in together? Did it look like they knew each other?"

"Hard to tell."

"Tucker. So maybe Craig didn't kill her." Guilt washed over me. What if I'd been wrong all along? It seemed so obvious that Craig had killed her, but if Tucker knew her, too, that changed everything.

"Heard he ran off. Bummer for Hannah."

Old Town felt like a village, but I hadn't realized just how fast news traveled. "How could you possibly know that?"

"Mars came by this morning. Humphrey, too." He checked his watch. "Humphrey's probably at your place by now."

What if Tucker was the evil one and I'd tried to sic him on my sister? I recoiled at the thought. "If Craig wasn't the killer, I'd have expected it to be one of Craig's relatives, not Tucker."

"Odd that you should mention them. They were here that night, too."

Darby had acted surprised to learn that Emily was in town. Had she been pretending? "Did they speak to Emily?"

"They were here a little earlier. I can't say for certain whether they intersected or not."

Bernie's phone rang, so I asked him to keep me posted and left the restaurant. Craig's abrupt departure had dominated my thinking this morning. But since I was only a block and a half from the bed-and-breakfast where Emily stayed, I thought I should drop in to see what worried Wolf.

A wrought-iron gate marked the entrance. The lush garden, an oasis from the bustle of the city, lay beyond. As I walked through the walled garden, dappled sunlight sneaked through the leaves overhead to dance on a bistro table and chairs.

I knocked on a quaint door, and a disheveled woman answered. Hair the color of straw frizzed around her ruddy face. Holding a large wicker laundry basket, she said, "Hi Honey, I'm Polly. Your room isn't ready yet, but you can leave your luggage and have a look around town."

"I'm not a guest."

She squinted at me. "You don't look like a cop."

I introduced myself, but before I could finish, she said, "You must be the one they were teasing Wolf about. The girlfriend who keeps finding bodies, sister of the bride."

Teasing? No wonder Wolf had cooled off. It might be childish and worthy of elementary school, but I could just imagine the ribbing he would get for dating a woman who'd found more than one dead body. Unless I took a liking to Humphrey, it seemed my love life was doomed.

"Honey?" She shifted the basket. "Come on in."

I stepped inside and she closed the door.

"I'm never this late. The darned police have got me running behind, so if you want to talk about Lina you'll have to do it while I take care of getting the room ready."

Following her to a tiny laundry room, I said, "I wanted to ask you about Emily."

She tossed white sheets into the washing machine. "Yeah, Emily, Lina, same person."

EIGHTEEN

"Lina was very polite." Polly slammed the top closed on the washing machine and rested her arm on it. "Had that odd New Jersey accent, but then, I imagine they'd think I sounded funny in New Jersey. You meet all kinds when you run a B&B. That's half the fun."

I was barely listening, still hung up on what she'd said earlier. "Who's Lina?"

"The girl they're calling Emily in the newspaper called herself Lina Kowalski."

"You're sure it was the same woman?"

"Yeah, yeah." Polly bustled through the house and up the stairs into a bedroom.

I followed and watched her run a dust cloth over furniture. "Lina?" Maybe she was wrong. "Did you see any identification? A luggage tag, maybe?"

Polly paused. "Seeing as how it's your sister that's all tangled up with her killer, I'll be honest with you—I never ask for identification. The cops think I did, and I will from now on, of course. I never expected to have one of my guests murdered. Thank goodness it didn't happen here."

Did Tucker know her as Lina or Emily, I wondered. "Did she have a male visitor?"

"What do you think I'm running here? Do you think most madams look like me and do their own cleaning?"

"That's not what I meant. Did you see her with anyone?"

"Nope. Just a nice girl named Lina."

"I suppose the cops took all her belongings. Could I see her room?"

"You're lookin' at it, honey."

I gazed around. The bed had been stripped. The top of the dresser held only a crocheted lace runner. The closet door gaped open and revealed a narrow but empty closet. "How about a trash can?"

"Cops took my trash." She rested a hand on a generous hip. "There's nothin' left."

"What about her necklace? Did you find the diamond necklace?"

"That was a knockout, wasn't it? She was wearin' it when she left here."

I thanked her and saw myself out. Walking home slowly, I was oblivious to the world around me. Had Emily used the name Lina so Craig wouldn't find her? Had she changed her name to keep him from locating her? But then why would she come here? Was that what Wolf wanted me to discover? Had Emily come to warn Hannah about Craig? That didn't make sense. Darby said Emily adored Craig. What if Craig was right and she had come to stop the wedding because she loved him?

"You should have told me, you know."

I looked up to find Wolf blocking the sidewalk. He hadn't assumed the intimidating police stance, and his chocolate eyes regarded me with such warmth that I wanted to throw myself at him for a much-needed hug. But after the cold reception he'd given me earlier, I didn't dare. "How did you find out?"

"Your dad. Where do you think Craig went?"

"Oh Wolf, you're asking the wrong person. Have you talked to his best man, Kevin? He knows Craig much better than I do."

"Kevin hasn't been very forthcoming. Either he doesn't know much or he's a very good friend and isn't about to betray Craig."

A flicker of movement behind Wolf drew my gaze past him. Mordecai observed us from a window that looked out on the front part of his porch.

Wolf didn't turn to look. "Mordecai watching us?"

I shivered in spite of the heat.

"He's just a lonely old man." He glanced at Mordecai's porch. "Something happened to him long before I came on the force and he's been a recluse, afraid of the world ever since."

"That explains the clothes from another era." Suddenly I wished I'd been nicer to him. It wouldn't hurt me to spend some time with a sad old guy.

"He calls the cops a lot. Always afraid someone is breaking into his house. Some of the guys hate responding because of the tales about him. People have no shame. They don't know the facts, but that doesn't stop them from making up stories."

My throat constricted. The bitterness in his voice suggested that he wasn't talking about Mordecai anymore. Finally, the subject I'd wanted to know more about but hadn't been able to bring up. I had to handle it carefully. Lightly, I said, "Like the stories about what happened to your wife?"

"Exactly."

I hoped he would elaborate, but he didn't.

"If you get a handle on Craig's location, I hope you'll pass it along to me."

"I'm hoping he'll stay away and I'll never see him again. But I'll let you know if I hear anything. Does that mean he's definitely the killer?"

"Not at all. Innocent people don't usually run away, though."

"Wolf," I said softly, "thanks for sending me over to the B&B."

"I don't want to see Hannah end up like Emily."

My heart melted. He cared about people, even about my sister, who was acting like a pill. I wanted to get together but at this point I didn't know what we would do next since so many guests had already arrived. "Maybe when all this is over . . ."

A male voice called Wolf's name.

He could have discreetly brushed my hand, but instead he said, "When this is over, I think we ought to talk."

Oh no! Not talk. I knew what that meant. The big kiss-off was coming.

He walked toward the officer who had called him. Our little chat had seemed to be going well, but that last bit sounded ominous. With a deep sigh, I returned home.

Hannah leaned against the kitchen counter, talking with Mom, Dad, and Humphrey. When Hannah saw me, she defiantly raised her chin and made a beeline for the sunroom.

"Not so fast."

Hannah drifted to a halt and turned. Her chin still set in anger mode, she lifted a hand and admired her fresh manicure.

"Craig isn't a doctor anymore," I announced.

Hannah closed her eyes, and I knew she wished I would fall through a trapdoor and vanish.

"And he had a heart attack."

Dad swung around to face her. "Is this true?"

Her mouth twitched, and she edged back toward us. "He had the heart attack before I met him. But he doesn't want people to know. It's a matter of pride. He's too young to have had a heart attack. When they told him it would be too stressful for him to continue his practice, he had to find something else to do, and he's been very successful."

Mom collapsed into a chair. "So what does he do now?"

"He sells vitamins over the Internet. He has his own brand and puts out a health newsletter called *Dr. Craig's Nutrition News.*"

"He's that Dr. Craig?" Humphrey sounded impressed. "A woman at the funeral home swears by his vitamins."

"When were you going to tell us this?" asked Dad.

Her elbows on the table, Mom rested her head in her hands. "It doesn't matter anymore. None of this matters. Craig killed Emily and left." She lifted her head and looked straight at Hannah. "I'm sorry, honey. You have to face facts."

"This is all Emily's fault." Hannah clenched her fists. "If she hadn't shown up, none of this would have happened. Craig would be here now, and we would be getting married tomorrow."

I slumped onto the window seat next to Mochie. Poor Emily. Why had she come? She must have known how Craig felt. Must have realized that he could harm her.

Mom massaged her temples, and I felt terrible for her. The roller-coaster ride we'd been on had taken a toll. "I'll call all the vendors to cancel, but Natasha will have to notify the people she hired."

Hannah wiped her eyes. "No." Her head hung low as she walked to the door, and I couldn't help feeling sad for her in spite of her reluctance to be realistic.

Both of my parents looked like they wished the nightmare would end. Since Craig was gone, probably for good, I didn't bother telling them about Emily's use of the name Lina Kowalski. At least creepy Craig wouldn't be a member of the family.

Humphrey gazed around at us, then jumped to his feet and followed Hannah out the door.

I helped myself to a brownie from a platter on the table, and Mom didn't notice. I munched on it without guilt. No need to wedge myself into a bridesmaid dress or lose weight to be slender for Wolf.

Mom clicked her fingernail against a coffee mug. "I didn't expect this. First a death and now a missing groom. Do you think he left because he was afraid his family would find out he's not practicing medicine? They're very proud of him for being a doctor."

"Maybe he left because he's afraid of his dad," I said between bites. "Did you notice how distant they act?"

Dad slid his hand over Mom's. "I knew something like this would happen."

"We don't know what happened," she muttered. "After

all, his ex-wife, someone he once loved, died yesterday. He must be very shaken. Much more than we thought. Think about the horror this must be for him. We're all focused on the wedding, but his ex-wife died."

"She wouldn't have if he hadn't killed her." I was sorry the moment the words left my mouth. I'd been fascinated by Craig's relatives, but they'd lost someone dear to them. And Darby seemed like fun. I hated that she'd lost her friend.

By five o'clock in the afternoon, things around my house had settled to a dull roar. Most of the wedding guests were headed home. A few planned to stick around the rest of the weekend to visit the Smithsonian and enjoy a mini-vacation. Phoebe and the rest of the bridesmaids invited Hannah out to dinner and, instead of a bachelorette night on the town, a lucky-he-left-me night on the town.

I opted out of Hannah's fun since she still wasn't speaking to me. She needed time to recuperate, and her friends were the best medicine I could imagine.

While Mom and Dad entertained the few stragglers, Daisy, Mochie, Jen, and I holed up in the tiny den and I made the phone calls I should have made the day before to cancel everything. The florist, musicians, minister, rental house, ice sculptor, photographer, and caterer all took the news well. And why shouldn't they? They would all be paid anyway. I marked them off one by one after calling.

Mochie rode on Jen's shoulder while she danced in and out of the den to the sunroom and back. "Somebody's in the shed."

"Uh-huh." I punched numbers into my calculator, sick over the wasted money.

"They must be looking for something."

"What?"

"Somebody is in the shed looking for something."

Someone looking for the knife he'd left in there last night? I flew through the sunroom and out the door. My Keds thudded softly against the grass as I ran across the lawn. I jerked open the door to the potting shed and found Hannah wrapped in a man's arms, engaging in a hot smooch—the kind I longed to share with Wolf.

NINETEEN

Dear Sophie,

Unlike the brides I see on TV, I'm on a budget. How do I get the most bang for my buck in reception decor?

—Not Rich in Northlakes

Dear Not Rich,

Table linens go a long way in adding a punch of color. Avoid all the fancy toppers and gauzy overlays that drive up the price. Votive candles don't cost much, but they're used at expensive weddings because they're versatile and effective. Buy simple glass votives on eBay or at your local craft or dollar store. Group four or five together for maximum impact.

—Sophie

The man embracing Hannah had hair so blond it verged on white.

I slammed the door shut. Humphrey? And Hannah? It took a minute to get used to the idea. Could be worse. Wasn't Craig. Wasn't Tucker. I couldn't help giggling.

Half my relatives ran across the lawn toward me, Jen and Daisy leading the way.

A chorus of "What is it" and "What's going on" pelted me.

"Nothing. Everything is fine."

But cute little Jen persisted. "Who's in there?"

When I felt pressure on the door behind me, I gladly moved aside to let Hannah suffer the consequences.

She stepped out, her hair mussed. Humphrey followed, and for the first time in my adult life, I saw rosy color in Humphrey's face.

The little crowd of relatives stared at them in silence until Dad began to chuckle. "At least it's not Tucker."

The pressures and ups and downs of the last two days were finally released as everyone broke into spirit-cleansing laughter. Tears ran down Mom's face as she guffawed. A stranger walking in on us would have thought we'd all gone mad.

"It's cocktail hour," I announced. We had an abundance of ingredients for Wedded Blitz Martinis to use up.

Near the shed, Dad, more relaxed than I'd seen him all weekend, embraced Mom and planted a quick kiss on her lips.

I swung an arm around Jen and walked back to the house with her. In the kitchen, we found Phoebe staring daggers at Joel.

"I wondered where everyone went," said Phoebe. "I hope you don't mind that we let ourselves in. All the girls are coming over here to get dressed. You know, to distract Hannah a bit."

It seemed to me that Hannah was plenty distracted.

"Hannah just got caught playing kissy-face with Humphrey out back."

Phoebe sputtered. "Humphrey? Oh, she'll regret that." She tossed her purse, a dress bag, and a small duffel onto the chair next to the fireplace and ran outside.

"Everything okay?" I asked Joel, as I took food from the refrigerator.

He stopped midway out the door. "Phoebe's mad at me because I said everything turned out for the best. It's a good thing Craig showed his true colors before they tied the knot."

"I think so, too." He ambled off, and I sliced chicken breasts into chunks and tossed them in fiery Jamaican jerk spice. While I cut a pineapple and red peppers, Jen threaded pieces onto long skewers. I dropped fresh tomatoes into the food processor and added basil from my garden, sweet Vidalia onions, jalapeño peppers, a red pepper, garlic, and lime juice. It whirled into a crimson salsa in minutes. Jen dumped organic white and blue corn tortilla chips into baskets that we loaded onto a large wooden tray along with the bowl of salsa. When Nina arrived with Hermione, I immediately enlisted her help in bringing the food outside.

She elbowed me as I arranged food on the patio table. "Is that adorable?"

I followed her line of sight to Mars. He was perched on a chair with Daisy between his knees, talking with Joel, who rolled a ball for Hermione. It was a cute scene, and I knew it made Nina happy to see Hermione wag her tail and bravely bring the little ball back to Joel. But I didn't understand why Mars kept turning up at my house. It wasn't as though I wanted to throw him out. Our divorce hadn't been acrimonious. Nevertheless, a person like my mom could get the wrong idea. She was already watching Hannah and Humphrey with a gleam in her eye.

Nina and Phoebe offered to carry out beer, and as the

three of us returned to the house, Nina said, "Phoebe and Joel are having a spat."

"It's more than that." Phoebe's fair complexion turned rosy. "He's been so weird since we got here, ignoring me and hanging out with the guys. I thought this would be a romantic weekend, but all he's interested in is the Civil War and guy stuff."

She wasn't the only one who mistakenly thought the weekend would be romantic.

I'd just finished pouring a tray of Wedded Blitz Martinis when Hannah's bridal party arrived in full force. They pounced on the martinis, shrieking and carrying on. I mixed more as they thundered up and down the stairs between the bathrooms and Hannah's large attic room, getting dressed and made up for their evening out.

I didn't think Hannah had actually forgotten Humphrey, but when I saw him on the window seat in my kitchen, he seemed alone and forlorn, watching the girls have fun.

Tucker rapped on the door and ambled in, yawning. "Sophie, doll, do you have any coffee?"

"Please tell me you didn't just get up." I'd never met another adult who managed to sleep past noon and party all night.

Hannah bounced in, clearly feeling better, and Tucker wasted no time sweeping her into his arms, waltzing her around the kitchen and dipping her. Hannah giggled and went along with his silliness, but I thought silent Humphrey might explode.

He'd turned a ghastly shade of pewter. "My good man, just because Craig has left doesn't mean you can swoop in and claim Hannah as yours."

Hannah bit her lip, probably to keep from laughing, but Tucker, still holding her in a dip, stopped monkeying around. "Craig left you?"

Shooting a killer look at Humphrey, Hannah stood up

and explained what had happened. Tucker fell to one knee and clasped Hannah's hand in his. "Come away with me, my fair damsel."

Humphrey sputtered. He rose from his seat, his fists clenched, his elbows flapping like a nervous chicken. "Unhand her!"

"Oh, Humphrey, calm down. It's just Tucker's baloney." Hannah bent her head close to Tucker. "And no, you cannot have your grandmother's diamond brooch back."

Tucker stood and hid his dismay quickly. "You wound me to the core."

Hannah brushed him off and when I handed him a cup of coffee, he moseyed outside, muttering something about not being appreciated.

Lowering her head bashfully, Hannah met my eyes and asked, "Truce?"

Every bride was entitled to be a Bridezilla and even though Hannah had taken it to new heights, she'd also faced more dilemmas than the average bride. Besides, no matter what she did, she'd always be my kid sister. "Truce."

We hugged and when I released her, she said, "What a worm. You know Tucker would sell that brooch."

I was surprised that Hannah would have kept his family heirloom. "Do you still have it?"

She whispered, "I gave it back to his mother years ago." Wiggling her eyebrows as though thrilled with her little deception, she asked, "Can I borrow your fuchsia top? The silk one? And the earrings you wore last night and . . ."

"Oh, yes! I am so sick of your colorless clothes. Raid the closet." I released a deep breath, relieved that the Craig phase of her life was over. She tore out of the kitchen, and I could hear her dashing up the stairs as someone knocked on the door.

Humphrey opened it for Darby. She deposited her purse on the chair by the fireplace next to Phoebe's items. "I wanted to say good-bye. Since there won't be a wedding,

I'm taking off. All of you have been so nice to me. I'm sorry Hannah went through this with Craig. She didn't deserve that kind of treatment."

I offered her a Wedded Blitz.

"I've got a taxi waiting, hon." She brushed her hair out of her face and fanned herself with her hand. "Well, maybe a very quick one."

I handed her a drink. "Are Robert and Stan leaving, too?"

"I don't know their plans. I drove down with them but I figured I'd just take the train home. I gotta tell ya, I'm still very shaken by Emily's death."

This was my last chance to ask her anything about Craig. "You've known Craig so much longer than we have. Do you think that's why he ran off? Because he murdered her?"

She downed the last of her martini and spoke carefully, as though she were considering her words. "I would like to say Craig could never, never do anything like that. But he's surprised me before, so as much as I'd like to count him out, I'm not sure you can." Her demeanor changed and she turned into the old, enthusiastic Darby. "Hey, if you're ever in Jersey, I hope you'll look me up."

She jotted down her phone number, and I gave her mine.

As Darby left through the kitchen door, Natasha barged in and I began to feel like I should install a revolving door.

The mere sight of Natasha's stormy expression tired me. We were all feeling so much better now that Craig was out of our lives. Natasha was probably upset that I hadn't laundered and returned her linens yet, but I couldn't be bothered with her nonsense. I braced for the storm. "Wedded Blitz?"

Natasha waved away the drink I held out to her. "Where is my mother?"

I hadn't expected that. "I'm sure I have no idea. Have you checked my backyard? Maybe she's having drinks with my parents."

Carrying a tray of martinis, I accompanied Natasha out back, where most of my family had gathered. Wanda wasn't present, but Mars still stroked Daisy and chatted with Joel and Nina.

Natasha's nostrils flared when she saw Mars. Trilling sweetly, she called, "Mars, may I have a word?"

I stood slightly behind Natasha and made a monster face at him when he walked over.

"Why," she hissed, "must you be here when we have guests of our own to entertain?"

Mars held up his hands innocently. "Your mom went out, and Kevin's getting ready to take off. What's the big deal?"

"The big deal," she waved at my mom but she clipped her words angrily, "is that Mordecai is supposed to arrive for drinks in fifteen minutes and no one is at our house."

Mars groaned. "Mordecai again? Just bring him over here."

"I will not. He's our guest and deserves to be entertained accordingly, not at some makeshift backyard barbecue."

I opened my mouth to defend our impromptu cocktails, but a bloodcurdling scream shattered the happy gathering.

TWENTY

From *"Ask Natasha"*:

Dear Natasha,

My cousin has three brats that will ruin my wedding. She and her mother refuse to attend unless the nightmare children are invited. My niece and nephew will act as flower girl and ring bearer, and my cousin insists that means I can't exclude her children. I'm having an elegant black-tie dinner with dancing, hardly something that would interest children anyway. What do I do?

—Not a Bridesmaid Anymore in Angier

Dear Not a Bridesmaid,

It's quite common and sensible to establish a "no children" policy for a wedding. Only the most daft, addled mothers would think for a moment that children in the wedding party

wouldn't be exempt from that policy. Be firm and provide a
trusted babysitter at the hotel.

—Natasha

Everyone looked around in confusion, searching for the source, but one of us knew exactly where the scream originated. Daisy galloped to the kitchen door. Trusting her instincts, I raced behind her. Inside, she bounded up the stairs, didn't pause at the landing, and ran up to the third floor. She lost me at the second floor but I heard her growling. Forcing my leaden legs and gasping for breath, I clambered up the last flight.

Phoebe stood at the top of the stairs, her hands shaking. "He . . . he's in the closet," she stammered.

Warily, I peeked into the bedroom. Daisy snarled at the closet door, her upper lip lifted into scary wrinkles, baring her teeth.

I could hear people churning up the stairs. Moving slowly, I entered the little bedroom, afraid I might find blood. She'd said *he*. Craig's father? Uncle Stan? Kevin?

Phoebe had jammed a chair under the doorknob of the closet. Good thinking for a panicked person. Dreading what I would find, I slid the chair away.

Mars, Joel, and Dad pressed into the bedroom with me.

I reached for the doorknob but before I touched it, it turned by itself.

The door swung open and Craig stepped out, perfectly fine and looking sheepish. "I think I frightened Phoebe. I just wanted to have a moment alone with Hannah."

Hannah pushed us aside and melted into Craig's arms.

When I recovered from my shock that he'd returned, I was furious that he'd slithered into my house and had the nerve to hide himself. Why hadn't he come out to the garden? What kind of person hid like that? Maybe he hadn't been waiting for Hannah at all.

Dad sounded angrier than I felt. "Now look here, young fellow. We've had about enough of this nonsense. First your ex-wife is murdered, then you run off and abandon Hannah, and now you reappear like some kind of fugitive, scaring us to death."

If Hannah heard him, she didn't show it. She clung to Craig like he was her last friend in the world.

"You two," Dad pointed at Mars and Joel, "don't let Hannah out of your sight."

He tugged my sleeve and motioned to the door. In the hallway he whispered, "Call Wolf. I'm not having any more of this. If Wolf has something on that man, he'd better say so now."

Mochie crouched in the hallway, ready to pounce or run depending on what happened. Cautiously, he stalked to the doorway to see what was going on.

Dad was right, of course. Even though Hannah would treat me as a traitor again, I hurried to my bedroom and made the call to Wolf, who promised he'd be right over.

I took a second to run a brush through my hair and apply a little eye makeup. When he didn't arrive immediately, I pawed through my closet until I found a cute turquoise sundress that belted at the waist. The skirt flared out and made my waist appear a bit smaller. I swapped the Keds for sparkly white sandals and hurried back downstairs.

Agitated by the scream and subsequent commotion, Mochie ran through the house at top speed, bouncing off furniture and turning at walls like a swimmer. When the knocker sounded, I scooped him up so he wouldn't fly out into the street.

Wolf did a double take when I opened the door. Did I look so shabby the rest of the time? I hoped for a peck on the cheek, but Dad interrupted, his jaw set with determination.

"Is he a suspect? Are you going to arrest him?"

"Sorry, Mr. Bauer. He's still only a person of interest. There's just no evidence tying him to Emily's murder."

"None?" A chill ran through me. Would he get away with it? A lot of murders went unsolved, didn't they? "Do you have evidence tying anyone else to the murder?"

"Nothing definite yet. Where is he?"

I pointed upstairs and was ready to lead the way when Natasha barreled into the foyer. Dad led Wolf upstairs and left me to deal with Natasha, who demanded answers.

"Is it true that Craig came back? I told you he wouldn't leave Hannah. I knew it. I have a feel for people, you know. I can see right through them. Oh, I am so excited!"

She'd lost me. "And why would that be?"

"He's back—the wedding is on again." She pressed her fingers against her cheeks. "There's so much to do. Oh no! I have to stop Kevin from leaving." She opened the door and fled down the short walk.

"Did you find your mother?" I called after her.

She stopped for a split second, turned, and said, "No. If you see her, send her home."

I closed the door and set Mochie on the floor. He scampered up the stairs, no doubt eager to be part of the excitement.

But neither Mom nor Humphrey looked excited. They watched from the arched opening to the kitchen.

Mom sounded tired when she asked, "He's really back?"

Humphrey put an arm around her shoulders, tentatively, like he wasn't sure if he dared. "At least there won't be a wedding. We have time to prove to Hannah that he's a rogue at the very least, if not worse."

Phoebe trotted down the stairs, her face flushed. "I'm afraid not, Humphrey. We're all supposed to be at the hotel in an hour for the rehearsal."

Someone banged the door knocker. I opened it to find Darby.

"I got all the way to the train station and realized I left my purse here."

"It's your lucky day," said Phoebe. "Craig's back and the wedding's on."

Darby's mouth fell open. "Fate. It was fate that brought me back. Oy, now I have to check into the hotel again."

"If you can tolerate the sleep sofa, you can stay with us," I offered.

"I would love that. You people are so adorable. I think I'd feel much safer here." She peered past Mom and Humphrey into the kitchen. "There's my bag. I'll just pay the taxi." She scurried into the kitchen and returned in a flash, holding her wallet. "Doll," she said to Humphrey, "would you help me carry my suitcase in?"

He blushed, and I wondered if Humphrey was beginning to come out of his shell.

The next hour flew by in a crazy rush of people borrowing clothes, jewelry, and scarves to dress up their outfits. Hannah's friends called people on the guest list, and I spent the hour with a telephone glued to my ear trying to reach my vendors. Natasha might have made deals with other vendors but she would have to deal with them.

Only Wolf and Craig were exempt from the mayhem. I knocked once to get some clothes for Jen, but when I walked into the room, silence hung over us like a murky gloom. Neither of them said a word until I left. Hannah flitted about like a butterfly too nervous to land on anything. Wolf and Craig reappeared in time to leave for the hotel—both poker-faced, so I couldn't tell what had happened.

Our caravan of cars wound through Old Town to a hotel just outside the historic area—a towering structure, tall and slim, the kind that makes you wonder why it doesn't topple over. The lobby could have been anywhere, elegant and modern with lots of shiny surfaces, as appropriate in Hong Kong as in London or New York. I missed the graciousness and southern charm of Carlyle House but reminded myself that it wasn't my wedding.

Someone must have gotten word to Natasha's mother. She waited for us in the corridor outside the ballroom with Craig's father, Uncle Stan, and the minister. Friday evening weddings were about to start in the ballrooms on both sides of us. Guests in wedding finery loitered in the massive hallway that served the ballrooms. Three boys close to Jen's age and wearing suits dodged through the guests and raced the length of the long foyer in a noisy game. Our crowd bunched together to make room for them when they flew back by us making engine noises, their arms extended out to the sides.

Curiously, Wanda hadn't bothered to dress for the occasion. Her hair actually looked better than it had the day before, since she'd brushed out all the spray and it no longer looked like wax hair. But I had a feeling that Natasha would have a word with her mother about her attire. The rings and jangling bracelets had returned. Skinny bird legs stuck out of a skirt that was too short, and her top revealed cleavage that had surely been bronzed in a tanning bed.

Natasha stopped dead when she saw her mother. She parked a large box on the floor and, holding her head high, marched over to Wanda and insisted she slip on Natasha's elegant jacket. It didn't help the outfit, but it did cover up a bit of cleavage.

Mom told me to get things going, but as far as I was concerned, this was Natasha's show. I had no idea what else she and Hannah had cooked up. I was along for the ride, like the rest of the bridal party.

The minister latched on to Natasha, and the two of them herded everyone into the ballroom.

I knew it had the potential to be elegant, but at the moment the ballroom was at its worst. Partitions on both sides had been drawn closed to accommodate the other weddings, and hotel employees worked around us, unfolding chairs for another function.

Following Natasha's instructions, we lined up just inside the door. On her command, I gave Jen the signal to start the processional.

I walked along our imaginary aisle toward Craig, who appeared no worse for wear. Had he been hiding somewhere? Had he gone away to grieve for his former wife? Or had he killed her? Mom stood off to the side watching him, her lips mashed in disapproval.

I reached my position near the minister and turned to watch Hannah process toward me with Dad.

Not prone to showing his emotions, Dad usually appeared calm and in control, but today he stared daggers at Craig. I doubted that Craig noticed, because he and Hannah were beaming at one another as though Craig had never disappeared.

They reached the minister and as he explained what would happen in the ceremony, a shot fired.

TWENTY-ONE

From "The Good Life Online":

If you invite children to your wedding, ask your caterer if child-friendly food can be provided. Hot dogs and pizza are often available at a substantial discount. Keep the kids together, preferably seated at the edge of the floor plan so that they're not underfoot. Provide entertainment like coloring books, puzzles, and favor bags of munchies. A movie shown in a room nearby with popcorn will make you the coolest bride ever. And hire a couple of responsible teenagers to keep the kids busy so the adults can enjoy your big event.

—Sophie Winston

No one appeared to be injured. A sizzling sound worried me as I looked around. Familiar popping noises in quick succession came from the foyer, but I couldn't quite identify them. A tiny sparking missile shot into the ballroom and hit the ceiling over our heads.

It all happened so fast that everyone still stood in the same positions. Before we could take cover, more missiles zinged their way toward us. Three bored holes through the partitions to the weddings going on beside us.

Water began gushing from the ceiling, all over Hannah, Natasha, and Craig as though a downpour from a single cloud drenched only them. But as missiles and sparks continued to fly and we all ducked, the deluge spread and got the rest of us, too. In seconds the entire wedding party was soaked.

A couple of steps propelled us out of one waterfall and into another as the sprinkler system let loose. Natasha's perfect eye makeup ran down her cheeks in black rivulets, and the hair that was never out of place draped on her head in dark webs.

Soaking wet, I leaped toward Jen, the carpet squishing with every step I took. I tugged her into the hallway, but water rushed down on us there, too.

The stench of sulfur overwhelmed me, but even more worrisome, the acrid smell of smoke hung in the air. I hustled Jen toward the exit, looked back, and saw Natasha's box burst into flames. Crackles and whistling noises filled the air as fireworks exploded like a war zone.

I shoved Jen through the door to fresh air. Guests in wedding finery emerged, every bit as wet as we were. The little boys I'd seen earlier were propelled out by an angry woman who held two of them firmly by their collars. A siren howled and a man holding a cell phone to his ear propped a door open and urged everyone to evacuate.

Two stunned brides swathed in layers of soaked silk, tulle, and lace advanced on him. Natasha complained to him with indignation. A sour look on his face, he informed us that a sprinkler puts forth twenty-five gallons of water a minute and if Natasha thought she was staging a wedding in his hotel the next day, she would be sorely disappointed because it would take days to clean up and dry out, not to mention the smoke damage.

Which brought forth another torrent of water, this time salty and from Hannah.

Two women, who must have been the wedding planners for the other weddings, demanded explanations. The manager was at a loss. I couldn't help noticing that Natasha had been silenced. As far as I could tell, the box Natasha left in the hallway had contained fireworks, and something had set them off.

Sirens grew in intensity and in a matter of minutes, firefighters rushed in.

Standing next to me, Wanda chanted, "Monday for health, Tuesday for wealth, Wednesday best of all, Thursday for losses, Friday for crosses, Saturday for no luck at all."

"They never should have scheduled the wedding for a Saturday," said Robert, offering Wanda a handkerchief to wipe soot off her face. "Did Hannah ever find her engagement ring?"

I was surprised by his question. I'd forgotten that the loss of the engagement ring meant loss of the husband. Surely Robert didn't believe that.

Wanda batted her lashes at him as she wiped her face. "How thoughtful."

"A gentleman always carries a handkerchief for occasions such as this."

As I surveyed our wet and dirty group, I felt a twinge of guilt for being one of the few people who weren't upset. If they couldn't have the wedding in the hotel, they were out of luck and would have to postpone the wedding indefinitely.

~~~

An hour later, we were home. I'd pulled on dry clothes and skipped a shower so the others could use the sole shower in my house. Now that there clearly wouldn't be a wedding, the pressure was off. For the first time in days, I relaxed with my feet up.

Bernie, who'd heard about the catastrophe, lit a blaze in the fire pit in my backyard. Nina, Humphrey, Bernie, and I settled in with martinis.

Everyone else was still changing into dinner clothes. Hannah's girlfriends insisted that she, Craig, Darby, and Kevin go out with them to take their minds off the wedding that wouldn't be, but I'd begged off.

Daisy lay at my feet and pricked her ears at the sound of high heels on the brick pavers.

"Well, well, if this isn't the hang-Craig posse." Hannah planted her hands on her hips and a pashmina slid down over her bare arms. Now that Craig was back, she'd ditched my bright clothes and changed into the pastel maiden again.

I bit my lip. It wasn't over yet. We still had time to find evidence tying Craig to Emily's murder.

"This is a little hard to ask, knowing how you feel, but, Sophie, could we have the wedding here tomorrow?" Light from the fire flickered across Hannah's face. She wasn't kidding. I wanted so badly to point out that if she had stuck to our original plans, the wedding would still be on at Carlyle House. But that would have been cruel.

Fortunately, Mom appeared behind her, dressed for dinner. "Honey, I think it's time to accept that it wasn't meant to be. At least not this weekend."

Hannah's chin tilted upward in defiance. "We still have the caterer and the florist, and our families are here. We just need a place. Natasha's backyard would be beautiful, but it's got police tape around it and everyone would be thinking about Emily and what happened there."

Phoebe wandered into the firelight and stood by Hannah as though she'd come to support her.

Hoping to put a quick stop to this nonsense, I hauled out

the big guns. "Did you know that Emily checked into the B&B under the name of Lina Kowalski?"

I heard Mom gasp.

Hannah counterattacked. "Why do you insist on casting Craig as an ogre?"

"Because he killed his ex-wife?"

"He did not kill her. And for your information, Miss Know-It-All, Lina Kowalski was Emily's maiden name."

Mom scowled. "No one changes a first name when she gets married."

"Emily did." Hannah pulled the pashmina up. "She didn't like the name Lina."

That didn't make sense. "If she didn't like it, why did she go back to it?"

"It was her middle name or something. I'm sure I don't understand the workings of the mind of a troubled woman. Is this your way of saying that we can't have the wedding here?"

Phoebe looked out into the dark yard. "Do you think you could accommodate everyone back here?"

I wished they would shove off to their dinners. "Good point, Phoebe. It would be cramped."

"How many guests are still in town?" Bernie asked. "We could set up eight rows of chairs, about eight across with a small aisle in between. If you did that way back in the yard near the potting shed, there would still be room for long tables near the house for the dinner after the ceremony."

I shot a dagger-filled glance Bernie's way.

Hannah didn't wait for anyone to argue. "Wonderful! You're my hero." She bent to kiss Bernie and flounced off quickly with Phoebe, no doubt so I couldn't refuse.

"Good job, Bernie," I said, sarcasm dripping from every word.

Mom groaned. "Don't blame him. Hannah is determined to marry this man. We might as well get it over with. Putting it off is just delaying the inevitable." She ambled away, muttering, "I don't know where Hannah got that stubborn streak."

The news that the wedding was on again probably ratcheted up the festivities at the last-night-of-freedom parties, but it put a damper on the rest of us. Voices died away and car doors slammed as they left.

"We have to stop her." Eerie shadows danced across Humphrey's pale face. "I could detain the minister."

Nina snorted. "You mean kidnap him?"

"Not permanently. I could offer to drive him and simply get lost for a while."

Bernie shook his head. "Sophie's mum is spot on. You'd only delay the wedding. Hannah needs evidence."

Nina tipped her head back to empty her martini glass. "We could have a look around."

"You mean Natasha's yard?" I asked. "The cops have searched it thoroughly, I'm sure."

Bernie tamped down the fire. "Let's go."

"Right now?" Humphrey's voice squeaked.

"Why not?" Bernie beckoned to Humphrey. "Natasha and Mars went to dinner with Natasha's mum and that Mordecai chap, and Kevin is with Craig."

I jumped up. "I'll grab a couple of flashlights and meet you out front."

I went into the house, located two flashlights in a kitchen drawer, and grabbed a box of freezer bags. I didn't bother locking up because we would be right across the street. But I clicked a leash on Daisy and met the others on the sidewalk.

Nina pointed at the freezer bags. "Are you out of dog poop bags?"

I handed her a flashlight. "We're looking for evidence. We don't want our fingerprints on anything we might find."

The four of us trooped along the sidewalk past the yellow police tape that still hung in front of the house. Since

Bernie resided in back, we theorized that he had every right to bring his friends over for a visit, but we rounded the corner and walked down to the alley to enter from the rear.

Natasha and Mars had built a red brick garage with an apartment above, where Bernie currently resided. An arched gate led into a covered passage on the south side of the garage. It creaked when I swung it open. A huge trash can sat just inside. To the left, a door led somewhere, the garage, I presumed, and to the right, a sliding glass door opened into a gardening room, complete with running water. Stairs led upward to Bernie's apartment.

I slid the door open to check out the gardening area in greater detail. Specifically, I wanted to know if Natasha's wired ribbons were readily available to anyone who happened by.

Bernie flicked on an overhead light.

"The woman has more ribbons than a craft store." Nina peered at rainbows of ribbons mounted on the wall.

"Do you see a coil of brown ribbon?" asked Humphrey.

Spools of ribbons hung on dowels in five wide rows. Every color in the universe appeared to be represented, even the much maligned pink.

If there had been a matching brown ribbon, and there must have been once because she'd made the topiary with one, it wasn't there now. Other shades hung in abundance, but nothing matched the ribbon on the topiary.

Daisy pawed at the glass door, and Bernie let her out.

"Better hang on to her leash," I cautioned him. "Natasha will pitch a fit if Daisy poops out there."

He grinned. "Natasha doesn't frighten me. I think it irritates her that I refuse to be at her beck and call like Mars."

We followed Daisy into the backyard, the two flashlights radiating bright orbs that roamed about against the dark house. Yellow tape still wrapped the doomed pergola.

"How come they didn't tape the garage?" I asked. "Seems likely the killer could have strangled Emily back there. No one would have noticed."

"I thought the same thing. But mine is not to question the authorities," said Bernie.

"Do you suppose he grabbed her when she was walking by, or did he kill her somewhere else and bring her here?" I mused aloud.

Bernie took the flashlight I held and shone it on the grass. "There aren't any drag marks. If he strangled her elsewhere, he must have carried her in."

Nina pointed a flashlight at the flower beds that ran along the brick side walls of the garden. "Why would anyone bring her to Natasha and Mars's pergola? Especially Craig. If he killed her elsewhere, he'd have left her body as far away from here as possible. You'd think a doctor would be smart enough to figure that out."

"That would mean he saw her, either on the sidewalk or in the back, grabbed her, strangled her, and then strung her up." Humphrey spoke with the objectivity of a person who deals with death on a daily basis, but I shuddered at the thought.

Bernie kneeled on the grass next to Daisy and detached her leash.

I grabbed her collar immediately. "I don't want her trampling Natasha's flowers."

"She saw everything." He pointed the flashlight at the basement window. "She was right there. She saw the killer hang Emily. Let her go. I want to see what she does."

She did what I expected. Squatted and did her business. I pulled out one of the freezer bags and collected it.

Meanwhile, Daisy wandered toward the flower beds, as I'd feared. She didn't trample anything, though. She delicately picked her way through flowers, sniffing care-fully.

Unfortunately, Bernie's theory didn't pay off. If Daisy had seen the murder as Bernie suspected, she wasn't giving us any clues.

Bernie snapped the leash on her again, and we returned the way we'd come.

I closed the gate behind us. "We knew it was a long shot."

We trudged along the alley, but when we turned onto the sidewalk, Bernie couldn't coax Daisy along. He let her pull him over to the fence, and she began to scratch at the soil in between old rosebushes. Nina turned a flashlight on her. Daisy dug with furious energy, her rump in the air, her front paws churning.

I grabbed her collar.

"Wait! Stop." Nina angled her flashlight. "Do you see that?"

I didn't see anything except the mess Daisy had made.

"Right there," said Humphrey, "in the bush next to your left foot."

The three of them watched me, their heads all cocked in the same direction.

I kneeled on gravel and cold dirt Daisy had dislodged and saw it. A thin gleam of silver glinted under the glare of the light. Reversing a plastic freezer bag over my hand, I said, "One of you bring me a piece of ribbon so we can flag the location for Wolf in case it's important." Reaching my bare arm deep into the thorny stems, I felt smooth metal.

Nina tapped my shoulder and handed me a ribbon. "It's pink. I'm hoping Natasha will be appalled."

Grinning, I looped it over the branch, certain the thorns would hold it in place, grabbed the silver thing, and yanked. Thorns scratched my arm and caught my hair. I pulled back and staggered to my feet.

Bernie kicked the dirt back where it belonged, and Nina held out her hand.

I removed the freezer bag from my hand so that the item was encased inside and dropped it into her open palm. Both flashlights shone on it. The initial C was attached to a matching silver chain, which had been broken near the latch.

TWENTY-TWO

From *"Ask Natasha"*:

Dear Natasha,

I'm trying to figure out how to allocate my wedding funds. What's the one thing I shouldn't skimp on?

—Breaking the Bank in Banner Elk

Dear Breaking,

Professional lighting is a must. Color washes on the walls, pin spot lighting on ice sculptures and floral arrangements, and special spots for your first dance are things you can't achieve without a professional. Lighting creates a mood and ambiance that you and your guests will never forget.

—Natasha

Had I broken it when I pulled it off the rosebush? Or had Emily done it when she ripped it off her killer's neck?

"It looks like a man's, but it's not Mars's, that's for sure," said Nina.

I giggled at the idea of starchy Mars wearing a macho chain.

Bernie ran a hand through his messy hair, looking rather ghostly lit by the beam below his face.

"I guess we've got him now. No wonder he took off." I gripped Daisy's lead tighter and told her what a good girl she was.

Running his fingertips across the top of the bag to seal it, Bernie said, "To tell the truth, I didn't think Craig would be so daft."

It did seem rather obvious. "I guess he killed her in the heat of the moment." Had Lina said something that angered him? Was her mere presence enough for him to be violent?

"Then why did Craig come back?" asked Humphrey. "You don't think he intends to whisk Hannah away and hide with her?"

Despite the warm night air, I couldn't help shivering. "Stop that!"

"No, Humphrey's right," said Nina. "If Craig murdered Emily, why would he leave and then return? What did he do while he was gone that gave him the courage to come back?"

"Maybe he worked out an alibi," I suggested.

Humphrey picked up the bag and borrowed Nina's flashlight for a better look. "She cannot marry him. We have to stop her. That vile man has such a hold over poor Hannah that she can't see the truth. If this doesn't convince her of his guilt, nothing will."

One kiss in the shed and Humphrey was smitten. I felt terrible for him. Humphrey wasn't Hannah's type. To her detriment, she gravitated to men who were wealthy or flashy, the type women fawned over and other men envied.

Even if she dumped Craig, poor Humphrey wouldn't stand
a chance with her.

We walked home somberly.

I called Wolf immediately but got his voice mail. My
desires and fears about our relationship played havoc with
my mind, and in the end I babbled about finding a potential clue.

Even though it was early summer and too warm to need
a fire, Bernie insisted on building a tiny one in the kitchen
fireplace. Meanwhile I boiled water for linguini and Humphrey set the table. Nina poured each of us a glass of Our
Dog Blue Riesling.

I sliced a loaf of Italian bread so that it was still held
together by the bottom crust and spread piquant garlic butter between the slices. The bread warmed in the oven while
I tossed a salad of young mesclun lettuce leaves, chunks of
juicy mango, crunchy red pepper, and sweet mango vinai-
grette.

"I've been trying to think of other people with names
that begin with C," said Humphrey. "But I can't come up
with anyone. Unless it was a stranger, that necklace points
to Craig."

"He must realize he lost it. Bernie, did you hear anyone
prowling about in the yard last night?"

"I didn't hear a thing. You think Craig was looking
for it?"

While we talked, I poured olive oil into a large sauté
pan. When it warmed, I sprinkled in chopped garlic and
stirred until it infused the oil and the scent drifted to my
hungry friends.

I added salt and leftover shrimp from the night before
just long enough to coat and warm it. The al dente linguini
went into the sauté pan next to soak up all the zesty flavor.
A few turns mixed it and I poured the pasta into a large
bowl from which everyone could serve themselves. Bernie

pulled the bread from the oven and set it on the table next to the steaming bowl of pasta and the colorful salad.

We stuffed ourselves with comforting linguini, yet managed to indulge in leftover Chocolate Mousse Cheesecake while we engaged in wild speculation about Craig and the mysterious Emily/Lina.

Mom and Dad returned with Jen, surprisingly gloomy after their dinner out. My parents joined us but picked at their cheesecake without enthusiasm. Jen plopped in the middle of the floor, cross-legged, and let Daisy lick a bit of the nonchocolate portion of the cheesecake off her finger.

"What's wrong?" I demanded.

Dad shifted uncomfortably in his chair. "We ran into Wolf. One of the neighbors claims he saw Hannah walking in the vicinity of Natasha and Mars's house at the time of the murder."

"It must have been someone else," I blurted. "Hannah was here with Nina and me."

"Which neighbor?" asked Nina in a suspicious tone.

Dad toyed with his fork. "Wolf wouldn't say."

"Honestly," huffed Mom, "even if it was Hannah, it's meaningless. Being seen on the street doesn't mean one has committed a crime."

Humphrey's fingers coiled into fists. "Does this mean Hannah is a suspect?"

Mom rubbed her forehead. "I'm beginning to believe Wanda's ridiculous nonsense about bad luck. It's like we're cursed. Every time I think things might work out, something goes haywire."

Dad sighed. "Let's get this wedding over with tomorrow and put it all behind us."

Only one problem with that, Dad. The murderer will be part of our family.

Mom sagged, her eyes weary. "It's time for bed, Jen."

Jen protested, but Nina caught on fast. Claiming fatigue, she prodded Bernie and Humphrey to see her home safely. Promising they'd arrive early in the morning, Nina turned the silver necklace over to me and departed. When I turned, Dad comforted Mom, her head leaning against his shoulder.

I debated taking the chain up to my bedroom, but since someone had searched my nightstand, I hid it in a low kitchen drawer where I kept cake-decorating items. I couldn't imagine anyone poking around there.

I considered calling Wolf again but decided against it. I didn't want to be a bother. Maybe he imagined I had called him to vent about the neighbor who said he'd seen Hannah the morning of Emily's murder. Or maybe he was avoiding me. I tamped out the fire and trudged up to my bedroom, wondering how I'd managed to make such a mess of things with Wolf. I'd foolishly thought this weekend would bring us closer together. Instead, the possibility of a relationship had fizzled to a dim ember. The next time I saw him, I would be witty and clever and charming. I climbed into bed and as I drifted off to sleep, I wondered if Mom could be right about wearing makeup and sexier clothes.

I was up at the crack of dawn. As I pulled on a denim skort, a striped cotton shirt, and comfortable old Keds, I harbored ill thoughts toward Natasha. Hannah's wedding day could have gone swimmingly if we hadn't lost Carlyle House as a venue. Natasha thought she knew better than anyone else, yet I was the one picking up the pieces of the wedding I'd planned so carefully. I pushed my ire aside. I had far too much to do and couldn't dwell on Natasha and her fireworks.

Jen bounced into my room full of energy. My admonitions to be quiet worked until we hit the kitchen. Jen bubbled with excitement about the fancy dress and shoes she would wear later in the day.

I asked her to set the table and put out some extra plates and silverware, because I wasn't sure who might show up. Meanwhile, I put on coffee and tea, poured orange juice, and mixed flour, milk, eggs, and blueberries for pancakes.

In short order, spicy turkey sausages sizzled in a pan and the aroma of fresh coffee waltzed through the air.

Bernie tapped on the window in the kitchen door. Jen unlocked it and let him in and Daisy out while I spooned pancake batter onto the hot griddle.

Bernie poured coffee into persimmon Fiestaware mugs for us and fetched a pitcher of milk from the fridge.

I flipped pancakes onto a matching plate and handed it to him. "Thanks for being such a good sport and pitching in."

He helped himself to sausages. "Mars is coming in a few minutes."

I almost sliced myself with the knife I had picked up to cut a cantaloupe. "Mars? The man has two left hands."

Bernie grinned and opened the door for Mars. Daisy trotted in behind him, followed by Hermione, Nina, and Humphrey. Mochie and Hermione touched noses, which appeared to satisfy both. Mochie jumped onto the window seat, waiting for his share of attention and, no doubt, a bite of turkey sausage.

Nina passed out tiny bags of kibble. "I want everyone to try to give Hermione treats today so she'll get the idea that people can be good and she doesn't have to be afraid."

"Won't that be too many treats?" asked Jen.

Nina smiled at her. "You're gonna be a veterinarian, kiddo. It's the kibble she would have eaten for breakfast with a teensy treat or two mixed in for variety."

Bernie pocketed the kibble. "Sophie, when you call the chair rental guy, ask if they have some kind of arch we can use for the ceremony. It would make a big difference to have a backdrop."

Nina held up her cell phone. "I hereby appoint myself

vendor liaison. Bossing people around is one of my specialties." I handed her the list of numbers and she dialed immediately. "Mars, would you bring me a cup of coffee? Milk and sugar, please."

Mars sniffed the air. "I'm starved. Last night Nat insisted on a pretentious restaurant that served food the size of a quarter. They think they can charge more because they draw a design on the dish with a useless sauce the color of grass."

Humphrey slumped next to Mochie. "Can't we stop this disaster from taking place? What if we refused to help?"

Jen piped up, "But Aunt Hannah wants to get married."

While I cut juicy mango and ripe kiwis to add to the fruit salad, Mars heaped pancakes onto plates and passed them to the others. "So what's the plan?" he asked. "Nat will be over here to help a little later."

Nina paused between mouthfuls. "Oh swell, a show! I missed the one at the hotel. What's she going to set on fire this time?"

Still wielding the knife, I whirled toward Mars. "Call her right now and tell her she's not needed. I'm not working like a maniac so she can come over and change everything."

The furrow between Mars's eyebrows deepened. "I think it would be good for her."

"Mars, we wouldn't be in this mess if she hadn't canceled Carlyle House or taken those ridiculous fireworks to the hotel."

"The fireworks weren't her fault. Those boys who were running wild set them off. She couldn't foresee that. She wanted to light them later, as a surprise for Hannah and Craig."

I sighed and helped myself to pancakes. Natasha ought to feel responsible for the disaster at the hotel. I knew I would have. Mars probably thought it would make her feel better to contribute. It would be kind of me to put up with Natasha, but we were sticking to the original pink color scheme if I had to lock Natasha in the shed to do it. I plopped the bowl of fruit salad in the middle of the table, sat down, and poured blueberry syrup over my pancakes, glad Mom wasn't up yet to pour on the guilt.

Craig strolled in, all smiles, and took some ribbing about his last day of freedom in a good-natured way. He sat down to eat but avoided my eyes when he asked, "Did you need something from my room last night, Sophie?"

TWENTY-THREE

Dear Sophie,

I can't believe the cost of flowers. Everyone says not to do them yourself, but I don't see any way around that. Is it tacky to use flowers from my mother's garden?

—Tossing the Bouquet in Basye

Dear Tossing,

It's never tacky to use flowers from your garden! They don't have to come from a florist to be beautiful. Time your wedding to coincide with flowers you love. On the day before the wedding, invite friends to an informal flower-arranging party. Use seashells, marbles, or glass vase gems to weigh the vases down so they won't tip over. For a country wedding, choose canning jars and wildflowers. There's no end to the possibilities—wicker baskets, terra-cotta bowls, tiny galvanized buckets, or wrap empty tin cans with anything from satin ribbons to bundled twigs.

—Sophie

I nearly choked on a pancake. Was that Craig's oh-so-subtle way of telling me he'd noticed that I went through his closet before he left?

"No." I hoped I sounded convincing. After all, I hadn't snooped in his room since his return—though his question made me wonder if I should.

"The door to that little cabinet in the corner was open, I thought it might have been you."

It certainly hadn't been me, but that news, coupled with the fact that I'd found my nightstand drawer open, suggested that someone was looking for something. Someone too sloppy or too hurried to bother closing everything. Darby and Craig's father had both been in his room at some point. I looked up at Craig, who was already laughing about an incident at dinner the night before. Was he devious enough to make this announcement in front of people so we wouldn't suspect him of snooping in my bedroom?

The rumble of a truck and screeching brakes signaled the arrival of the party rental delivery van. Carrying my cup of coffee with me, I went out the front door and something hard smacked me in the forehead. I stumbled, but even though I regained my footing, coffee spilled down my shirt. I looked back, rubbing my head. Someone had hung a rosary from the door frame. Of all the silly things. I snatched it down and left it on the console in the foyer. My head still smarted as I ventured out to the street to show them the way to the garden.

Bernie met us in the backyard with a diagram. "I ran up a plan last night."

Bernie never ceased to amaze me. His general

appearance probably made me underestimate him. He reminded me of a grown-up Dennis the Menace. Spunky,
sweet, and more clever than anyone might suspect.

He took over, and in minutes two neat rows of white
garden chairs began to form. I verified the presence of a
runner but told them we would roll it out after the rest of
the work had been completed.

My heart sank when the delivery guys hauled in the
wedding arch. It was the right size, but that was the only
thing about it that worked. Finished in matte bronze that
looked more like rust, the top arched in swirls that ended
in a gaudy heart. Somehow, I didn't think that was what
Hannah had in mind when she'd asked for a garden wedding. But it was too late to make changes. It was that arch
or none at all. I tried to look at the bright side. Hannah and
Craig would have some unbelievable wedding stories to
tell their children.

I set up the ladder in the potting shed so I could reach
storage boxes. Carrying a coffee mug, Mars arrived just in
time for me to hand him an enormous box of Christmas
lights and tiny fairy lights on white strings. When I climbed
down, he moved the ladder so he could change the bulb in
the overhead light.

"Be careful," I cautioned as he climbed up. Mars wasn't
exactly the handiest guy. I held the replacement bulb to
give him in exchange for the one that had burned out.

"That's odd, it was loose like the other one. Try the
switch."

I flicked the switch and the light came on.

Mars shook his head like I was incompetent and began
the descent. His foot slipped off a tread and I rushed toward the ladder to prevent him from falling. He slid into
my waiting arms and stopped.

For a long moment, we stood in a horribly familiar clutch.
The scent of his skin evoked a rush of memories, and it felt
like the world had dissolved and left just the two of us.

A discreet cough from the doorway caused us to jump apart. Wolf leaned against the door frame. "Sorry to interrupt."

To make matters worse, Wanda stood next to him.

"We were changing the lightbulb . . ." My voice faded under their disbelieving glares. I still held the lightbulb we hadn't needed. Painfully aware of what they must have been thinking, I set it on the table and picked up the box of lights. Wolf and Wanda parted as I walked toward them, but I knew that one innocent moment would cost Mars and me.

When I emerged, Bernie seized lights for the wedding arch and Kevin showed up. Craig and Kevin took the rest of the lights and started stringing them overhead.

I motioned to Wolf to follow me. The walk across the lawn and into the kitchen was so awkward, it felt like miles. I was desperately trying to think of an explanation for what Wolf had seen, but everything seemed lame.

Mom was putting away the last of the breakfast dishes when we entered the kitchen. She winked at me, clueless about Wolf and me. I hurried to the drawer and, to my utter shock, found it hanging open.

"Why is this open?" I blurted.

"I guess you left it that way, sweetheart," Mom said, drying a plate.

My heart thudded in my chest as I lifted the lid on the icing-tip box where I'd stashed the evidence. Fortunately, whoever had gone through the drawer hadn't found it. I handed it to Wolf as Mom looked on.

"You didn't touch it?" he asked.

"No. And we left a ribbon to mark the spot where we found it."

"You realize that you were compromising a crime scene by going behind the yellow tape."

I explained that we did not enter the area marked off by yellow tape and that Daisy had alerted us to the item in the alley.

He held up the packet, and Mom studied it. Even Mochie jumped to the counter to peer at it. Wolf stuffed the package into his pocket and ran a hand over Mochie's gleaming fur. "I doubt that it has anything to do with Emily's death. My men did a thorough sweep. They would have seen it."

"Are you saying someone put it there afterward? Like to throw everyone off?" asked Mom.

"I don't think we'll even be that lucky. It was probably there for years and no one noticed."

"Impossible," I pronounced before realizing that contradicting Wolf's professional opinion probably wasn't the way to endear myself to him. "It's sterling silver, it would have tarnished."

"How do you know it's sterling silver?" asked Wolf.

Mom laughed. "My girls know their jewelry. It would be marked 925."

He pulled the package out and peered at the necklace. His gaze flicked to me and I knew he'd found the sterling mark. He tucked it away again and let out a long, slow sigh. Saying good-bye very politely, Wolf let himself out the kitchen door, and I had the horrible feeling that my last chance at dating him had just burst like a soap bubble.

When I returned to the backyard, Craig was proudly handing out the knives he'd purchased for the men in the wedding party and, to my surprise, they turned out to be very practical for cutting ribbons and wires.

Dad planted shepherd's hooks along both sides of the aisle between the chairs and hung baskets of hot pink gerbera daisies I'd ordered from a local nursery.

Prompted by a desperate call from Nina, my favorite florist showed up early with flowers for Bernie and Dad to twine onto the ghastly arch.

I stopped by the potting shed to retrieve the coffee mugs Mars and I had left there and found Joel looking around, a large shovel in his hands. "Planting something?" I teased.

Joel returned the shovel to the corner and leaned the handle against the wall. "Nosing around, actually. Do you think the shed predates the house?" He walked out with me and gazed up at my house. "It's just so cool to think that people lived here during the Civil War."

I asked for a hand and cringed when Mars volunteered. He followed me to the kitchen to deposit the mugs and then to the basement. I debated whether to bring up that awkward moment earlier, but in the end, he didn't say anything about it and I chickened out. We both knew it was nothing and best left alone. We found boxes of mirrors and crystals hung on clear filament that I had used at a formal black and white function, but when we emerged from the basement, Natasha waited in my kitchen, arms crossed over her chest, her face taut.

Wanda must have told her about Mars and me in the shed. I collected myself and waited for her to yell at us for being alone together in the basement.

"I don't suppose you saw my mother down there?"

"Took off again, did she?" asked Mars.

"I don't know why no one wants to be at our house. I fixed a lovely brunch of scallops in tarragon and wine, goat ricotta blintzes, and strawberries Romanoff. The cute pots of herbs in my tablescape took me three months to grow. But the only one who bothered to show was Mordecai. He fed his little dog my scallops and blintzes."

"No strawberries?" I joked.

"Seems the dog doesn't care for strawberries. And neither does Mordecai."

I felt sorry for Natasha. I knew how much work she'd put into her fancy brunch. It must have hurt that Kevin and Mars chose to help us instead of appreciating her efforts.

But then she said, "Honestly, Sophie, don't you have any clothes that aren't worn out or grubby? What is that brown spot on your shirt? If you need money, you could try to write a more sophisticated column. Mine was just picked up by newspapers in North Carolina and Georgia."

My moment of compassion passed.

When we walked outside, Craig and his lighting team were working on the small passage that led from the gate to the backyard. Humphrey helped them but scowled at Craig and, for once, didn't even notice me walk by.

Hannah, Darby, Phoebe, and the bridesmaids launched themselves at the boxes of mirrors and crystals. Everyone in the wedding party seemed to be in good humor and enjoying themselves, except for Phoebe and Joel, who were barely speaking to each other. Even Hermione didn't seem to mind the chaos. Darby crouched and patiently held out a piece of kibble. Hermione debated the risk but after a few seconds, she couldn't ignore the lure of food, grabbed the morsel, and ran.

Natasha sidled up to me. "What a pity everything is in pink tones. My pheasant feathers and curly willow branches will arrive in a few hours. We can swap them out then."

It took all my self-control not to lash out at her. Calmly, and in as sweet a tone as I could muster, I said, "If you even try a swap, I swear I'll toss you out of here on your fancy fanny. If you want to pitch in, then please do. But I am not going to let you criticize when everyone else is working so hard to make this a lovely day."

She craned her neck, flabbergasted. "I believe I have some hanging votive holders that would be darling suspended from tree branches. I'll bring them by as soon as I find my mother."

She strode away, but I didn't have time to give Natasha or her missing mother any more thought because the linens had arrived.

Bernie had arranged rectangular tables in a large U shape on my patio. Unfortunately, the tablecloths were round. With Phoebe's help, I spread them so they overlapped and we pinned small bouquets of blossoms where they joined.

"Joel seems nice," I said, pinning blooms.

"I was hoping the wedding might make him think about popping the question but now I'm having second thoughts."

"Problems?"

"He's been different, moody and distant." She shifted to a whisper. "Last night we had a big argument about whether Hannah should marry Craig after all that's happened, and he's completely against the wedding."

"Oh, Phoebe, he's not the only one."

Phoebe flushed. "I'm beginning to think he's not the marrying kind. It's his dream to reopen the family jewelry store, and I had fantasies of working together. But when he was talking about Hannah and Craig, he might as well have been talking about us."

"Have you met his family?"

She pinned a bouquet onto the tablecloth. "They're wonderful people. His father died of a heart attack a few years ago. Joel says it was the stress of a lawsuit that caused them to lose the family business, but I've seen pictures and his dad was more than a little portly. I nag Joel about getting exercise and eating right. That kind of thing can run in the family, and he is far too devoted to French fries and any meat that comes from a pig." Phoebe straightened up and wiped her cheek with the back of her hand. "I guess I won't have to worry about that anymore. We're barely speaking at this point."

I glanced up at Joel, who stood on a ladder and wrapped a strand of lights onto a tree. He was out of shape, but his thick neck suggested he'd worked out. "Did he play football?"

"He didn't want to be known as the girlie jewelry boy growing up, so he was very involved in sports."

Even though he wasn't tall, I would have considered

him brawny. The additional pounds rounded out a sweet face, and I could see why she found him appealing.

She nudged me. "Don't tell Hannah we're breaking up. I don't want to spoil her special day."

Uncle Stan and Robert arrived carrying boxes, which Natasha had sent over. Mom filmed giant, macho Stan relaying Natasha's explanations to Hannah and her bridesmaids. Stan held up a completed example of a plain tin and glass lantern tied with a broad pink ribbon to suspend it from a tree limb. A pink votive candle rested inside.

I could hardly believe my eyes. No feathers and not even a whisper of brown.

The girls assembled the lanterns, and Robert patiently hung them where they directed.

By one in the afternoon, the backyard had been transformed into a wedding wonderland. More lovely than I'd ever imagined and not a bit tacky. Perfect for a gracious southern garden wedding.

Wanda must have turned up at Natasha's house because the two of them surprised us by spreading blankets on the grass and serving homemade gourmet pizzas for lunch. Smoked-salmon pizza, shitake and crimini mushroom pizza, even a Tex-Mex pizza with a punch of jalapeño peppers was dished out, along with freshly squeezed lemonade.

I hated it when Natasha demonstrated thoughtfulness. It made it so much harder to deal with her haughtier side. Nabbing a piece of mushroom pizza, I settled on the blanket and almost croaked when Mars sat next to me. Jen plopped down on the other side. Sipping refreshing lemonade, I looked around. It was almost like we'd thrown a special party. Natasha and Wanda were the only ones who didn't look a little bit grubby, but everyone seemed to be having a good time.

Between bites of pizza, Jen said, "This is the best wedding I've ever been to."

That wasn't saying much. At ten, I doubted she'd been to many.

But Mars leaned over and said, "Me, too."

Uncle Stan rose and clinked a fork against his lemonade glass. "I would like to take this opportunity to welcome Hannah into the Beacham family. And to show our love for Hannah, we would like to present her with a token of our affection. That all-important something new to wear on her wedding day. Hannah?" Stan held out a box so small that it could only contain jewelry.

Hannah stood up, kissed Uncle Stan's cheek, and accepted the box. She pulled off the ribbon and opened it. Her eyes bright with excitement, she removed a necklace and held it up for everyone to see.

On the end of a gold chain a diamond sparkled in the sunlight. Just like the one Emily had worn.

TWENTY-FOUR

From *"Ask Natasha"*:

Dear Natasha,

My daughter wants a white reception. White linens, white flowers, white chairs, white china—you get the very stark picture. I'm afraid it will look too sterile. What can I do to make it festive?

—Color-Crazed Mom in Colomokee

Dear Color-Crazed Mom,

The trick to working with white is to add a metal. Gold, silver, bronze, or copper will add the spark of interest you're looking for. Use metallic balls in centerpieces. Adorn place cards with a tiny glint of metal. Use it on napkin rings or ribbons or tablecloth overlays. You can buy sheets of 24-karat gold leaf that are perfect for this kind of application. The hint of sparkle will make all the difference.

—Natasha

While the others admired the necklace, I stared at it in horror. My flesh crawled and I could only think of Emily. Was it the one she had worn? Or the necklace in Craig's tuxedo? Were there three different necklaces or only one?

I sat on the blanket, paralyzed with fear for Hannah. The necklace was a lovely gesture, but to me it symbolized Emily's tragic demise. I longed to yank it off Hannah's neck and had to convince myself that it didn't mark her for death.

Phoebe, Joel, Jen, and my parents admired the generous gift. Nearly salivating, Wanda and Natasha edged in for a closer look.

But Nina, who'd seen the similar necklace on Emily, crouched behind me and said, "Think that's the necklace of a dead woman?"

Mars leaned to the side to see Nina's face. "Why would you say something so awful?"

"She means Emily. She was wearing a necklace like that when we met her."

Lowering his voice, he asked, "And you think that's Emily's necklace? Oh, that's too morbid. You two are sick."

I hoped he was right. Still, the necklace scared me. Hannah basked in the attention she was receiving as the bride, but the diamond that lay in the hollow of her neck seemed as sinister as a poisonous snake.

Mars's expression of disgust turned to amusement. "Nat's not going to be happy when she realizes she lost her boy toy." He cocked his head toward Kevin, who was gazing at Darby with more than a passing interest.

"At least someone is happy," I grumbled. "You're upset with Natasha, Phoebe and Joel aren't speaking, my relationship with Wolf is down the tubes, and poor Humphrey's hopes have been dashed—altogether a lousy weekend for relationships."

Our workers scattered to rest, shower, and dress for the wedding. Near the hydrangea that climbed the wall of the potting shed, Hannah and Craig shared a romantic kiss that made me itch to get into Craig's room again to find out if the diamond necklace was still in his pocket. I sprinted to the house, but the two of them followed. Puttering around the kitchen, I surreptitiously kept tabs on Craig. When he called Hannah and Jen into the living room, I thought my chance had arrived and I started up the stairs. Unfortunately, Mom spotted me and pulled me into the living room with the rest of my family.

In front of his little audience, Craig said, "I want to apologize for leaving yesterday. I know this won't make it up to you but I wanted you to have these." He handed Hannah and Jen white boxes.

Jen ripped hers open faster than I'd have thought possible. "Ohhh, it matches my dress." She lifted a small silver tiara set with faceted rose and clear crystals and placed it carefully on top of her auburn hair. Twirling like a ballerina, she asked, "Do I look like a princess?"

I had ordered a special crown of pink and white roses for Jen to wear, pinned on with sparkly hair ornaments. I hated for it to go to waste, but Craig's heart was in the right place.

Hannah lifted a similar but larger tiara from her box. I had to hand it to Craig, the tiaras were the perfect touch of bling. Not too flashy or pretentious and they fit the pink theme of the wedding.

Tears rolled down Hannah's cheeks, and I thought I might be ill at the way she gazed adoringly at Craig. I turned to find Humphrey looking as sick as I felt.

"We have to put a stop to this," he muttered as we retreated to the kitchen where Wanda watched Mochie eat kibble out of an open-toed white satin shoe adorned by a swirl of Swarovski crystals. I'd been with Hannah when she paid a small fortune for them.

"What on earth?" I reached out to rescue the shoe, but Wanda caught my arm.

"Don't disturb him. It's good luck to have a house cat eat out of your shoe."

"Is it bad luck if he chews up the shoe?" I asked.

Wanda clucked at me. "Don't be silly. Cats don't chew shoes like dogs do. And the way things have been going, poor Hannah needs all the good luck she can get. Natasha even hung a rosary over the door for good weather."

I rubbed my forehead. "I banged into that thing this morning."

Wanda smiled. "But the weather is great. Natasha is hanging a horseshoe out back right now."

If I knew Natasha, she was ripping out all our hard work and replacing everything with feathers. Ignoring Humphrey's pleas for my attention, I whipped outside, Daisy running alongside me, and barged into the backyard.

To my utter amazement, Natasha was draping boxwood swags on the shed, attaching them with light pink grosgrain ribbon. I sputtered, at a complete loss for words.

"I hope you don't mind my dressing up the shed. It's so plain."

On the window facing the wedding arch, she'd hung a large heart-shaped wreath covered with blooms of pink in every conceivable shade and shape. I had filled the window box below weeks ago, but now a horseshoe nestled, open side up, among the rambling petunias.

At this point, I felt decorating the shed was overkill, but it seemed entirely too ungracious and unkind to say so.

"No feathers?" I asked.

Natasha stopped fussing with the swag. "Honestly, Sophie, I don't know how you deal with vendors all the time. They promised me they'd be at the hotel early this morning, but when they arrived and realized no functions would be held there, they took my feathers back to the warehouse and didn't even bother to call me. They're supposed to be here any minute, but I have my doubts."

I wanted to chew her out again, but at this point the yard was decorated to the hilt and I couldn't imagine where she thought she could use feathers. I thought I might get further with praise. "Thanks for the swags on the shed. They must have been a lot of work."

"You're the only one who appreciates my efforts."

If only she would appreciate *my* efforts. "I think everything looks absolutely perfect just the way it is. I wouldn't add another thing."

I spoke firmly, hoping she would get my message. Daisy and I returned to the kitchen, where Mom and Wanda sorted through place cards, trying to figure out who was still in town.

Tucker slouched in one of the chairs by the fireplace and held a bag of frozen peas to his head. "Soph, sweetheart, could I trouble you for some aspirin?"

I fetched the bottle and handed it to him with a glass of water. "Too much partying last night? Craig was up early."

"Speak softly, please. Craig wussed out and left. I spent the wee hours of the morning with the hardy boys—Uncle Stan, Kevin, Joel, and a few other lads."

"Not Robert?"

"He took off. Got any hair of the dog? Scotch would be nice."

Wanda patted his shoulder. "I'll make you my special tonic."

I crouched next to Tucker. He wasn't doing his job. I hadn't lured him to Hannah so he could party all night. "This is your last chance to woo Hannah away from Craig."

"As soon as my head clears."

Wanda mixed tomato juice with clam juice, added a generous dose of Tabasco sauce, then whisked in a raw egg. "This never fails." She handed him the drink.

Tucker choked on the first sip. "That's brutal."

None of us had any sympathy for him.

Humphrey sidled up to me. "Could I please have a moment?"

But I ignored him when I saw Natasha leading men past

the kitchen door. Visions of feathers propelled me outside, but it was worse than I imagined. She was bringing the ice lounge into my already crowded backyard.

"Excuse me. Stop!" I shouted, but they kept going with gigantic blocks of ice.

"It's okay, Sophie," called Natasha. "They're bringing in the bar." Waving her arms and shouting directions like a crazed traffic cop, she directed two men to place the blocks of ice ten feet from the dinner tables and another two men to set the wedding cake she'd baked as a gift to Hannah a bit farther into the yard.

Natasha flicked her hands at me. "You'd better shower. I'll handle this end of it."

Had she intentionally waited to bring her contributions when we had finished and no one was watching?

There was no way her ice lounge would fit. But I had to tackle one problem at a time. The round table holding Natasha's four-tier cake sat squarely in the sun. As if it weren't enough to bake the cake herself, she'd also made the monogram topper linking H and C. Silver crystals sparkled on the initials.

"The cake is going to melt there," I said. Blunt, but to the point and not argumentative.

"But the ice lounge has to be in the shade."

Just the opening I needed. "The cake is more important than an ice lounge." I murmured, "Besides, there's not room for it."

A voice rang out of the sky. Natasha and I turned our faces upward.

Hannah leaned out the window in Jen's room. "I love it! The ice bar stays, Sophie."

Natasha smiled at me. A condescending I-win-again smile that irritated me.

Happily, I recognized the guys assembling the bar. At lightning speed, I ran past Humphrey and out to the street where I found Laurie, owner of the ice sculpture company.

We'd worked together before on events, in fact, I had ordered our martini luges from her.

"Please tell me you don't have the rest of the ice lounge in your truck."

"What's going on?" she asked. "Are you merging functions with Natasha?"

I explained the situation, and she agreed that the ice lounge would not be a good idea in my crowded backyard.

"What about the sculpture Natasha ordered?" Laurie pulled back a freezer blanket that wrapped a cupid sculpted from ice.

What was with the hearts and cupid? Did Natasha not realize that Hannah had a stargazer lily theme? "Will it fit on the bar?"

"It'll be a tight squeeze with your martini luges, but she ordered the biggest bar we offer."

At that moment, Darby walked down the street from Natasha's house, a delivery van drove up and blocked traffic, and Natasha emerged from my backyard.

"Is that the cutest thing," gushed Natasha. "I love the cupid."

Darby chimed in. "Adorable. And so perfect for a wedding. What a clever idea. Did you order that, Natasha? No wonder you have a TV show. You're so original."

Horns honked and some guy shouted out his car window. Oblivious, the truck driver hauled out a box.

Natasha crowed, "My feathers! Take them inside, please."

Sometimes it's just best to acknowledge that you've been licked and give in. "Just the sculpture then." I followed Laurie's crew to the backyard to be sure Natasha didn't give her a hard time about the rest of the lounge she'd ordered.

The ice bar had been assembled on top of a light box fitted with a tray. A pump hidden under a table on the side of the bar would suck water out of the tray as it melted and the light box would illuminate the bar.

Brawny guys lifted the cupid and set it in the center of the bar as Natasha rounded the corner with a skinny five-foot-tall vase filled with gigantic ostrich plumes. "Aren't these perfect centerpieces?"

The table had already been set with lavish white peonies in short vases. Humphrey and Joel, neither dressed for the wedding, placed more of the mirrors between the flowers and glass votives. The lush peonies already infused the reception area with their sweet, clean scent.

"They're too tall, Natasha. The slightest breeze will knock them over." They might have been impressive in her hotel ballroom setting, but they couldn't have been more wrong for a garden wedding.

A rapping sound interrupted my thoughts, and Daisy barked at something behind me. I turned to see Tucker in the sunroom, brandishing some kind of weapon in one hand and pretending to fence, while eating what looked suspiciously like our chocolate truffle favors with the other.

Natasha huffed and ignored me, still carrying around her gigantic feather centerpiece.

It seemed like hundreds of details flashed through my head every minute, and I wished I weren't wasting time on Natasha's nonsense. I hurried to the house to retrieve the cake knife and server of ornate sterling, one of the few items my grandparents had brought from Germany. Mom dragged them out for every special occasion. The long blade had been honed to a sharp point over the generations, but it connected us as a family. I found them in the sunroom, where the cake would have rested safely out of the heat.

When I returned to the yard and set them on the table next to the wedding cake, the two martini luges I had ordered had been positioned on opposite ends of Natasha's ice bar. It was crowded, though, with the cupid in the middle, and I walked away when Natasha fussed over the placement of the cupid.

Uncle Stan and Robert rounded the corner, still dressed in casual clothes. "Need a hand?" asked Robert. "No charge!"

I enlisted their help in setting out place cards, and we were almost finished when I heard a crash.

TWENTY-FIVE

From "The Good Life":

Dear Sophie,

My great-grandmother's diamond pin would be perfect on my son's fiancée's wedding dress, but I'm not ready to part with the brooch. I would be thrilled for her to wear it, but how do I tell her I want it back?

> —Mother of the Groom in Mount Crawford

Dear Mother,

Surprise her with the pin and include a note welcoming her to the family. Explain that the pin is to serve as "something borrowed." I can think of few lovelier ways to let her know she's a trusted member of your family now.

> —Sophie

Natasha squealed and cupped her hands over her mouth. The cupid sculpture lay at her feet in large shards, surrounded by tiny diamondlike bits. I dashed to the basement and retrieved two coolers. If the ice melted, the guests would have to stand on a soggy lawn to get drinks.

Natasha kneeled next to me and helped with the laborious task of picking up chunks and bits of ice and putting them into the coolers. I fought the urge to say something nasty. It wouldn't change anything.

Rushing, we dragged the coolers to the shed. I opened the door for Natasha and heard her shriek.

Peering inside, I made out Wanda and Robert in a clutch so passionate I felt like I'd intruded on something that ought to be private. What was it about the potting shed that made everyone so amorous?

Natasha rarely lost her composure, but her throat muscles grew taut and her shoulders trembled. She sucked in air and pulled the cooler into the shed. Standing up straight, she wiped a strand of hair out of her face and hissed, "Mother! You have no idea what I went through to sweet-talk Mordecai out of his house to meet you. Meanwhile, you're sneaking around in a garden shed like a hormone-crazed teenager."

"I can't imagine what you thought I would see in a man who dresses in sixties clothing and carries a little dog with him everywhere like a doll," Wanda shot back.

"He owns one of the most fabulous houses in Old Town." Natasha's cheek pulsed as she glanced at Robert. "You couldn't have fallen for the doctor?"

Although their squabble provided amusing entertainment, I didn't have time to hang around. I needed to shower and change. I left Natasha to pull the other cooler into the shed while I threw an outdoor rug over the wet spot left by the broken cupid and hurried inside to change.

White-coated catering employees had taken over my kitchen. In the midst of the confusion, the florist handed me Hannah's bouquet of pink roses and stargazer lilies. He had slipped diamondlike crystals into the center of each rose, and the entire bouquet sparkled.

I wedged it into the refrigerator and raced for the stairs. But once I passed the clanking and bustle in the kitchen, an eerie quiet possessed the house in spite of all the people in it. Something was wrong.

An angry male voice drifted to me. On the third floor, I found Phoebe and Craig standing outside the door to Hannah's room.

"She won't let me in," he said.

"I've told him she's already in her wedding gown," explained Phoebe. "Hannah doesn't want him to see her until she walks down the aisle."

From the other side of the door Hannah yelled, "I don't know what you're talking about."

Craig leaned his head against the door. "Please come out here. I need to see your face."

"What's going on?" I asked.

Phoebe thrust a sheet of paper at me. Written on hotel stationery, it read, "Sweetest Hannah, How I've longed to be in your embrace again. I treasure the hours we spent together yesterday and cannot bear to imagine life without you. Come away with me, dearest, and we shall bask in romantic bliss. Yours forever, Tucker."

Hannah continued to protest her innocence from behind the door.

Craig swung around to face me. "Were they together while I was gone? Tell me!"

Time crawled to a slow tick while I considered my options. If I said Tucker and Hannah had gone off together, would Craig leave? A darker notion made me nix that idea. If he'd killed Emily, he might murder Hannah out of jealousy. On the other hand, this did seem to be an opportunity to throw a wedge between them.

Hannah solved my dilemma by insisting that she loved Craig, and if she was going to have an affair, she'd do it with someone more interesting than Tucker. That wasn't quite true. Bad boy Tucker won over Humphrey in the interesting category, but she'd been caught in a compromising kiss with bland Humphrey.

Hannah's sarcasm appeared to alleviate Craig's concerns. He stomped down the stairs to the foyer, and we heard the front door slam shut.

I read the message again. I'd hoped Tucker would cause problems between Hannah and Craig, but this was far better than I'd imagined. Guilt nagged at me for luring him to my house. If I knew Tucker the way I thought I did, he was up to something.

Phoebe rapped on the door and assured Hannah that Craig had left. I was trotting down the stairs to my bedroom when I heard a shout. Would there be no end to the minor crises?

Following the sound of angry scolding, I discovered Natasha in my family room, surrounded by feathers. They covered the hardwood floor and wisps floated in the air. Mochie leaped high in an effort to catch them, but Daisy and Hermione tucked their tails between their legs and cowered. Bits of white ostrich feathers clung to their fur. Two cardboard boxes lay on the floor, their sides torn away. They'd had fun ripping into them.

"Look what your beasts did!" Natasha held her hands against the top of her head as if the pressure inside might cause it to blow. "You insufferable curs!"

Hermione whimpered and fled to the kitchen. I scooped up Mochie, who had a pheasant feather clamped firmly between his teeth. Daisy didn't need any coaxing to leave. She stuck close to me. Natasha continued her tirade even after we left the room. I found Hermione shaking under the kitchen table and wondered if Natasha had managed, in one moment, to undo the progress poor Hermione had made. It wasn't easy, but I clutched Hermione with one arm and Mochie with the other and walked upstairs to my bedroom, followed by Daisy. With the door safely closed behind me, I gave each of them a kiss and told them what smart babies they were to have destroyed Natasha's feather plans.

I showered, donned my shabby robe, and was about to blow out my hair when Mom stuck her head into my room. "Are you ready for hair and makeup?"

Sure. Better than wrestling with it myself. I was delighted to have a minute to rest with my feet up.

Mom sat on my bed while the hairdresser and makeup pro worked their magic on me. Mom's hair pouffed out more than normal, and her violet mother-of-the-bride dress brought out her blue eyes. "Honey, the other day, Dad found the bottom drawer of that organizer in the bathroom open. We didn't think anything of it but this afternoon, when we came in to dress, we discovered a small drawer in our room hanging open."

"You're not the only ones. Someone was snooping in Craig's room and in mine, too."

"Why would anyone do that?"

I couldn't shake my head because four hands were at work on it. "I haven't the faintest idea. Someone must be looking for something."

"Did Hannah find her engagement ring yet?"

"Do you suppose it's Hannah looking for the ring?"

"That doesn't make any sense. She might think you would hide it, but she knows Craig wouldn't hide it from her."

In the commotion, I'd completely forgotten to look for her ring. If I had a few minutes before the ceremony, I would run a broom handle under the furniture downstairs. The floors in my old house canted to the outer edges, and if Mochie had played kitty hockey with the ring, it was very likely in a dark corner.

The hairdresser finished ten minutes after the makeup expert. I turned around and barely recognized myself in the mirror. She'd fluffed out my hair so that it doubled in thickness. It framed my face but still brushed my shoulders. The makeup woman had emphasized my cheekbones. I would have to ask how she did that, because it slenderized my face. But the smoky eyes were something I wouldn't be eager to repeat.

Nevertheless, my mother cooed about how beautiful I looked and urged me to hurry.

When they left the room, I stepped into a strapless coral dress. Hannah, having worn a few too many hideous bridesmaid dresses, cleverly chose three styles and three coordinating colors that ran from geranium pink to coral to tangerine for copper-haired Phoebe, so each of us could wear a color and style that suited us.

I zipped it up, clipped on the preapproved mobe pearl earrings and gold bracelet, and slid my feet into caramel slingback shoes.

Leaving Mochie, Daisy, and Hermione in my bedroom, I returned to the foyer, where I found Mom wrestling with Hannah's bouquet.

"I'm trying to attach this pin," she explained, fumbling with a delicate butterfly made of periwinkle-colored stones. "It's old because I wore it when I was married, borrowed because I want it back, and blue." She held the bouquet, and I pinned the butterfly onto a rose.

But the bouquet didn't smell like roses. I bent my head and sniffed. Garlic. Peering closer, I could see that someone had stuck garlic cloves down between the flowers.

"Robert did that," whispered Mom. "Something about warding off evil spirits."

Good heavens. I could hear Hannah and Phoebe coming down the stairs. I couldn't remove the garlic without making a mess of the bouquet. Thrusting it at Mom, I said, "You'd better hand it to her."

Her eyes opened wide. "She'll blame me for the smell."

"Tell her about the pin. That's charming. Maybe she won't notice the garlic." *Fat chance*. But she was far less likely to chew out Mom about the odor.

We crowded in the foyer, out of the way of the caterers. I fetched the bridesmaids' bouquets, cherry and white medleys of lilies, roses, and peonies, and handed one to Phoebe. She wore the same style dress that I chose, but hers fit much better on her slender figure. When I handed out the bouquets, I saw the adorable crown of roses that had been made for Jen to wear and felt a tiny pang of disappointment.

I could hear Hannah asking, "What stinks?"

Fortunately, the string quartet chose that moment to begin playing, which launched Hannah into a frenzy. "I have to speak to the minister."

Mom stroked Hannah's shoulder. "Calm down, honey. The minister is here and everything is going perfectly."

"You don't understand. I have to talk to him before the ceremony."

Dad and Jen emerged from the living room. Jen wore her tiara and asked Hannah, "Can Daisy be a flower girl with me?"

Natasha, wearing a formfitting dress in her signature robin's-egg blue, every bit the beauty queen, looked scandalized. Bending to Jen, she said, "Daisy isn't that kind of dog, honey. It would be different if she were a cute little Pomeranian like Mordecai's Emmaline."

Poor Daisy. She'd landed with a wicked stepmother who clearly couldn't stand her. But Hannah winked at Jen, and that was all the encouragement she needed to dash up the stairs to fetch Daisy. I could only hope that Daisy had spent enough time outside earlier so that she wouldn't relieve herself when they walked down the runner.

But Hannah's good cheer didn't last long. "I still need to talk to the minister."

She headed for the door, but Natasha stopped her. "You can't go out there. I'll get him."

Hannah sniffed as Natasha stepped outside. "This place reeks. I hope that's not what they're serving for dinner."

Mom's eyes met mine, but we were smart enough to keep mum.

Natasha returned with the minister, and Hannah seized his arm.

"When you do the wedding vows, I do *not* want you to say the part about 'speak now or forever hold your peace.' " And then she glared at me.

I might not like Craig, but I wouldn't intentionally ruin their ceremony. Hannah had made up her mind several times over. I couldn't think of any bride who'd had as many great excuses or opportunities to bow out graciously. If the groom killing his ex-wife didn't change Hannah's mind, an objection from me in the middle of the ceremony certainly wouldn't deter her.

Mom and the minister left for the backyard, and Natasha lined the bridal party up in the kitchen. Catering staff dodged around us.

"Ready?" I asked.

On Hannah's nod, I turned to Jen. She'd found the rose crown and fastened it onto Daisy's head. It was corny, but there was something very sweet about Jen in a lacy white dress with a huge cherry sash and the glittering tiara, holding a basket of pink and coral roses, and the leash of a hound wearing a crown of flowers.

Natasha checked her watch and stopped us at the door. "You have to wait seven minutes."

"Everyone's here. What are we waiting for?"

"Sophie," she sighed, "you have to be married when the hands are moving upward on the clock. Maybe that's what went wrong with your marriage—the hands were moving down when you were wed."

It was ridiculous, but I waited, which gave Hannah a

minute to come over and hiss into my ear, "If you say one word to Craig about my little indiscretion with Humphrey, I swear I will never speak to you again."

She had to be kidding. I'd worked like a fiend all day just to make her happy. I should have been a sweet sister and said something reassuring, but I was tired of her imperial behavior. I said, "Thanks for the idea," and urged Jen out the door, Natasha protesting behind me. The quartet changed to Mendelssohn's "Wedding March," and I signaled Jen to start.

As I waited to walk down the aisle, my gaze drifted over to the dining tables. Someone, and I suspected I knew who, had placed fist-sized cut glass diamond paperweights at selected spots. Natasha joined me and instructed the first bridesmaid to go.

"What's with the diamonds?" I hissed.

"Aren't they cute? I thought it would be fun to give one to each of the single men."

Just what every man hoped for.

Phoebe processed along the aisle, and then it was my turn. I forced a smile as I walked and took in the scene. The garden bloomed as though it had waited for this day. Natasha's green swags on the potting shed were a charming touch, and Bernie had transformed the horrible arch. Roses, peonies, and lilies twined around it. The dreadful heart at the top had turned out better than I ever expected once it was covered with blooms.

I took my place and watched as Hannah emerged from the service alley with our father. She glowed, no doubt amazed that she would finally be married in spite of all the problems. Under her bustline, a cherry inset embroidered with lace and pearls adorned her strapless A-line wedding gown. Her blond hair had been swept up into a sophisticated chignon, perfect with Craig's tiara. She made a beautiful bride.

But Dad, on the other hand, seemed pensive. I wondered

if he was considering running in the other direction with
Hannah. I wished Mom could be the happy mother of the
bride. She was looking on, twining her fingers so vigor-
ously I thought they'd be bruised. Humphrey stood behind
Mom, paler than normal. It wouldn't have surprised me if
he'd fainted. For once, Tucker seemed somber, almost unhappy. Even Mars looked a little queasy. Natasha and
Wanda beamed. Wanda sat next to Mordecai with little
Emmaline squirming on his lap. Behind them, Joel seemed
apprehensive.

Craig's side of the family watched in fascination. They
seemed almost gleeful. Darby, in a striking black and
white outfit, sat next to Tucker. In a last-minute change,
Robert had taken the place of the best man and stood next
to his son. I wondered how it was possible that a tuxedo
could turn a withered little man into a dashing, debonair
fellow. Kevin, in a tuxedo that strained at the seams around
his massive arms, stood next to Robert.

When Hannah arrived at the floral arch, she kissed Dad
and turned to face Craig. I should have paid attention to
the traditional ceremony, but all I could think was that my
sister was marrying a killer.

The minister droned on and had just made it to "Do
you, Hannah," when Humphrey jumped up and shouted, "I
object!" I saw my mother close her eyes as if she wished
she would wake up and find that the whole weekend was
only a nightmare. The other guests faced Humphrey, who
had, amazingly, turned the exact color we were calling
cherry.

"Well, ah . . ." The minister looked to Hannah for guid-
ance. "What is your objection, sir?"

For a moment, I thought the strength to stand and object
had been too much for him, but instead of falling back into
his seat, Humphrey proclaimed boldly, "The baby is mine!"

My mother's eyes popped wide. Heads swiveled toward

Hannah, and I knew they were searching her fitted bridal dress for signs of a pregnancy.

Hannah did not look amused, and Craig stared at her in shock. Humphrey's protest came as a surprise, but at least it rocketed an expression onto Craig's face.

The minister asked Hannah in a low tone, "Would you like a moment to discuss this with the gentleman?"

In the loud and unhappy voice of an irate schoolteacher, Hannah demanded, "Humphrey, sit down!"

I doubted that I was the only one who was sorry that he did just that. For Hannah's sake, I hoped Robert and Stan wouldn't make a fuss when the rings were exchanged and it was obvious that Hannah hadn't found her engagement ring yet. But the rest went smoothly and minutes later, Hannah and Craig were married.

Walking next to Robert, I followed Dr. and Mrs. Craig Beacham down the runner, thinking we'd done every possible logical thing to keep this from happening. Whether I liked it or not, Craig was a member of the family now. I made up my mind to accept him. After all, Hannah saw something in him. I would have to rely on her judgment. Forcing myself to get past my personal reservations, I kissed Craig on the cheek, hugged Hannah, and wished them well.

The photographer whisked Hannah and Craig aside for photos in front of the floral arch, while Mom and I steered the guests toward the ice bar. Wedded Blitz Martinis ran through one ice luge into martini glasses rimmed in sugar. For those whose taste ran to the less sweet, lime mojitos ran through the other ice luge. Two waiters appeared from the house bearing trays of coconut-encrusted shrimp and tiny Italian herbed meatballs.

When Phoebe sought me out for photos, I reluctantly joined the family for pictures and forced myself to think cheerful thoughts. I might not like the fact that my sister had married Craig, but for her sake, the pictures ought not reflect my gloomy feelings. The photographer's assistant arranged us in front of the wedding arch. She placed Jen in front of me, and I smiled for the camera.

And then Jen screamed.

TWENTY-SIX

From "THE GOOD LIFE":

Dear Sophie,

My reception will be outdoors with loads of flowers. We're having a buffet, but I'm worried that it will look too much like a church supper. It will be in the afternoon, so candles won't make a difference. What can I do to add a little class?

—Counting Pennies in Cooperstown

Dear Counting Pennies,

Choose festive tablecloths so it won't look like a fish fry. Write the buffet menu in a fancy script on your computer. Print it and insert it in the fanciest crystal or gilt picture frame you own. It will add instant glamour to the buffet table.

Buy tiny gilt picture frames at your craft store to use

as place cards. They'll add a touch of glitz to the tables
and double as favors.

—Sophie

Jen wailed, "Daisy's bleeding and someone stole her
crown."

I saw it a second later. Blood marred the white socks on
Daisy's front paws.

Jen and I rushed toward her. I fell to my knees and
picked up one of her paws but couldn't find the source of
the blood.

"She doesn't have it on her anywhere else," said Jen.
"But her crown is gone."

I lifted the other paw and searched for a cut but found
nothing. The tops of her paws were bloody but the bottoms
seemed muddy. Reaching up, I cupped her head in my
hands and examined her. She appeared to be fine.

Mars dashed over to us. "Is something wrong with
Daisy?" He ran his hands over her back. She wagged her
tail and when Mars kneeled by me, she licked his nose.

Despite my assurances that I couldn't find any cuts on
her paws, he checked them himself. When he was done,
Daisy had had enough poking and prodding and romped
merrily off toward Mordecai. She snuffled at Emmaline,
who finally broke Mordecai's death grip on her and sprang
to the ground, and the two dogs ran for the potting shed.

Mordecai's empty arms flew into the air and he loped
after them, crying, "Emmaline! Come back."

It was awful of me to find the scene amusing, but I did.
In the interest of maintaining some semblance of dignity, I
hurried toward Mordecai. "She'll be fine. Let her play with
Daisy a little bit."

He rasped, "Look what your monstrous beast has done
to my Emmaline."

Their rumps in the air, the dogs scratched at the doors to the shed and dug in the grass. Emmaline's fur bore dark spatters. But they weren't fighting. Whatever was on her fur hadn't come from a bite.

Mars grabbed Daisy's collar and pulled her away from the shed at the same time that Mordecai snatched up Emmaline.

A stream of red trickled out underneath the doors, and I flung them wide open.

Craig's Uncle Stan sprawled on the painted brick floor. His tuxedo jacket had fallen open, and a strawberry stain saturated the front of his white shirt. A handgun touched the fingers of his right hand as though he'd reluctantly released it.

I held my breath as I stared at him. How could this possibly have happened? I should have checked for a pulse, but I had a bad feeling it was too late for Stan.

Dad, Mars, and Bernie crowded behind me. A chill ran through me in spite of the warm evening air. "I'll call Wolf. Keep everyone out of here."

But precisely as I said that, Robert ran to the doorway. "Stan!" He launched himself at his brother and started CPR.

It was the right thing to do, so I didn't stop him. Darby knelt on the other side of Stan to help. I brushed past Craig and ran up the lawn toward my house.

Breathless, I flew into the kitchen, pushed past the catering crew, grabbed the phone, and dialed 911. I spewed information at the woman who answered. Unless I missed my guess, Wolf would arrive in a matter of minutes. Still short of breath, I hung up the phone and took ten seconds to calm down in the foyer, out of the way of the noisy kitchen. As I took deep breaths, Tucker emerged from my powder room, wiping his trousers with a towel.

"Will you look at this? Some oaf spilled his mojito on me." His brow furrowed. "Are you all right?"

"Uncle Stan's dead."

"What?"

"I have to get back." I flew through the sunroom and out the door but slowed down and walked to the shed so I wouldn't create a bigger scene than we already had. Guests milled about but spoke in hushed tones and stared at the shed as though something dramatic might happen. Stepping inside, I said to no one in particular, "The rescue squad should be here shortly."

Humphrey squatted beside Stan's lifeless body. "I'm afraid he's past needing rescue."

Robert hovered above his brother, looking even smaller and more wizened. Darby made a cross over her chest, and Craig wrapped a tentative arm around Robert.

"What do you suppose happened?" asked Dad.

Humphrey stood up. "From the looks of things, I'd say he was either stabbed or shot in the abdomen."

"Anyone hear a gunshot?" asked Mars.

We shook our heads.

"Surely someone saw Stan enter the shed. He wasn't in here earlier this afternoon." I wished I knew exactly what time Natasha and I had left the shed.

My heart thudded a little harder when I heard Wolf's voice. "Step back, please. Sophie, I'll need a list of names of the people who entered the shed." But despite my thudding heart, Wolf was all business. There was not so much as a shared glance or a brush of my arm.

Unfortunately, Detective Kenner accompanied him. We'd had an unpleasant encounter before, so I was none too happy to see him. Behind his back, locals called the sly-eyed cop Defective Kenner, and I had to agree with their assessment. He turned beet red at the sight of me.

Fortunately we didn't have to put up with each other for long because Wolf and Kenner shooed us out of the shed and guests on the lawn stepped aside to open a path for the rescue squad jogging toward us. Standing next to me, Mordecai kissed the top of his little dog's head and held her so tightly I thought he might squash her.

"For goodness' sake, Mordecai," said Natasha, "we'll just hose her off and she'll be fine."

He acted as though she'd suggested roasting the dog on a spit.

"Did I say *hose*? I meant *bathe*. Maybe a day at the doggy spa?" Behind his back she made a face at me. "Come up to the house and we'll bathe her sweet little feet."

I watched her escort Mordecai past Hannah and my mother, who looked like they might need the rescue squad. Jen wasn't anywhere to be seen. I hoped she wasn't in the shed watching the cops.

"Where's Jen?" I asked Mom.

"Nina took her up to the house. Jen protested, as you can imagine, but she's too impressionable to be here right now."

I nodded with relief and realized that a crimson stain smudged the hem of Hannah's beautiful wedding dress. She must have been inside the shed.

Wanda drifted over and shook her head somberly. "Married in pink, your spirit will sink."

"Oh, please, Wanda. This isn't the time for your ridiculous superstitions." The last few days had worn Mom's nerves thin.

"Really, Inga, you of all people know that I had the most awful marriage. My husband walked out on us. I only want Hannah and Natasha to benefit from my misery. Natasha is the only good that ever came of my wedding."

Hannah ran trembling fingers over the bodice of her dress, flattening out imaginary wrinkles. "This is my fault. I don't know what I was thinking. I wanted so badly to be married to Craig that nothing would stand in my way. And now we're married and it's a nightmare. None of this would have happened if I hadn't insisted on going ahead with the wedding. I just didn't want to imagine that anyone I knew had killed Emily." She screwed up her face and her breath came erratically, but no tears fell.

"Hannah," I said, "no one could possibly have foreseen something like this. Stan isn't dead through any fault of yours."

Mom nudged her. "You're married now, don't you think you should comfort your husband?"

"I thought he needed some time alone with his dad and cousin. Imagine what they must feel. They came here for a reunion with Craig and now . . ." Her face stiffened as she watched Darby hurry to the house.

Her shoulders hunched, Darby held a tissue to her nose and avoided making eye contact with anyone. Craig followed behind her and motioned to Hannah. I searched for Robert and found him slumped in a chair. His rounded shoulders and sagging head said everything.

Mom murmured, "Why would anyone kill Stan? He seemed like a fine man."

Wolf cut through the crowd and joined us. "This is a logistical nightmare. The guests are trampling a crime scene, but there's nowhere to put them."

"Maybe we can fit in the house." In the sixties Faye had built a substantial addition onto the house, expanding the dining and living rooms to accommodate large gatherings. Mars and I had thrown our share of parties for his business, but I hadn't prepared for this crowd to be inside. Still, a lot of people went home yesterday. I didn't think we had anywhere near the hundred-plus guests who were originally invited.

"Sophie, would it be unseemly if we served dinner?" asked Mom.

I shouldn't have been a bit surprised. Poor Stan. Not ten minutes had passed since we discovered his body, and the talk had turned to food.

Wolf shot me a questioning look. "It would keep the guests busy while we collect names and find out if anyone saw anything suspicious."

Serving dinner at a murder—we would be the talk of the town. But it was the only reasonable thing to do. "Give me fifteen minutes to set up."

In a murmur, Wolf continued, "You have a guest list in case anyone takes off before we can talk to them, right?"

"No. There was a guest list once, but we have some guests who weren't on it and a lot of others aren't here."

Wolf moaned. "Detain everyone as long as you can."

I headed straight to Dad and Bernie. After explaining that we needed to move inside, I left them to mobilize the bridal party, and I ran into the house and shoved living room furniture against walls and out of the way. With one last glance at the backyard, I swung the floor-length saffron curtains closed. Walking as fast as I could, I intercepted the waiters with hors d'oeuvres and asked them to serve inside the house.

"Can we set up dinner buffet style?" I asked.

After a short discussion, we agreed to arrange it something like an omelet bar. Each guest would have to retrieve his or her own food, but the plate would be prepared by a cook who would hand it to the guest—sauce, side dishes, and all. That would distract the guests a little bit and keep them busy. We would offer tea and coffee with dinner instead of the wine we'd planned to serve. Once the police finished their questioning, we could offer wine to all.

Amid the clanking of pots and pans, I skirted through the family room, intending to return to the yard by way of the sunroom, but the sound of Craig's voice stopped me.

"Your parents and Sophie can take care of everything. You know Wolf. If we don't leave now, we'll be stuck here for days."

What a cold man. His own uncle had been killed, and he was willing to run off and enjoy himself. Or maybe he was willing to run away from a second murder he'd committed.

I waited for Hannah's response. If I interfered, she'd go with him for sure, just to spite me.

"We can't leave now. Don't you see, Craig? We've tried . . ." Her voice cracked. "We've tried so hard to have a beautiful wedding, but nothing has gone right. This isn't the same as having it rain on a wedding day. Two people have been killed. My ring is lost. The hotel is drenched. This isn't how it's supposed to be."

I sagged against the wall. Hannah was finally coming to her senses. She might not believe that Craig could be a killer, but at least she wasn't willing to run away.

Hannah let out a little sob. "Oh no. There's blood on my dress. That does it. We never should have pushed to be married. Wanda was right. It wasn't our destiny. If you'll excuse me, I believe I'll change into something less . . . bloody."

I could hear her crossing the sunroom, and I scooted forward just enough to peer at Craig. With his back to me, he looked out over the yard, his hands in his pants pockets. I wished I knew what he was thinking.

I didn't want him to know I'd been eavesdropping, though. Luckily the clatter from the kitchen covered creaking floorboards as I sneaked through the kitchen to the foyer. But at that moment the front door opened and Darby entered, looking surprised to see me.

"I'm so sorry, Darby," I muttered, at a loss for comforting words. "I didn't know your uncle well, but he seemed like a nice man."

She spoke wearily. "Just before the wedding I asked if anyone had seen Stan, but then the music started and I forgot about him. If I'd only said something, maybe we could have found him. Maybe it wouldn't have been too late."

"You can't blame yourself."

She wiped her eyes with trembling fingers. "We shouldn't have come. We never should have come here."

It finally dawned on me that half of the four uninvited people who had come to see Craig had been killed. "Are you afraid?"

She swallowed hard. "I guess I can say it now. I thought Stan killed Emily. I was so certain. But this changes everything."

Her revelation shocked me because she knew Craig and his family far better than anyone else. "You have to tell the police. Why did you think that?"

But Bernie and Mars interrupted our little talk by carrying in the first of the long tables. Darby fled to the den, and I was stuck directing. We lined the tables up in the living room with little space between them. Although the sunroom overlooked the backyard, we decided we would have to place a couple of tables there as well. Half an hour later, with the magic of so many helping hands, everything from chairs to flowers had been moved indoors.

A table covered with one of my gingham cloths had been set up for the entrees. The waitstaff plated a choice of Pepper-Crusted Filet Mignon, Asparagus Tips with Hollandaise, and Duchess Potatoes, or Pan-Seared Salmon with Wild Mushroom Risotto and Parmesan Spinach. Guests stood in line and if police hadn't been swarming through the yard, it might almost have seemed like a normal wedding buffet.

Mom intercepted me in the sunroom. "What should we do about Jen? We can't keep her cooped up." Together we walked up the stairs to my bedroom. I opened the door carefully and peeked inside.

"Mochie has been a perfect kitty," Jen announced from the bed. She still wore her fancy dress and the tiara. "Hermione was scared at first, but I think she's okay now."

Nina looked up from a magazine. "Jen has taken

excellent care of them so they wouldn't be underfoot in the kitchen."

Mom sat down next to Jen and told her what happened. Turning to me, she said, "Do you think you'd be okay if we packed Jen up and drove home?"

"No!" cried Jen. "Aunt Hannah will need me when they arrest Uncle Craig."

TWENTY-SEVEN

From *"Ask Natasha"*:

Dear Natasha,

My mother is appalled at the thought of my Papillon at my wedding. He's my baby, and I can't marry without him. How can I convince her?

—Pixie's Mom in Pawley's Island

Dear Pixie's Mom,

I understand your mother's concerns. If you must include your dog, be sure he receives a full spa pampering on the day before the wedding—bath, trim, and painted claws. Sew a special outfit for him that matches your dress. If you're not an accomplished seamstress, Pixie can be custom-fitted for his wedding attire. Don't forget the bling. Swarovski crystal jewelry, hairpins, and tiaras dress up any dog. Visit http://www.barronshouseoftreasures.com.

—Natasha

I gulped. Poor Jen had probably overheard far too much of our anti-Craig chatter.

"Why would you think that, honey?" asked Nina.

"Uncle Craig and Stan had a big argument. They were really mad, worse than my mom and dad ever are."

Mom frowned at her, evidently unaware of problems in my brother's marriage.

Her little face earnest, Jen continued. "Uncle Craig said he just wanted to live in peace. But Uncle Stan said he should have thought about that a long time ago and it was too late."

"Where were you when you heard this?" I asked.

"Gramma sent me to the basement for extra paper towels and when I opened the door, I could hear them yelling, so I didn't go down."

"Are you sure it was them?"

"I waited in the kitchen and saw them come up. I couldn't hear everything, but Uncle Stan said something about icing. I didn't say anything before because it was just an argument, but . . . isn't that another word for killing?"

Mom clutched Jen and stroked her silky hair, giving me a can-you-believe-this look. "No more TV unless I approve it. We'll go home as soon as we can, baby."

"Did you hear them, too?" I asked Mom.

"No," said Jen. "She was busy telling Humphrey that you still think he's sexy."

"What?" I studied Jen doubtfully. Mom had strange ideas sometimes, but she surely wouldn't say such a thing to Humphrey. Out of the corner of my eye, I could see Nina lean forward, a huge grin on her face.

"It's no big deal, Sophie," Jen explained with the sophisticated aplomb of a fourth-grader. "Humphrey thinks you love Mars and it's hopeless for him, so he thought he should get Hannah on the rebound and he kissed her in the shed. But then Craig came back and Hannah dumped

Humphrey, but he knew you'd seen him kissing Hannah and thought you wouldn't like him anymore."

"That does it. We're going home. Maybe they can pack a dinner for us downstairs." Holding Jen close, Mom whispered, "I had no idea she heard all that."

"I don't want to go home," whined Jen. "You promised we would stay the whole weekend. I want to stay with Aunt Sophie."

"Things are different now. The wedding is over." Mom flicked dog fur off Jen's dress and stood. "Pack your bag."

Jen folded her arms over her chest and averted her eyes.

"Oh, Jen," sighed Mom. "She didn't get this stubbornness from our side of the family," Mom insisted before turning back to Jen. "We'll go downstairs to have some dinner, but I want you to stay away from the garden shed and the police."

Jen's face shone again. "I'll be very good, but I have to tell Wolf about Craig, okay? Maybe he won't get into trouble if he killed Stan in self-defense."

Mom inhaled a deep breath. "What do you know about self-defense? Honestly, I can't imagine what your parents are thinking when they let you watch adult television programs."

We left Mochie and Hermione in my bedroom so they wouldn't be underfoot, and Jen led the way downstairs. Mom pulled me aside for a second and whispered, "She's a huge fan of Nancy Drew and liable to be inclined to do some sleuthing, so help me keep her out of it."

"We'll tell her it's her job to watch Daisy." But I never implemented that idea because Hannah reappeared in a pale yellow sheath and grabbed my arm with a strength that made me nervous. What had I done now? She'd taken off the tiara but left her hair in the becoming chignon. All traces of the feted bride had vanished. Even the wedding ring. Belying the tension I could feel in her fingers, she chirped cheerily, "Sophie, I need to borrow you."

I followed her outside and around to the front of my house. She intertwined her fingers so tightly that her knuckles shone white. "I know I've been a pill and that I have no right to ask anything of you after the way I've acted. But, oh . . . I can't believe I'm saying this. When I was getting ready, I looked out the window to check the progress in the backyard and I saw Craig come out of the shed."

Goose bumps rose on my arms. I stood before my sister, totally confused. Did she want reassurances that Craig must be innocent? Did she want me to tell her what she already knew—that she had to tell Wolf? I took the easiest route and hugged her.

Her head on my shoulder, Hannah half-whispered, half-sobbed, "Did I marry a killer, Sophie?"

My poor sister's body trembled, and even though we were in open view of anyone passing by, I let her cry on my shoulder to get it out of her system. She lifted her head, and although I suspected that she had indeed married a murderer, the thing that surprised me was how well her makeup had stayed in place. She didn't even have raccoon eyes. Making a mental note to ask the makeup artist what brand of mascara she'd used on Hannah, I said comfortingly, "Is there any other reason you're worried?"

She sniffed, but neither of us had a tissue. Waving her fingers in front of her face like a beauty pageant winner, she said, "Before the wedding, it didn't mean anything. I didn't know Stan was in the shed. He was afraid of Stan. I could see it in his eyes. And now he wants to run away. Not even attend the funeral. Like he needs to get out of town."

How she was able to see anything in that poker face of Craig's was beyond me.

"You have to help me, Sophie. I can't face going anywhere with him until I know the truth."

That was easy enough to accomplish. "We'll just say that Wolf insists you stay in town until they've solved the case."

Tears welled in her eyes, and she choked out words. "I don't want to be one of those women who disappears on her honeymoon."

"Calm down, Hannah." I admit to the fleeting thought that we could have avoided this mess if she'd only put off the wedding in the first place. But I quickly banished it and said instead, "You'll stay here with us. We'll make a little slumber party of it. You and Jen and I can sleep in the family room tonight. We'll," I searched for something to say, "make popcorn and watch a funny movie."

"It's my wedding night," she wailed. "How could I possibly explain that to Craig?"

"We'll think of something." I said it with false confidence, since I hadn't the foggiest notion what kind of excuse we could concoct. "But first, you have to inform Wolf." We dodged around the side of the house and spied Humphrey scuttling ahead of us. I had a hunch he'd been watching. Too bad he hadn't kept as close an eye on Craig.

Hannah stuck by me like a frightened child as we made our way into the backyard. Mars and Dad watched the police from a safe distance. Near the potting shed, Craig spoke animatedly with the dreadful Detective Kenner, but Wolf came toward Hannah and me as soon as I beckoned to him.

Surprisingly, Hannah kept her emotions in check while she told Wolf what she'd seen. When she finished, I relayed Jen's story about the argument between Craig and Stan.

Wolf ran a hand over his face. "What is it about your potting shed? Everyone and his brother was in there today. Are you sure of the time, Hannah? Most people don't seem to be able to remember if they saw someone in the morning or later in the day."

"Someone must have seen the killer," I insisted. "The people with the ice bar or—what about the string quartet?"

"None of them noticed anything unusual."

Hannah swallowed hard. "It was after I went upstairs to get dressed."

"Was it before or after you shouted down to Natasha and me?"

"After," she murmured. "Here he comes."

Craig slid his arm around Hannah, and she stiffened at his touch. "Hannah, darling, I feel like I've neglected you. We can't let this mar the start of our lives together." He pulled her closer. "The good news is that Detective Kenner has some ideas on the identity of the killer. I don't think it will be long before they make an arrest. Maybe we can leave for our honeymoon after all."

I thought Hannah might be sick. "Dad," I called. "Isn't it time for you and Hannah to have a bite to eat? Hannah's looking a little peaked."

She tensed, but I knew she'd be okay with Dad. Besides, I wanted a minute to speak to Wolf.

My little plan didn't work. Instead of taking Hannah into the house, Dad and Mars joined us.

"Think whoever did this is the same person who killed Emily?" asked Mars.

If Wolf had any hunches, he didn't let on, saying only, "It's too early to tell."

"It looks to me," said Craig, "like whoever did it killed Stan in self-defense. After all, Stan had that gun in his hand."

I couldn't help wondering if that was what Craig had intended. Had he placed the gun by Stan's hand after he was dead?

Wolf listened to Craig's statement passively. "It's getting dark out here, Sophie. Do you have any spotlights you could turn on?"

Since Dad hadn't taken my cue, I rescued Hannah myself by asking her to help me turn on lights. She readily agreed and minutes later, the tiny lights on the sunroom ceiling twinkled, along with the festive lights the guys had strung across the backyard earlier in the day.

Hannah met me midyard when we were done. "It's gorgeous," she whispered. "Like a garden wonderland. The hotel never would have been so magical."

"Next time," I said.

Hannah laughed so hard that tears flowed again. I figured it was cleansing for her.

Mom found us laughing. "Girls! That's hardly appropriate. Hannah, some of the guests are ready to leave, given the circumstances and all. Would you come cut the cake, please? After what we've been through, posing for lots of pictures would be morbid. At least the photographer can get a decent photo of you and Craig cutting the cake. Oh, but you've changed out of your dress."

I could tell Hannah was panicking at the thought of being near Craig with a knife. "Play along," I said softly. "Mom will be with you every second."

Mom and Hannah crossed the yard to the cake with Craig, and I strolled over to Wolf. The cops had set up lights inside the shed, and they silhouetted his broad shoulders. I tapped his arm, and he instinctively moved away from the shed with me.

"Hannah's scared. Craig wants to leave for the honeymoon, and she doesn't want to go. Could you tell them not to leave?"

"I'm sorry, Sophie. I can ask, but I don't have the authority to prevent anyone from leaving the area yet."

"So fake it. If you don't, I'll pretend and tell Craig you said so." Under the romantic lights, thoughts of Stan and Craig faded. Wolf stood close enough for me to smell the fresh scent of soap. I wanted to clarify what he'd seen between Mars and me. I longed for a sign. A hint that things weren't over between us.

My fingers brushed his in the semidarkness, and I turned my face upward to him.

His expression had been benign when he observed Craig, but I could see a mixture of pain and resignation now. "I have work to do. And you need to figure out what you want."

Natasha's shrill trill cut through the dark. "Sophie, we need a hand. Stop flirting with Wolf."

He winced, and I knew he'd take ribbing for that. I wished we *had* been flirting. "I should get back."

He nodded and I took off my slingback wedding shoes and walked across the lawn to Natasha, who waited by the wedding cake. "Where did you put the cake knife? I can't find it anywhere."

It had been a very long day. I was tired and hungry and in danger of becoming grumpy. "It's next to the cake, Natasha. If you had bothered to look, you would have seen it."

"Really, Sophie. It's not like you baked the cake or did any of the hard work for the wedding. If I hadn't been around to pick up the pieces, this never would have come off. And now you can't remember what you did with the cake knife?"

I hadn't lost my mind entirely. The server lay on the table where I'd left it. But the long knife that had cut wedding cakes in our family for generations was gone.

TWENTY-EIGHT

From "The Good Life":

Dear Sophie,

I have looked at every cake topper in town. They range from shabby to gaudy. Are fresh flowers the only alternative?

—Topless in Topsail Beach

Dear Topless,

Make your own topper. Initials and monograms are always in style. Dress them up with rhinestones for bling, or diamond glass glitter for subtle sparkle. Or wrap them with ribbon for a classy look.

—Sophie

I fetched a knife from the kitchen, certain the cake knife had been brushed off the table in the commotion. We'd find it in the morning when the light was stronger. The lights that sparkled above provided a romantic glow but weren't strong enough for a major search.

I handed the new knife to Hannah, who stood by the cake, a safe arm's length from Craig. The photographer told Craig to place his hand over hers. I thought Hannah might spit up on the four-tier cake adorned with sugar blossoms and delicate string work that must have taken Natasha days. In spite of the photographer's efforts to coax a smile, the toll of Uncle Stan's death showed on Hannah's strained face. The entwined C and H topper seemed almost ironic at the moment.

I backed away, wondering how on earth I could help Hannah. And then, in what felt like slow motion, the second cake tier slid forward, initiating an unstoppable avalanche of buttercream, raspberries, and spice cake. The interlaced initials crashed to the ground and broke in half. Icing covered the photographer's shoes. My mother held her hands over her mouth in horror, and Natasha immediately shouted, "What happened? Who pushed it?"

Daisy wagged her tail and closed in on the yummy dessert that splayed across the grass. When Jen tugged her away, buttercream frosted Daisy's dark lips.

I held my breath, wondering how Hannah would take another wedding disaster, but she broke into gales of laughter, which clearly offended Natasha. But I suspected they reflected hysteria, not mirth.

Biting back the impulse to remind Natasha that I had warned her the cake would melt, I displayed my worst side by leaving the cleanup to Natasha. I fled to the sunroom, where I heard thumping in the den.

I peered in and found Darby crawling on the floor amid the contents of her suitcase. "Lose something?"

She shrieked and clapped a hand to her chest. "You

scared me!" Her face twisted like she might cry, and she plopped onto the sofa. "Y'all," she said southern style, "are such nice people. I'll always be sorry we brought our troubles into your lives."

"What do you mean?"

"Uncle Stan was never an easy person to get along with. I guess it's not a nice thing to say, but I'm not surprised that someone wanted to kill him."

"Do you know something?" I sat in the desk chair. "Do you know who murdered him? Was it Craig?"

"I don't know what to think, except that none of this would have happened if we hadn't come."

"Did you tell Wolf about Stan?"

"Who?" she asked.

"The detective."

"The cute one with the silver temples?"

"Yeah, that one." The one I'd thought I'd have a romantic weekend with.

"He and that other detective grilled Robert and me."

That figured. They knew Stan best. "Are you saying he had enemies and that one of them followed him here?"

"Honest to goodness, Sophie, I don't know. I'm as confused as you are. What you don't realize is that Stan—"

Just then Robert appeared in the doorway. In his slow odd way, he said, "Darby? I hope you're not boring Sophie with old stories."

"Of course not." She straightened her skirt in a nervous gesture. It was clear she knew something, and I had to get it out of her before Robert whisked her back to New Jersey. But I couldn't pry in front of him. I bowed out as gracefully as I could and found myself caught in the foyer with Mom and Hannah, saying good night and apologizing to guests as they left with favor boxes.

I closed the door behind the last one and heaved an enormous sigh of relief. The day couldn't end soon enough.

"Where's Jen?" I asked.

"In your bedroom with Daisy, watching a Disney movie." Mom wiped cake frosting off her sleeve. "Your brother has told me a million times how gifted she is and I know she's one smart little girl, but, honestly, I don't think it's good to expose her to mature material. Where did she ever pick up *iced* as slang for murder?"

Hoping to find a leftover filet mignon, I ventured into the sunroom. The food had been cleared away, but Mars, Nina, and Bernie lounged on the wicker furniture. Wineglasses rested on nearby glass-topped wrought-iron side tables. They ate their entrees watching the backyard, which had taken on an eerie quality. The lovely lights strung overhead twinkled in a light breeze. But underneath, a harsh glare lit the potting shed and dark figures moved about as if in a horror film.

"Good show?" I asked sarcastically.

"Best seat in the neighborhood." Mars craned his neck to look back at me. "Pull up a chair."

Macabre as it was, I did just that. But before I sat down, I dragged my weary legs to the kitchen and loaded a plate with leftovers from the bulging refrigerator.

I returned to the sunroom and cut into the cold steak. It was still juicy and unbelievably tender, and the asparagus was perfect.

"Eww, Sophie, I know you ignore Nat when she criticizes your housekeeping, but there's crud in the bottom of my glass," complained Mars.

Like I needed a lecture on cleaning right now. "So get a fresh one."

"Yuck. I drank some of this stuff."

Nina took the wineglass from Mars and peered into it. "It's not one of Sophie's wineglasses. These are the wedding rentals. And that's not just crud. Someone must have dumped this into your drink."

"Mars?" I asked, afraid of his answer, "how do you feel?"

"Fine."

"Did one of the waiters pour your wine?" asked Bernie.

Mars shifted uncomfortably. "Natasha brought it to me. You know, suddenly I don't feel so good."

Déjà vu set in. I wondered if I could stay awake and on my feet long enough to get Mars to the emergency room. "Why would she poison you?"

Nina held her wineglass elegantly but lifted an eyebrow in a rascally fashion. "Wanda seems to think marriage is on the agenda."

Mars sputtered. "Marriage? To a woman who flaunts a bodybuilder in my face? Come on, don't any of the rest of you find her obsession with Kevin the Hulk and Morbid Mordecai a bit odd?" He cupped a hand to his forehead. "Sophie, feel my head. Am I hot?"

I set my plate on the table in time to see my mother in the doorway looking in at us. She didn't say a word, but from her satisfied expression I knew she'd heard Mars's request. She winked at me and retreated along the hallway.

I picked up Mars's wineglass. Tiny balls and plantlike bits rested in the bottom. I sniffed. The wine overpowered another familiar smell. Using two fingers, I scooped out some of the detritus and rubbed it between my fingers. "Chamomile," I announced.

Mars smelled my fingers. "Are you sure?"

Bernie leaned over to sniff and declared, "Definitely chamomile."

"Like you would know," Mars grumbled.

"Actually, I do. It grew on a farm where I lived as a child. I used to pick it with the gardener and sip the tea on cold winter nights."

Mars felt the sides of his face. "You're certain?" he asked me.

"I'm certainly astonished that you think Natasha would try to hurt you."

"I was being silly, but . . ."

His voice faded as Craig's rose in anger. "Why are you being so difficult? Uncle Stan would want us to go."

"No, he wouldn't." They must have been in the foyer. Hannah's voice also came through loud and clear. "Any normal person couldn't enjoy a vacation the day after a family member was killed. Stan would expect his loved ones to give up a vacation, bury him, and find out who killed him."

"Darby and my dad will take care of that."

"How can you be so cold? Aren't you the least bit upset?"

Craig sounded as tired as I felt when he said, "You can't begin to know my pain."

Uh-oh. Would Hannah fall for that softer, beset-upon Craig?

"I'm not going and that's final." Someone pounded up the stairs and we heard a door slam.

Seconds later, the front door slammed, too.

Bernie sipped his wine and said, "I rather enjoyed the ceremony, especially Humphrey's contribution."

The situation wasn't funny, but the four of us cracked up, laughing with enormous guilt about Humphrey and his paternity announcement.

Nina stretched. "Never a dull moment around here. I believe I've had enough excitement for one day. You fellows feel like walking me home?"

I followed them to the foyer. When Nina and Bernie collected Hermione from Jen, Mars hung back. "You're sure it's chamomile?"

"Want your stomach pumped?"

He considered my question seriously. "Not particularly."

Hermione, Daisy, and Mochie raced down the stairs ahead of Nina and Bernie. It took a treat to capture the dachshund, but Nina succeeded and the three of them left.

I closed the door and wandered back to the sunroom. A little shout drew the attention of the police in my backyard, and I went outside to see what had caused the excitement.

A young cop held my mother's cake knife in a gloved hand. A red substance smeared the blade, and I didn't think it was jam.

TWENTY-NINE

From *"Ask Natasha"*:

Dear Natasha,

So many weddings seem the same. Vows and then a boring reception. What can I do to liven up my wedding?

—Jazz Girl in Jasper

Dear Jazz Girl,

Provide entertainment at your reception and build your theme around it. Live music is a given. Acrobats, mimes, caricaturists, dance troupes, belly dancers, hula dancers, and magicians are only the beginning. And don't forget to provide a dance floor and lounge for an after-reception party where you and your friends can dance the night away.

—Natasha

The red stain covered the long knife blade. Unlike a modern cake knife, it ended in a sharp point and made a vicious weapon.

"I found it in the neighbor's yard, on the other side of the fence," said the young cop, displaying it with pride.

I shivered at the thought of Stan being killed so brutally. But I realized with a start that the killer hadn't planned ahead. It must have been a crime of passion, because clearly he'd grabbed the knife from the cake table and lured Stan into the potting shed.

"Did any of the guests note anything suspicious?" I asked Wolf. "Someone must have observed Stan going into the shed."

Detective Kenner looked down his nose at me. "I've never encountered so many people ready to admit they were inside the murder site. A lot of folks are afraid their fingerprints are in there."

"Well, we were in and out of the shed all day. Everyone in my family went in there for something. Besides, won't the fingerprints on the knife give away the identity of the killer?"

Kenner leered at me. "I don't suppose *you* touched it?"

Chills ran along my spine. "I placed it on the table. My mother packed it and brought it with her. I hope you won't suspect her?"

"I never exclude anyone," said Kenner with an ugly smirk.

Wolf flinched, apparently pained by our exchange. "Why do you bother?" he said to Kenner. "There isn't a person alive who hasn't watched enough TV shows to know to wipe the murder weapon clean. If there are prints on it, I'll be amazed."

It had to be irritating to work with Kenner. Wolf jumped up a notch in my esteem for not strangling the guy.

Although I wished I could hang around and listen,

exhaustion overtook me. I'd had a long day and could finally hit the sack, but poor Wolf had to work.

I muttered good night and trudged to the house. The
second I entered the kitchen, the salty aroma of popcorn
hit me. Jen, with the enthusiasm of a grade-schooler who
never needs sleep, said, "Go upstairs and change. Hannah's
making popcorn and we're going to have a slumber party
in the family room."

Hannah mouthed to me, "Hurry."

"What did you tell Craig?"

"That the murder upset Jen and she's afraid of the
dark."

All things considered, it wasn't a bad excuse. "Leave a
light on for Darby. I think she's outside." I thought Craig
was, too, but thought better of saying so.

I wanted to fall into my bed and sleep. But Hannah
needed me. My legs felt like weights were attached as I
climbed the stairs to my bedroom. I reached for a leopard-
print nightshirt that Hannah had given me "to make up for
the spots that Mochie, the Ocicat, doesn't have." Cute,
comfortable, and snuggly. I gazed longingly at my bed
and gave thought to sliding between the covers, but in the
end, I knew I had to be there for Hannah. I took the pil-
lows off the bed, retrieved a blanket from the closet, and
joined the girls, Daisy, and Mochie in the family room.

I munched a handful of popcorn while an old black-
and-white horror movie started. A gloomy voice intoned
about an exotic princess and as a shadow crossed the wall,
the music rose to a frightening crescendo. Thinking that
my mother would surely not approve of the film for Jen, I
fell asleep.

～※～

A paw patted my forehead. Groggy, I halfheartedly swat-
ted at it, but Mochie's gentle prodding continued. I peered
at the clock. Two-thirty in the morning. If he thought I was

going to feed him just because I was sleeping near the kitchen, the poor little guy would be sorely disappointed.

But a strong light blitzed through the doorway to the sunroom. Trying not to step on Hannah or Jen, who slept on the floor, I stumbled into the sunroom and squinted against the light that shone in from my backyard.

A gurney, laden with a dark mound, was being rolled across the grass. Mere feet from Stan's passing body, Darby, Craig, and Robert watched. I could only imagine their sorrow.

Single file, they fell in line behind the gurney, and like a sad funeral, they followed the corpse out of my sight. Someone pulled the cord on the lights Craig and his team had strung across the yard, and suddenly it lay in darkness, quiet again.

I sank into the wicker settee, and Mochie hopped into my lap. I was so tired that I thought I might drift off, but the horrors of the last few days pummeled me. Every time I closed my eyes, I could see the desperate fear in Hannah again. Not that I blamed her. The killer had strangled Emily and stabbed Stan in broad daylight. Loads of people had been milling around when Stan was murdered. Clearly the killer had no inhibitions, no fear of being caught. And now that Stan was also a victim, the list of suspects had become woefully short. Only Craig, Darby, and Robert even knew the victims.

Mochie pricked his ears. Voices murmured. It was probably Craig and Darby coming in. Seconds later, Darby tiptoed through the sunroom.

"How's Robert holding up?" I asked.

Darby stifled a screech, which brought Daisy running. Darby staggered toward me. "Where did you come from? You nearly gave me a heart attack."

"Sorry."

She slumped into a chair. "Robert is devastated. This has been such a horrible weekend. I thought I'd come down here, see Craig, tweak him a little bit about getting married, and go home. Never did it cross my mind that Stan or Emily would end up dead. You know, it's almost too much to absorb it all."

With everyone in bed, it was my chance to pick up where we left off earlier. "Why did you think Stan killed Emily?"

She flicked her hand through the air. "She left him! And you don't run off on Stan."

That shook the sleepiness out of me. "Left him? You mean Uncle Stan had a relationship with Craig's wife?"

Darby's eyes darted to the side as if this was an uncomfortable topic for her. "Yeah." She said it slowly, like she was trying to remember something. "Then she left Stan the same day that Craig disappeared. Stan was crazy mad because he thought they ran off together."

"Ewww. Stan dated his nephew's ex-wife?"

She brayed like a horse and stood up. "Sounds so creepy when you put it that way. Love the nightie, hon, a real fashion statement."

Darby disappeared into the den, and I could hear her moving around. She didn't seem to realize what a bombshell she'd handed me. No wonder she'd been distressed when I asked her if Craig could have killed Emily. Families hid some scandalous secrets. That juicy tidbit explained Craig's estrangement from his family. If Stan and Emily had an affair, Craig's ire with Stan would be understandable. It hadn't been fear of Stan that Hannah thought she'd seen in Craig, it had been suppressed fury. The news about Emily didn't account for Craig's alienation from Robert, though. Nevertheless, it put the murders in a whole new light—and meant Craig was even more dangerous than I'd thought.

"Hon?"

The light from the den lit Darby from behind. She held a suitcase. "You and your family have been adorable." She set the bag down and walked over to hug me. "I'm so sorry that we brought our troubles here to you. I will always regret that. Listen, I called a cab and I'm takin' off. Do me a favor and don't let on to anybody that I'm gone. At least not until morning. That'll give me a head start."

"It's the middle of the night."

"I know. It's better this way."

"Who are you running from?" It had to be Craig or Robert.

"I wish I knew. Hey, give Kevin a kiss for me. When this blows over, I'd like to get together with that strapping hunk of man. If you're ever in Jersey, don't forget to look me up."

She seized her suitcase, tiptoed out, and the front door clicked shut behind her.

I stretched and Mochie jumped off the settee. But before I was on my feet, a movement in the backyard caught my eye. A mere shadow of a person unfolded himself from a chaise longue, strolled to the back, and let himself out the gate to the alley.

THIRTY

From *"Ask Natasha"*:

Dear Natasha,

My son and his fiancée want us to host a brunch at our home the morning after the wedding. I'm going to be worn out, so I guess we'll have it catered. Is the brunch treated as a formal extension of the black-tie wedding, or will people graze on muffins and coffee cake?

—Tuckered Out in Tuckertown

Dear Tuckered Out,

The postwedding brunch has become a part of our wedding ritual. Make a centerpiece that reflects the new couple in a special way. A coffee and latte bar is a must with whipped cream and chocolate-covered spoons. Serve crab cakes, Quail Eggs Benedict, or seafood crepes. Be sure one food like butter, waffles, or toast is in the shape of hearts. Serve a signature drink made with champagne and bake cupcakes as favors for your guests to enjoy as they travel home.

—Natasha

I considered dashing out after the person, but I didn't particularly want to catch up to him alone. If I woke someone to go with me, he'd already be a block or two away in any direction. I did, however, sprint to the kitchen to peer out the window at Darby. She was sliding into the backseat of a cab. Whoever the shadow was, he hadn't caught up to her.

My second wind began to wane and, as disturbing as that person in the garden was, the sofa beckoned. I tried to convince myself that Wolf had left a cop behind. Maybe to watch our behavior? I snuggled onto the couch and pulled the blanket over my shoulders. I would ask Wolf in the morning.

⚜

Fortunately, I wasn't the only one worn out by the wedding and the murders. Everyone in the house slept late. When I padded into the kitchen yawning, Mars and Dad sat in the chairs by the fireplace reading the newspaper. I scowled at Mars, not that he noticed. I didn't bother saying anything, though. Now that the wedding was over, Kevin and Wanda would be leaving and Mars wouldn't have to hide in my house anymore.

Mom, wearing an elegant floral bathrobe, measured coffee. "How many do you think we'll be this morning? Should we use the coffee samovar?"

With all the commotion, I hadn't given much thought to Sunday brunch. I rubbed my eyes. "I guess we'd better. I imagine Hannah's friends will be coming by. The caterer should be here soon." I fetched coffee mugs for the four of us. "I think the body's gone."

Mars turned the page of the newspaper. "Your backyard has yellow tape around it."

That made sense. We wouldn't be eating outside.

Mom poured milk into a creamer. "I gather there's a problem between your sister and her new husband since she slept in the family room?"

I slipped my arm around her waist to give her a little hug. Hannah ought to be the one to explain everything.

"I can't believe we slept so late," said Mom. "Hannah and Craig will have to leave for the airport soon."

"They're not going," I said.

The newspapers lowered simultaneously. Dad nodded his approval. "I'm glad they decided it was more important to show respect to Uncle Stan. I imagine they'll be heading to New Jersey when his body is released."

I figured I'd better fill them in about Stan and Emily before Craig came downstairs. But I stopped short of telling them that Hannah was worried about Craig and didn't want to be alone with him. She'd better be the one to break that news.

Mom sank into a chair. "Good heavens. We have to protect Humphrey."

Not exactly the reaction I expected. "Humphrey?"

"After that little display at the wedding yesterday, Craig might bump him off, too."

"Get Wolf over here right now," said Dad. "I don't want us alone in this house with Craig."

"Wolf has to work. I can't just call him and ask him to babysit us. But I do have to let him know about Stan and Emily's relationship."

Trying to remember the things I needed to tell Wolf, I returned to the family room, crouched next to Hannah, and shook her awake. "Did Craig ever wear a necklace with the initial C on it?"

Hannah groaned and pulled the blanket over her head. "Too tired," she murmured.

"Hannah, this is important."

She lowered the blanket to her chin. Her eyes closed, she muttered, "He doesn't like to wear jewelry."

I nudged her. "You never saw a necklace like that at his house?"

"Don' know."

"Hannah! You must know. You married the man yesterday."

"Mmffp. Don' remind me." She drew the cover over her head.

Giving up, I headed into the den and picked up the phone to call Wolf. Mochie jumped onto the desk and rubbed his cheek against the computer screen.

Darby had thoughtfully stripped the sofa bed mattress and left her linens in a pillowcase by the door. Poor Darby hadn't had much of a guest room. Boxes of Natasha's dishes and assorted serving pieces cluttered the floor.

I left a message for Wolf. But before I was through, a jingle played somewhere in the den. I hung up and searched for the source of the sound, but Mochie found it first. He thrust his paw between sofa cushions, trying to reach it. I moved him and discovered a cell phone that looked a lot like mine. It stopped jangling precisely as the knocker sounded on the door. Assuming Darby had left it behind, I placed it on the desk. I would have to call her later to let her know I had it. Maybe Robert could take it back to her. I hustled through the sunroom and down the hallway to answer the door. Humphrey stood on the stoop, half-moons of exhaustion under his eyes.

"Sophie!" He said my name softly but with undisguised lust. "You're not dressed . . ."

I yanked him inside. If a long T-shirt nightie excited him that much, he needed a girlfriend—but not me. I felt a little bit guilty, but I invoked Mars's name anyway to quell his eagerness. "You look like you could use some coffee. Mars is already here." I pointed Humphrey toward the kitchen and ran up to shower and dress before Humphrey got any more ideas.

I was stepping into a sleeveless print dress the colors of mangos, lemons, and papayas, when Hannah burst in, wearing nothing but a towel.

"I'm trying to avoid Craig," she whispered.

"He's staying here," I whispered back. "I don't think that game plan will work very long."

She sat on my bed, her skin damp. "What am I going to do?" She didn't cry, but she was breathing so hard that I could see her shoulders move with each breath.

"First go through my closet and find something to wear. Then come downstairs and help me with brunch." Her head sagged. "Hannah! He doesn't have a reason in the world to hurt you." I sat next to her, wrapped my arm around her, and told her about Uncle Stan dating Emily. I thought it would reassure her and that she would be comforted by the thought that Craig had no reason to knock her off, but Hannah tensed and said, "Then why did Emily come here?"

I could only imagine one reason. "To warn you about Craig."

Hannah shivered. "If that's true, then everything he said about her was a lie."

"Probably. Can you think of anything that would help Wolf?"

She sat up straight. "That's the key, isn't it? That's my only way out of this mess—to remember details that might tie him to the killings."

The door knocker sounded again downstairs, reminding me that the caterers and hungry guests were arriving. After a quick look in the mirror, I put on gold earrings, urged Hannah to find something cheery in my closet to wear, and bounded out the door.

But footsteps overhead stopped me cold. Jen didn't weigh enough to make that kind of clomping sound. I made it no farther than the first step when Tucker traipsed down the stairs from the third floor.

"Good morning, dear sister-in-law. Have you seen my sweet Hannah?"

I intended to grill him, but the door to Craig's room opened and I was caught in a bind.

"I think you'll find what you're looking for in my bedroom." To Craig, I feigned friendliness. "Was that your father I heard downstairs? I'm so sorry about Stan. How is Robert taking it?"

Thankfully, Craig followed me down the stairs and, as much as Hannah probably didn't relish being alone with Tucker, at least she didn't have to fear being alone with Craig right now.

The caterers, as well as Phoebe and Joel, had just arrived, so I solved the problem by sending Phoebe up to rescue Hannah from Tucker. Joel joined the growing crowd in the kitchen, bubbling about seeing Robert E. Lee's boyhood home. He helped himself to coffee, and I couldn't help noticing how different his mood was from the rest of us.

He high-fived with Jen about something and asked if she'd been to Lee's house.

Mom smiled at Joel's fervor and murmured to me, "He's such a nice man. Why can't Hannah meet someone like that?"

"He's available," I whispered.

"No! They broke up? What a shame. Hmm, now what can I do to bring them together again?"

"Mom," I warned, "stay out of it."

She ignored me. "Paul, we have all that champagne left. How about pouring some and splashing a little bit of leftover peach schnapps in it?"

"Do they have a name?" Dad asked.

Jen chirped, "Schnappinis? Schnapeachies?"

As I poured coffee into the samovar, Joel opened the

kitchen door for Nina and Hermione. Hermione sniffed Joel's feet and looked up at him hopefully. "Sorry, I don't have any doggy treats today." He stooped to pet Hermione, who wagged her tail and didn't run away.

Humphrey hovered near me, too close for comfort. "I need to talk with you. Privately."

I didn't have time for Humphrey, but he pleaded with sad eyes and I let him tow me into the family room.

Whispering, he said, "I know Mars holds your heart, but I think Wolf is interested in you, too."

I didn't care which one he thought I was involved with as long as he left me alone. "Humphrey, when everyone goes home, we'll work on introducing you to some women."

"They found your fingerprints on the knife that was used in Stan's murder. Kenner wanted to bring you in for questioning, but Wolf wouldn't hear of it and walked out on Kenner. Everyone's talking about it down at the morgue."

For a second, my heart beat a little faster. Maybe it wasn't over with Wolf. "Of course they found my prints. I didn't wear gloves when I put the knife on the table. Did they find any other prints?"

"They haven't identified them yet."

They would be as inconclusive as mine. Any number of people might have handled the knife. "Thanks, Humphrey. I appreciate the update."

He beamed but his eyelids sagged, and I wondered if he'd slept at all. "Did you get any coffee?" He followed me into the kitchen, and I poured him a mug.

Craig leaned against the kitchen counter, a glass of orange juice in his hand. "Is Hannah up?"

I tried to buy her time. "She's getting dressed."

"I need to check on my father. It would be nice if my wife came with me."

All conversation came to a halt. I could see apprehension on my parents' faces. Hannah would panic if she knew

Craig wanted to be alone with her. We needed to give her a reason to stay with us.

"Shouldn't she stick around here to entertain her guests?" I hoped I'd said it casually and immediately poured orange juice into a pitcher.

Mom jumped on it. "Craig, dear, it would be impolite if she abandoned the people who worked so hard for you two yesterday."

"Very nice—my own wife won't go with me to console my father." He gazed around at us. "Where's Darby?"

THIRTY-ONE

From "The Good Life":

Dear Sophie,

I'm conflicted. I'm a do-it-yourself kind of gal, but I keep reading that I should leave my wedding to experts. It seems like I could save a lot of money by doing things myself, like baking my own cake and arranging the flowers.

—Labor of Love in Lovedale

Dear Labor,

It's easy to create your own table numbers, menus, save the date announcements, and place cards ahead of time. You can prepare favors in advance, too. But food, flowers, and cake need to be fresh. Do you have a refrigerator large enough to accommodate the cake? Where will you store the flower arrangements if you make them the day before?

It's a lot of work setting everything up, especially if

you have the ceremony in one place and the reception in another. You will be very busy on your wedding day. Don't wear yourself out trying to do everything. Hire the pros to do some of it for you.

—Sophie

Pretending to be unconcerned, I said, "Darby left."

Craig banged his glass down on the granite countertop so hard I thought it might shatter. "Darby!" He raced out of the kitchen, and I could hear his heavy footsteps heading for the den.

Feeling anything but calm, I strained to show a placid outer demeanor and checked on the caterers setting up a buffet in the dining room. It was an odd assortment, the result of a compromise between Mom and Hannah—white cheddar grits and peppered ham biscuits for the southerners, hash browns, scrambled eggs, bacon, spinach quiche, pasta with artichokes, and assorted pastries.

As I passed through the foyer, Jen raced down the stairs. "Someone stole my tiara. It's gone!"

Craig swept back through and overheard. His stormy expression changed to amusement. He reached into his pocket, crouched, and fastened a diamond necklace on Jen's neck. "This is much better," he whispered.

The necklace looked like Emily's. Jen ran off to admire it in a mirror. "Is that real?" I asked, wondering if it *had* been Emily's.

"I was going to give it to Hannah as a wedding gift, but then Stan gave her one. The way things stand between us now, well, Jen will probably appreciate it more." He took a great breath. "When did Darby leave?"

"Early this morning." It wasn't exactly a lie. It had been morning, technically speaking. I hoped that would buy her more time. "She's probably still on the train." Moving with care so I wouldn't show my nervousness, I returned to the kitchen with him and offered him a Schnappini.

Craig's rigid stance betrayed his fury. It seemed as though everyone in the kitchen held their breath. Even Mochie and the dogs kept their eyes on Craig as if he might explode.

Mom came to the rescue. "Please be sure to express our sympathies to your father, Craig. We couldn't be more horrified by the tragic death of your uncle."

The others chimed in, murmuring condolences. Craig acknowledged them with a simple "Thank you" and left through the front door. From the kitchen window, I watched him walk away, his hands stuffed into his pants pockets, his head down as if deep in thought.

"Thank goodness!" said Nina. "That was frightening. Poor Hannah, to be married to such a man."

Dad jumped from his chair and peered out the window. "He's gone." He scanned those of us present. "I want to know where everyone was yesterday afternoon."

"And what you saw," I added.

Joel jumped right in, almost too eagerly. "Phoebe wanted to get dressed here and help Hannah, so we came back early. I hung out in the garden mostly. Humphrey was there, too. Sophie and Natasha were quibbling about the ice bar. Then I came in and watched golf on TV in the family room before I changed clothes. I passed through the sunroom on my way to the bathroom, and, I'm sorry to say this, but I saw Craig entering the shed."

That news startled Humphrey. "I didn't watch golf. I was trying to get a minute to talk to Sophie, but she was too busy. I remember Inga serving iced tea and handing boutonnieres to Robert to distribute."

"What time was that?" I asked.

Mom sipped a Bloody Mary. "Well before the ceremony. I felt so sorry for that young man who was taking care of the ice. You'd think he would have been freezing, but it was right warm outside."

"The ice guy," I mused. "Why didn't he see anything?"

Mom tsked. "I'm afraid that was my fault. I invited the ice fellow into the family room to cool off. He watched golf with the boys."

"What about the string quartet?" I asked.

"I didn't come over until I saw the musicians unloading their cars." Nina watched Hermione, who behaved surprisingly well. "I showed them the way, and a whole bunch of people were already in the backyard."

"Rather a fun parlor game." Tucker picked up his coffee and spoke dramatically, like a has-been actor. "On my arrival, Natasha's mother fed me a dreadful concoction—but now that I think about it, my head did clear up. I, too, witnessed the amusing squabble between Sophie and Natasha. I had to wait while Stan changed clothes in the den. When he left, I took my turn, then rested my weary self on the settee in the sunroom and dozed off. On waking, I joined the golfers in the family room." With a flourish, he took an elaborate bow.

"Joel, I presume you saw Tucker on your way through the sunroom?" asked Dad.

"Absolutely. He was snoring."

"Inga?" asked Dad.

"I think you can count out Hannah, the bridesmaids, and me," said Mom. "Between dressing, makeup, and hair, none of us were paying much attention to the backyard."

I paced the kitchen floor. "We're overlooking something here. Who was the last one of us to see Stan alive?"

Joel piped up. "Right before I went inside, Stan was checking out the ice bar. I remember that distinctly because he was kidding around about how your tongue would stick to it if you licked it."

"Inga," said Dad, "did you see Stan in the house?"

A frown wrinkle appeared in the middle of Mom's forehead. "I remember that he changed clothes in the den. But I was busy with Robert. He was so proud of Craig and tickled pink to be best man. He said hundreds of years ago, the bride was often stolen from another village, and the best man's job was to stand by with a sword and make sure her family didn't whisk her away on her wedding day."

"This is all irrelevant," clucked Tucker, slouched on the window seat. "The suspects aren't present. We should be asking where Darby, Craig, and Robert were."

Mom eyed him with irritation. "Robert took the box of boutonnieres to hand out to the men." Pointing at Tucker, she said, "And I distinctly recall you waltzing in here with a shameful hangover, young man."

Hoping they would think of something significant, I snagged Jen to help me set the table. We had so many beautiful flowers left that centerpieces would be a snap. I thought Hannah might have had enough of pink, so Jen picked a yellow tablecloth and helped me set it with white plates. The living room was a disaster area, full of tables and chairs from dinner the night before. I moved Natasha's enormous heart topiary to the desk in the den and dragged a folding screen to the opening between the two rooms in an effort to block off the unsightly view. While Jen folded multicolored French Provincial napkins into diamond shapes, as she'd seen on Natasha's show, the catering crew departed.

Phoebe poked her head around the corner. "Where is he?"

"He went to comfort Robert."

"All clear, Hannah!" Phoebe shouted up the stairs.

Hannah raced down as the phone rang. "You're sure he's gone?" When Hannah changed her mind, she didn't do it halfheartedly. She wore a dress the color of strawberries, bold hoop earrings, but no wedding ring.

Mom strode into the dining room, holding the phone in her hand. "Sophie, Wolf needs to see you. Down at Bernie's restaurant."

"Right now?"

Mom nodded, her eyes bright with excitement. "Put on a little eyeliner?"

I didn't bother with makeup. I grabbed my purse but when I looked for my cell phone, it wasn't in the charger where it should have been. Swell. Darby must have taken my phone by mistake.

On my way out, I said, "The food's ready, Mom. You can go ahead and eat."

She caught my arm. "Good luck, sweetie."

If she only knew the truth. "I'm sure it's about the murders. He, uh, I don't think I'll be seeing much of him anymore."

I could hear her saying, "What? Sophie, what happened?" but I fled out the front door.

Although I loved entertaining, this time I would be relieved when everyone went home. It had been a disaster from the beginning.

The walk to Bernie's place picked up my spirits. Horrible summer humidity hadn't descended on us yet, and the sun warmed my bare arms. It felt like the first day after school let out—the entire summer stretched ahead of me.

A small crowd waited for tables at the restaurant. I squeezed past them and told the host Wolf was waiting for me. He showed me to a table immediately. But Wolf didn't seem particularly happy to see me. A half-empty cup of coffee rested in front of him, so I guessed he'd been there awhile. When I sat down, he leaned back and said, "What's up?"

"I called to let you know that Stan and Emily dated."

His eyebrows shot up. "Interesting. And?"

And? What did that mean? What did he want me to say? I didn't think I needed to spell out the implications. Maybe I should clear the air. Maybe he would never want to see me again, but it was better to get it over with. "About yesterday. It wasn't what it looked like."

"You called me here for that? I'm working two murders.

Until they're solved, everything else goes on a back burner."

"You called me."

"Don't do this. You just said you called to tell me about Emily and Stan. I hate catty woman games."

Confused by his reaction, I said, "Gee, sorry. I thought you would want to know."

"Got anything else that concerns the murders?"

I should have been conciliatory, but his cool demeanor stunned me. "Are you making any progress?"

"Not while I'm sitting here." He left cash on the table and took off without another word.

I could feel my ears flushing hot and made my way to the front door. I was almost there when an arm wrapped my waist from behind.

THIRTY-TWO

Dear Sophie,

I cringe and run from the room when the groom removes the garter from the bride's exposed leg and one of his buddies has to slide it onto the leg of some helpless woman who doesn't know him. And frankly, I'd like to keep my bouquet and preserve it. Would it be awful of me to skip those two rituals?

—Garterless in Garfield

Dear Garterless,

It's your wedding. You're under no obligation to participate in anything that makes you uncomfortable. Besides, there are other fun rituals you can incorporate. Greek brides write the names of single female guests on the bottoms of their shoes. At the end of the night, the name that is most worn will be the next to marry.

Another charming alternative is to ask the married
couples to stand. Those married less than five years may
sit first, followed by those married ten years, and so on
until the couple married longest is the only one standing.
The newlyweds then reward the couple's devotion with a
gift of flowers.

—Sophie

Mars gave me a friendly squeeze. "Frighten another man
away?"

I gently jabbed my elbow into his stomach.

"Oof. Don't be so touchy."

"What are you doing here?" I asked, as we stepped out
onto the sidewalk. "You were at my house when I left."

"Natasha called and insisted I come down here to pick
up chocolate mousse. Is the plural of *mousse mousses*? So
many mysteries. I don't know why Natasha is so fascinated
with that Mordecai guy, either."

"She's trying to set him up with her mother, you dolt.
She said as much yesterday when she caught Wanda and
Robert canoodling in my potting shed."

"Before Stan died, I hope. Well, color me stupid! That
explains a lot."

We turned the corner and headed for home. "Don't you
two ever talk?"

Unfortunately, Wolf hadn't made it far. He glowered at
the sight of Mars and me but wasted no time in asking
Mars, "Do you know where Natasha was when Emily was
killed?"

Mars blinked. "At work?"

Wolf locked his gaze on Mars in a way that made me
want to squirm, but it didn't appear to faze Mars, who was
used to taking on politicians. "You were in a meeting with
half a dozen people who confirmed your presence. Ber-

nie's employees verified that he was at the restaurant, but oddly enough, we have no confirmation of Natasha's oblique explanation of her whereabouts."

"Surely you don't suspect Natasha of strangling Emily?" said Mars.

"I'm just saying we have a lot of peculiar issues that remain unsettled, and Natasha is one of them." Apparently satisfied that he'd unnerved Mars, Wolf said, "If you'll excuse me, I have work to do."

He strode away, and I suspected he'd been all too happy to slam Mars a fastball. "Do you know where Natasha was?"

"No. I didn't know she'd dodged giving the cops a straight answer, either."

"Your mousses are probably melting."

He lifted the box in his hand. "Guess I'd better go home and do a little interrogating of my own."

We walked in the direction of our homes. Birds chirped and proud parents pushed strollers past us. It was impossible to believe that someone had murdered Emily and Stan in our backyards.

As we passed Mordecai's house, we saw Natasha and Detective Kenner speaking with him on the front porch. He appeared agitated. Holding Emmaline, he pointed a quivering finger at me. "This is your sister's fault. I saw her walking right by here the morning she killed that woman."

I recoiled and Mars stepped in front of me as if to shield me. So Mordecai was the neighbor who'd reported seeing Hannah on the day of Emily's murder. "Hannah didn't kill anyone. Even if she did walk by your house, that's not a crime or proof of a crime."

Mars whispered, "We should go." He took my arm and coaxed me around.

Natasha surprised me by squeezing between Mars and me. She hooked her arm into Mars's and pulled him close as we crossed the street to my house.

As soon as I opened the front door, we heard happy chatter. Daisy, Mochie, and Hermione raced to the foyer to see who had arrived. Jen followed, carrying two leashes. "Gramps and I are going to walk the dogs." I held the door for them as they left.

I could hear Natasha in the dining room. "Mother! Kevin! What are you doing here?" I joined them and found my family and Hannah's friends still gathered around the table. Mars was already helping himself to the buffet. Wanda and Kevin exchanged a guilty look, and Wanda spoke slowly, like she was making up an answer as she went. "When you didn't come right home, we went looking for you."

"How thoughtful." Natasha peered at the selection of now cold dishes. "Sophie, couldn't you cook something special for the wedding breakfast?"

If she didn't eat barbecue, I suspected hash browns were beneath her, too. "I think there are hash browns, aren't there, Mom?"

Natasha's jaw clenched. I enjoyed her quandary a bit too much. Her mother served hash browns every day at the diner where she worked, and I knew Natasha wouldn't dare insult her by being haughty about them.

"None for me!" Natasha turned on her sweet TV persona. "I'm watching my weight." She scootched an empty chair over to Kevin and tried to wedge it between him and Phoebe. They grudgingly made room for her.

Mars surprised me by pulling out a chair for me. He hadn't done that in years. Naturally, that little gesture did not escape my mother. To make matters worse, he set a plate of food in front of me and brought me a mug of coffee.

Natasha's nostrils flared. Folding a napkin in her hand, she wiped an imaginary crumb from Kevin's mouth. I thought he might lose his breakfast. Instead he leaped to his feet, his chair scraping across the floor. "Thank you for brunch."

I couldn't blame him for wanting to escape, but I'd

managed two bites of quiche and wanted nothing in the world more than to sit and enjoy a meal.

Nevertheless, Kevin's departure signaled an end to brunch, and before I knew it, Mars, Tucker, and I were the only ones left at the table.

A melody played and Tucker clamped his hands over his ears.

Mom stuck her head in the dining room. "What is that? It's driving me nuts."

The soft jingle stopped playing as Jen and Dad returned. "Must be Darby's phone."

"Do you have Darby's landline number? She'll be looking all over for that thing." Mom brushed imaginary crumbs off her blouse. "I hope you don't mind if I skip the brunch cleanup. I need to pack if we're going to leave soon. Jen, honey, can you pack your own bag?"

Hannah emerged from the foyer, worry lines etching her face. "You're leaving?"

"Well, Hannah, I'm not sure there's anything more we can do. Craig is leaving for New Jersey, and Sophie will be here with you."

With an irritated glance at my mom, Dad wrapped an arm around Hannah. "If it would make you feel better, then we'll stay."

Mom tapped her fingernail on the buffet. "I could arrange for someone to fill in for me at the hospital volunteer desk, but your father has a Fourth of July parade committee meeting, and Jen would miss the first days of the children's summer theater group."

That was my mom. Micromanaging three lives.

"Hannah, we'll certainly stay if you need us. It's your decision." Hannah and I knew the answer when Mom used that tone.

"You should go." Hannah put on a confident face. "We'll be fine. Besides, it would be safer for Jen."

Tucker preened like a mating bird. "I'll take care of my

darling Hannah and drive her home to Berrysville whenever she likes." He wiggled his eyebrows at her.

"You needn't bother trying to seduce me. I know you
better than anyone, and I haven't forgotten the reasons for
our divorce."

At least Hannah wasn't being sucked in by him.

"Isn't it time you were on your way, Tucker?" asked
Dad. "There must be someone else you could irritate."

"I am duty bound to the winsome Hannah."

Dad shuddered. "Given the circumstances, Hannah, perhaps you ought to go back with us today." Glaring at Tucker,
he added, "It would remove you from harm's way."

Humphrey shyly sidled up to Hannah. "I can drive you
home whenever you're ready to go."

Hannah squared her shoulders and lifted her chin. "I
have a responsibility to Emily and Stan. They came here
because of me. I have the week off, and if it's okay with
Sophie, I believe I should stay and do whatever I can to
help in the search for their killer."

"That's my girl." Clearly satisfied, Mom went upstairs.

"Be careful." Dad followed Mom, saying, "Jen, you'd
better hustle. You don't want to keep Gramma waiting."

Humphrey, the wan ninety-pound weakling, said, "I'll
stay by your side, Hannah. I won't allow that dreadful man
to whisk you away."

Tucker laughed at him, which produced a beet red flush
on Humphrey's pale jaw.

But Hannah handled them graciously. "You're both very
sweet. We need to put our heads together and figure out
what happened. There must be something we're overlooking."

I didn't want to ask Hannah about Mordecai's accusa-
tion, but I had to know. "Mordecai says he saw you walking by his house around the time Emily was murdered."

Hannah frowned. "I was mad at Craig and got out of the
car three blocks away. But I came straight here."

That sounded like something Hannah would do.

They settled in the sunroom, but while they speculated, I excused myself to phone Darby at home. As I dialed, I wondered if Craig or Robert would bring her cell phone to her. She'd clearly been afraid of Craig. Maybe she wouldn't want him to come to her home.

An answering machine picked up the call. "This is Donata, you know what to do!"

THIRTY-THREE

From "THE GOOD LIFE":

Dear Sophie,

One of my daughter's bridesmaids has the most awful tattoo of a dragon on her breast. The tail comes up in the middle of her cleavage, and it looks like a creature jumped into her bra. The bridesmaid dresses aren't low cut, but we can't cover up that tail unless the girl wears a turtleneck. I've told my daughter that she has to pick another bridesmaid and write off Dragon Lady, but she refuses.

—No Lizards Please in Slaughter Beach

Dear No Lizards,

Kudos to your daughter for standing up for her friendship with Dragon Lady. Although ordinary makeup seldom covers tattoos, there are now companies selling kits that can cover the darkest dragon tails.

—Sophie

Donata? It sounded like Darby. I must have dialed wrong. I tried again. The same perky tape answered again. The Jersey accent sounded like Darby's. Maybe she had a roommate?

I debated leaving a message and finally said, "This is Sophie. Just wanted you to know that Darby left her cell phone at my house and I think she might have mine. Call me if you want Craig or Robert to bring it to New Jersey." If I had the wrong number, the Donata person could ignore the message. If Donata lived with Darby, I hoped she would pass it along.

I perched on the desk chair and typed the number into a reverse directory on the Internet. It turned up under the name D. Franchini. Donata Franchini, probably. There could be half a dozen explanations. Idly, I searched "Donata Franchini," but all the results were for women in Italy.

"Hannah," I called into the sunroom, "did Craig or Darby ever mention someone named Franchini?"

Hannah appeared in the doorway with Craig behind her. Where did he come from?

"Nope," she said, her jaw tense.

"Where'd you get that name?" asked Craig.

When did he return? I promptly shut down the computer. Darby's fear rushed back to me, and I wanted to protect her. It seemed imprudent to mention her name, and I was at a loss to explain my question. "Craig." I forced myself to sound pleasant. "How's your dad?"

"Torn up. He's taking it very hard."

Unlike his son, apparently. "Is there anything we can do for him?"

Craig placed a hand on Hannah's shoulder, and her eyes sprung wide. "You can convince Hannah to come to New Jersey with us. Meeting the newest member of the family might soften the blow of losing Stan."

Hannah gulped and appeared frightened but quickly

composed herself. "Not this time, Craig. We have some things to resolve first." She turned and pushed past him and must have been desperate to find something to do because my sister, who detests cleaning even more than I do, suggested that everyone pitch in to help clean up the brunch dishes.

I joined them in the dining room. Humphrey and Hannah carried dirty dishes to the kitchen, but Tucker, not used to lifting anything heavier than a poker chip, stared out the window at the street.

"Penny for your thoughts," I said, though I suspected they weren't worth that much.

"Saint Thomas Aquinas said 'Justice is a certain rectitude of mind whereby a man does what he ought to do in circumstances confronting him.'"

Maybe his thought *was* worth more than one penny. I stopped stacking dishes. Did that mean he knew something about the murders? "And what ought you to do in these circumstances?"

He held up a finger and bowed his head, as if deep in thought. The finger waggled and he said, "Atlantic City."

"What about it?"

He swung around to face me. "That's where I know Stan from."

"You knew Uncle Stan?"

"Well, not to speak to. I didn't know him by name, but he was a fairly distinctive guy, being so tall and all. I just couldn't place him until now. He hung with some unsavory types."

"You should tell Wolf."

He smacked a hand over his mouth, and for one fleeting moment I thought he'd remembered something. But he removed his hand and grinned. "I should have set up a poker game with him. Missed my chance."

I sighed. Why had I thought for even a moment that Tucker might think of something other than himself?

I carried the leftovers into the kitchen, wrapped them in foil, and stashed them in the fridge.

The reassuring murmur of Hannah and her friends in the kitchen followed me when I returned to the dining room. I paused to look out the window where Tucker had stood and saw Nina running along the sidewalk toward Natasha's house.

Fearing something was wrong, I rushed to the front door, slammed it behind me, and loped along the sidewalk. Little Hermione dodged back and forth across the street with Nina chasing after her.

I raced toward them, hoping to herd Hermione in Nina's direction. But the impish dachshund dodged both of us and wedged herself under Natasha's gate. I caught up to Nina at the yellow tape.

"She dashed out the front door. At first all she did was hide, but now she thinks she's the queen of the neighborhood." Nina fingered the yellow police tape. "I have to go in and get her."

She had no choice. It wasn't like she could explain the meaning of the yellow tape to Hermione.

Nina unlatched the gate and we slipped through to forbidden territory. All I could think of was Emily. When we rounded the corner, I half-expected to see her, but the beautiful pergola stood alone and abandoned.

"There she is." Nina pointed toward the garage in the rear, where Hermione was digging in the soft soil of Natasha's flower garden.

"You come around from the side and I'll go for her straight on." Nina flexed her fingers like she was ready to grab the little dog. "If we're very quiet, maybe she won't see us coming."

I stole across the yard, changed direction, and hurried to the rear. Crouching, I prepared to stop the clever dog if she bolted. Across from me, Nina stepped stealthily toward her.

As Nina bent to grab her, I heard heated voices.

A figure moved in the shadows of Natasha and Mars's garage, giving me a jolt. It turned out to be Mars, who scurried toward me, a finger pressed across his lips.

"It's not working, is it?"

"Obviously not." Natasha sounded angry. "I've done everything except howl at the moon."

Holding a wriggling Hermione, Nina joined Mars and me to listen.

"Maybe you should visit her again. I'll go with you this time."

"All right. But Mother, be careful. Mars saw the chamomile in his wineglass last night. He confronted me about it when he came home."

"No wonder it didn't do the trick. What did you tell him?"

"What could I say? I made up something about wanting to calm him. He was furious with me. And then this morning he ran straight to Sophie's house again. I'm getting desperate . . ."

The voices came closer. Mars signaled wildly and the three of us sprinted across the yard toward the passage leading to the front gate.

Once we were safely on the other side of the yellow tape, Mars asked, "What in the devil could they be plotting?"

I felt sorry for him. Of course, I wasn't the idiot who had fallen for Natasha. Considering the amount of time he'd spent at my house lately, I wondered if their problems ran deeper than I'd suspected. "Have you been fighting?"

"Not at all."

Nina shifted Hermione in her arms. "Want me to talk to her?"

"Oh, right," I said. "I forgot you were such good friends. I'm sure she'll reveal her darkest secrets to you."

"We could hide in the house somewhere." Nina sucked in a little breath.

Hermione pricked her ears and turned her long nose, looking about in alarm.

"Bernie's apartment. She and Wanda obviously talk out there. We could drop a microphone out one of his windows to pick up their voices." But as Nina spoke, a squad car drove toward us. "Oh, crud. Natasha called the cops on us!"

A shiver ran through me. Natasha might be up to no good, but the police car came to a halt directly in front of my house.

There weren't any flashing lights, which I hoped might be a good sign. Detective Kenner stepped out of the car and smirked. Surely he hadn't taken Mordecai's nonsense about Hannah seriously. *Dear heaven, they couldn't arrest Hannah!*

I broke into a run, but Kenner beat me to my front door and had already banged the knocker.

My heart pounded. "What do you want?"

His lips pulled upward in a cruel grin. "I'm just doing my job."

His answer irritated me. He could give me a proper response. The door swung open, revealing Hannah, sweet and vulnerable. Tucker and Humphrey crowded behind her.

"Tucker Bradford Hensley the fifth?" said Kenner.

Tucker stepped forward. "Good afternoon, constable."

"I'd like you to come down to the station with me for questioning."

"No!" shouted Hannah. She reached for Tucker, but Kenner swiftly steered him to the police car. Mars, Nina, and I stepped aside so they could pass us, but Hannah ran after them. As she caught up to them, Tucker leaned toward her for a lingering nuzzle on her cheek. Hannah nodded as if he'd said something. Then she watched him fold himself into the backseat of the squad car. When Kenner slammed the door, Hannah placed her palm on the window.

The police car drew away and Hannah marched into the house, her face grim. My parents and Jen peppered her

with questions until she finally threw her arms in the air
and said, "I don't know more than any of you."

Craig puffed out his chest. Wrapping his arms around
Hannah, he said, "It appears the police have their man. I'm
so relieved. Now you can go to New Jersey with me. Maybe
we can even get away on our honeymoon?"

Hannah wrenched loose. "I . . . I'm sorry, Craig. I have
to help Tucker. He doesn't have anyone else."

"But now you know it wasn't me, Hannah."

I held my breath, afraid Hannah would do an abrupt
about-face and melt into Craig's arms.

She stood her ground. "Do I, Craig?" Her eyes sparked
with fury.

I was relieved by her response but wondered what she
was thinking. She motioned to Joel, who trailed after her
into the sunroom. I followed to see what was going on, and
the others crowded into the sunroom, too. Hannah picked
up a designer duffel bag. "This must be Tucker's. As they
were taking him away, he said Joel could cash in the contents if we need to bail him out."

THIRTY-FOUR

From "THE GOOD LIFE":

Dear Sophie,

What two things does every wedding need? I'm on a shoe-string and can't decide what's most important.

—Cutting the Cake in Custer

Dear Cutting,

A written budget and a calendar. Once you see the numbers, you can adjust so that you'll spend less on things that don't matter to you and move your money where it counts. Don't be under the misimpression that a wedding has to be fancy or large to be special. A wedding in a national forest, by a lake, or in a small country chapel has every bit as much charm as a major production in a hotel or mansion.

—Sophie

"Your ex-husband murders my uncle and you're going to bail him out?" Craig stared at her in astonishment. "This isn't like you. You were always on my side. I thought you loved me."

Hannah ignored him and shook the contents of the duffel bag onto the floor. Along with Tucker's clothes, the tiaras tumbled onto the old brick.

Jen screeched with joy and launched herself at the small tiara while Hannah pawed through the remaining contents. "I don't see anything valuable. Do you think he meant the tiaras?"

Craig snickered. "He's an idiot, Hannah. Tucker doesn't love you. He's been cozying up to you so I'll pay him to leave."

Hannah's brow furrowed. "I don't believe you."

"It's true! Surely you don't think he came here to win you back. All he wants is money. It's probably not a coincidence that your engagement ring went missing at the same time Tucker showed up."

"Oh, that's low. He would never steal my ring."

"No? He stole your tiara. He's broke . . . again. Come on—pack up and let's head north."

Joel held the larger tiara in his hand. "Aw, he must have thought these were real. Why else would he stash them in his bag?"

"They're not real?" asked Jen.

"They're real tiaras," Joel said sweetly, "but not real diamonds."

Jen plopped hers on her head and said, "I don't care. I love mine."

"Poor Tucker! What are we going to do?" said Hannah.

Craig cleared his throat. "You, Mrs. Beacham, are going to go upstairs and pack your bag so we can leave. Tucker doesn't deserve your pity. He killed my uncle, and he stole from you."

Craig was right. But I understood Hannah, too. If Kenner had arrested Mars, I would have believed the best about him. "Maybe Tucker had a good reason for pinching the tiaras." I didn't know what that good reason might be, but I wanted to help Hannah.

Craig glowered at me. "Hannah, could I speak with you privately?"

"I'm not changing my mind. Go to New Jersey with your dad. When you're done, come back here and we'll talk."

His comb-over flapping, he left the room and we heard his feet, heavy on the stairs as he raced up them.

Mom and Dad closed in on Hannah, consoling and praising her. And Humphrey boldly assured my father he would look out for Hannah. *Like he would be of any help.*

The next half-hour passed in a flurry of suitcases being brought down. I carried a bag out to the car for my parents, and when I returned, Hannah and Craig were at it again in my foyer.

Hannah's lower jaw quivered, but her hands were balled into tight fists. Humphrey flitted around them like a mosquito who thought he was a prizefighter waiting for his chance to get in a good shot.

Craig simply ignored him. "I don't understand you anymore, Hannah. You wanted to be married and as soon as we were, you turned on me and acted like I was a stranger."

"You are."

"But why? I've done everything for you. Is it Tucker? Do you want to go back to him?"

"Don't be ridiculous."

"Then what? You loved me, I know you did. But being around your family . . ." Craig jabbed a finger in my direction. "They're a bad influence. You get around your sister and start acting like a suspicious shrew, exactly like her."

"Just a minute," said Dad from the upstairs landing. "I won't have you insulting us."

Craig stepped closer to Hannah. "Please, come with me. Everything will be okay when it's only the two of us again."

Hannah backed away. "Nothing can ever be the same. Don't you understand?"

Craig's gaze drifted over to me.

"My feelings have nothing to do with Sophie. Craig, I saw you. I saw you walk out of the shed."

"But I didn't kill Stan. Can't you grasp that? I swear I didn't kill him. How can you think it was me now that the cops have Tucker in custody? You're not making sense, Hannah."

She opened the front door for him. In a patient tone, Hannah said, "I need to help Tucker. I'm sorry."

Craig left in a huff, and the rest of us relaxed visibly once he was gone. Parading about proudly, as though he'd run Craig off, Humphrey proclaimed, "Good riddance. I shall make it my mission to see that he never troubles you again."

To my unending surprise, Hannah held the door open for Humphrey, too. "Thanks for protecting me. See you around." The poor guy stumbled out the door, and Hannah closed it before he could protest.

While Dad carried the last bag to the car and Jen hugged Mochie, Hermione, and Daisy, Mom beckoned me to the living room.

"Now listen, Sophie. It's abundantly clear that your relationship with Mars is not over. We can see what's going on, so there's no use in denying it. Your father and I would welcome Mars back into the family. We're both very fond of him, and you make such a lovely couple."

"Mom, you're misconstruing things."

She waggled a finger under my nose. "A mother knows. Natasha has a better eye for makeup and sexy clothes. But you're a pretty woman, Sophie. You just have to take the time to look alluring so you can steal Mars back from her." She cupped my cheek in her hand. "Now promise me you'll try."

A brief *yes* would have made her happy. But it would be

a lie. And though I didn't think her hopes could be raised any higher, I didn't want to mislead her. "Mom, it's not going to happen."

"I don't believe it. Open up to the possibility, sweetie."

Dad and Jen called her and they finally departed, prompting Hannah to say, "I thought they'd never leave."

She walked into the kitchen, shouting, "Joel?"

Mars and Nina were relaxing at my kitchen table with coffee mugs, but Joel held car keys in his hand.

"Are you going to see Tucker?" asked Hannah.

"Yeah. Now that Dad's gone, I guess that responsibility falls to me." He gazed around at us. "Tucker has his faults, but he's like family to me. And you always take care of family."

Kevin grumbled, "I feel like a traitor. I came to be the best man and now I'm going to help the groom's rival."

Nina laughed. "Oh, please! It's not like medieval times. You don't have to avenge his honor."

"Still, Craig is my friend."

Joel asked, "Are you coming or not?"

"Let's go." Hannah was out the kitchen door in a flash with Joel right behind her. Kevin followed and Phoebe took the time to wave as she left.

Once the cavalry had departed, Mars yawned and said, "I'm starved. I can't go home to eat. There's no telling what Natasha put in the food. What's on tap, Sophie?"

With a glance at the looming pile of dishes, I made a snap decision. "Chocolate mousse. Down at Bernie's."

After corralling the dogs in the kitchen, Nina, Mars, and I walked to Bernie's pub and nabbed a table on the terrace. I ordered a pot of English Breakfast tea, and since I had more of that heavenly chocolate mousse in mind for dessert, I opted for a curried pineapple and turkey salad. Nina and Mars went for the Pub Club, a sandwich stacked with three kinds of meat and two kinds of cheese.

Leaning back in the chair, I tried to shake off the horrors

of the weekend. Two people were dead and Hannah was married to the person who probably killed them. And instead of getting closer to Wolf, here I was with my ex-husband. Again.

Through the window, I could see Bernie rush into an agitated cluster of waitresses. He resolved the problem and was headed for his office when he spied us.

"Jolly good timing." He pulled out the fourth chair and sat down. "What a day. I haven't had a minute for lunch, and now half my female staff has gone goofy over Tucker. Was he really arrested?"

Mars nearly spewed the water he drank. "You mean all those pretty young things are in love with Tucker?"

"Hard to grasp, isn't it? Makes me consider buying a red sports car."

"Now, fellows," said Nina, "don't forget that Tucker still has those boyish good looks. It's not just the car. Plus, Tucker has a way of making every girl feel special."

"Now he can make the lady jail wardens feel special," Bernie quipped.

Mars toyed with his fork. "I don't think he's under arrest yet. Just in for questioning."

"The three young ladies who went to rescue him shall be sorely disappointed. I must say, though, while I can clearly envision Craig jabbing a bloke with a knife, I can't see Tucker going through with it. He might joke about using it as a sword, or even have mock fights with it, but I can't see him taking that final fatal step."

"Maybe it was an accident," I said. The waitress set my dish in front of me. Large chunks of turkey breast mingled with pineapple in a golden sauce. "Maybe he was playing around, as you suggest, and then he slipped, or Stan moved where he didn't expect, and suddenly Stan was speared."

Bernie asked the waitress to bring him a Laughing Dog and a Pub Club.

"Laughing Dog?" Mars plucked a strip of bacon from his sandwich and chewed it.

"English-style ale made here in the States."

"Not that I mean to interrupt what would surely be a fascinating discussion about beer, but does anyone know anything about Kevin?" Nina needed both hands to pick up half her sandwich.

"He said he works out with Craig."

"He told me he owns the gym where they work out." Mars sipped his iced tea. "Did Hannah ever find her ring?"

"Not that I know of."

Nina tried to mash her sandwich. "These are like a delicatessen inside bread. Umm."

The waitress brought Bernie's Pub Club and ale and set them in front of him. "Poor Tucker. All anyone can talk about is the murders."

"What are people saying?" I asked.

She cast a quick glance at Bernie, but he was already busy eating. "The speculation is that the bride killed the groom's ex-wife and the uncle found out, so she offed him, too."

I was *not* glad I asked. I could only imagine what they were saying about the fact that we'd served dinner after the murder.

When the waitress moved to another table, Nina sat back in her chair. "Let's look at this logically. We have Craig, who had more motives and opportunity than anyone else. Right?"

I had to agree. He remained my number one suspect.

"And then we have Tucker, who appears to interest the police. We know he had a motive to kill Stan, but what about Emily?"

I swallowed a savory bit of turkey. "He met her here—the night before she was killed."

"So he might have known her? No wonder he's a

contender. Who else? We can add Kevin to the list, but I don't think he knew Emily."

"He was supposed to be Craig's best man. Don't you think his best man knew his ex-wife? Bernie was my best man, and he certainly knows," Mars smiled at me, "Sophie."

"Good point. We'll keep Kevin on our list. What about Craig's dad?"

"He's a little small to strangle someone and hang her up on a pergola, don't you think?" I scooped up the last morsel of tangy, sweet pineapple.

"He could have stabbed his brother, though." Mars pointed at the half sandwich that remained on Nina's plate. "Are you going to eat that?"

Nina protected it with both hands. "You betcha. I'm just resting."

Bernie took a swig of his beer. "The first night, at the barbecue, I thought Wanda fancied Stan. But when we decorated the backyard, she catered to Robert. You don't suppose Robert killed Stan over Natasha's mother?"

Mars snorted into his iced tea. "Next suspect! How about darling Darby? She got out of Dodge very fast."

I poured myself another cup of tea. "I think you're on the wrong trail there. She was devastated by Emily's death."

"There you have it, then. A motley cast of three possibilities—Craig, Kevin, and Tucker," Bernie said.

A little cry went up in the restaurant. "What now?" Excusing himself, Bernie hustled over to the waitresses making a scene. They dispersed and Bernie returned to our table. "I'm afraid it's a bit of bad news. One of the waitresses just heard that Tucker's fingerprints are on the handle of the knife. And they found Stan's money clip and $5,000 in Tucker's car.

THIRTY-FIVE

From "THE GOOD LIFE":

Dear Sophie,

At the last wedding we attended, the bride gave glass Cinderella slippers as favors. You can imagine how much my husband cherished his. Our own daughter, in the feverish throes of wedding insanity, is wavering between conch shells and wax roses. My husband and I imagine these items going straight into trash cans. I'm pushing for an edible favor, but my daughter says I'm out of touch with the times.

—Out of Favor in Fayetteville

Dear Out of Favor,

Favors should be edible or usable. Perhaps the question each bride should ask herself when she considers favors is—would I buy this if I weren't getting married?

Unconventional favors, like tree seedlings, can be

charming, but a lot of them will end up in the trash. Edible favors are best. A guest shouldn't have to wonder what to do with the favor.

—Sophie

No wonder Kenner had picked up Tucker for questioning. Poor Tucker. Fingerprints on the knife would be hard to refute. My fingerprints and Mom's were to be expected, but Tucker didn't have a good reason to have handled the knife. But killing a man to steal his money? That wasn't Tucker's style. Was it?

We stuck around for the sinful chocolate mousse, but the news about Tucker dampened our spirits and we soon walked home.

Daisy and Hermione pranced in joy when I opened the door. I would have let them run in the backyard, but the yellow police tape still hung in place.

Mars roughhoused with Daisy. "Let's go for a walk." He snapped his fingers. "Hey, wasn't I supposed to have Daisy last week?"

"You're just noticing? Natasha didn't want her."

He clapped his hands over her ears. "Not in front of her."

"I think she already knows how Natasha feels about her. Poor Daisy," I cooed, "you have a wicked almost-stepmother."

"Almost?" asked Nina.

"They're not married. What does that make Natasha? A wicked paramour?"

Mars grabbed Daisy's leash. "I'll take the dogs down to Founder's Park for a run." He bent to speak to them. "We'll stop by my house for some tennis balls first."

He left with the dogs, and Nina stepped outside to go

home. "I hope I can find someone to adopt Hermione. She's a sweetheart, but she's very energetic."

I closed the door and leaned against it. *Disaster area* barely described my house. Dishes threatened to topple in the sink and coffee mugs cluttered the counters. I wandered, wondering what to do first. Long rental tables still crowded the living room. Darby had straightened up the den, but boxes of Natasha's plates and coffee carafes littered the floor and the gigantic heart topiary sat on the desk.

I grabbed the pillowcase that Darby had stuffed with her sheets. Balancing the box containing Natasha's coffee carafes, I made my way through the sunroom, tossing the glass diamond paperweights inside. I couldn't imagine why Natasha thought they would be appropriate for single men. The heavy diamonds slid in the box and it almost flipped. Leaving the rest for another trip, I passed through the family room to the door that led to the basement. Mochie sat in front of it, studying the crack underneath as though he'd spun something through it. I opened the door and descended six steps. Balancing the box carefully, I tossed the bag of linens down to be washed.

I grasped the box with both hands and turned. And from the dark beneath me, someone grabbed my ankle. I screamed as I fell. The box tumbled and I flailed, grasping for a hold that would prevent the weight on my ankle from tugging me farther down. Instinctively, I knew that disappearing into my basement would be the end of me.

Clawing at the stairs, I struggled to propel myself upward with my free foot. In the dim light that filtered through the open doorway, something glittered on a step inches from my fingers. Glass? Could I use it to defend myself? I strained for it and closed my fingers around a ring. Hannah's engagement ring. I slid it onto my middle finger but it was too tight. Wearing it below my first knuckle, I twisted, made a fist, and punched my hand into the head of the person below me.

It was a bad move. He seized my other ankle and I could only hold my position by wrenching myself around and hanging on with my hands.

I could feel him moving upward. I needed something, anything, as a weapon. I felt around with my right hand and encountered one of Natasha's ridiculous glass diamonds. It wasn't much, but it was all I had.

Summoning strength, I twisted abruptly. The top of a pantyhose-covered head neared my hips. That stocking-clad head scared me more than anything else. Whoever he was, he'd planned this.

I slammed the glass diamond onto his skull with all the force I could muster. He grunted, and for a split second the grip on my ankles loosened. I flipped onto my stomach, and was trying to scramble upward when I heard Natasha's voice.

"Sophie? Sophie! I know you're here."

Hearing another voice, the man propelled himself over me, stepping squarely on my shoulder. I heard him dash to the sunroom and out the door. Slowly I dragged myself up to the landing at the top of the stairs, my heart pounding. "Here, Natasha."

Doggy breath assaulted me and Daisy licked my face.

"Sophie? What are you doing? Did you break my diamonds? Oh, and my coffee carafes, too?"

"Someone was hiding in the basement. He grabbed me."

"Are you okay?"

She helped me stand and I limped into the kitchen. Collapsing into one of the fireside chairs, I said, "See if there are any bags of peas left in the freezer."

"Peas? You want to cook peas? You can barely stand." Hands on her hips, Natasha glanced around. "Is he still in the basement?"

"I think he ran out."

"Daisy would have found him by now if he were still here."

Daisy nuzzled me as though she sensed something was wrong. Her leash trailed on the floor.

"Just bring me the peas, please."

Natasha opened my freezer. "This is such a mess. How can you find anything? You should arrange your freezer according to food. Vegetables go in one bin, and meats should be together on a shelf. Oh, here they are."

I punched the bag of peas to loosen them up and was immediately sorry. I still wore Hannah's ring and had evidently hit my intruder hard enough to bruise my finger. I hoped the diamond had made a dent in his skull, but I doubted it.

"Are you sure you were attacked? You don't look any different. Your dress is a mess, but that's nothing new."

Holding the peas to my throbbing head, I assessed my ankles. Ugly red marks were starting to turn blue.

Hermione dashed through the kitchen, her leash clacking on the floor. "What are you doing here, anyway? Where is Mars?"

Natasha's dark eyes sparked. "I suppose you were planning to walk the dogs together? He brought them to our house and while he went up to change, I hurried them home to you. I can't have them destroying my house. It doesn't matter here at your place."

Frankly, I'd rather have Daisy and Mochie than a clean floor, but I was too shaken to take her on.

My thoughts returned to the intruder. Natasha and Mars had a key to my house, but how did the intruder enter? "I think I should call Wolf."

Natasha immediately brought me the phone, saying, "I'll clean up the kitchen. We don't want him thinking you're a poor housekeeper. Just don't let him look in your freezer." She checked the time. "Maybe I can reorganize it before he arrives."

Like Wolf would be interested in my freezer. I started to lash out at her but stopped. At the moment, the last thing

I wanted was to be alone. Having two dogs and Natasha in the house made me feel safer.

I phoned the police station, told them what happened, and asked them to relay the message to Wolf. Then I slumped back in the chair and closed my eyes. I could hear Natasha shooing away Daisy and Hermione and the sound of a broom whisking chunks of glass into a dustpan.

I sat up. "Stop cleaning! The cops need to see it untouched."

"Too late." Natasha dumped the contents of the dustpan into my trash. She peered out the window over the sink. "They're so prompt. Oh. It's that's dreadful Kenner fellow. Pity."

She opened the door for him before he knocked, and he strode into the kitchen, stopping in front of me. "Well, well. I hear Little Red Riding Hood wanted the Big Bad Wolf to come rescue her."

"Is it standard police procedure to poke fun when citizens need police assistance?"

He bent toward me. "You aren't acting wounded."

I struggled to my feet, sore all over, showed him to the basement stairs, and explained what happened.

Kenner switched on the light and explored while I waited upstairs. When he returned, he said, "I don't see any signs of a struggle. You do know that it's a crime to make a false report to the police?"

Was he implying that I'd made up the entire thing? I pointed to my ankles, which had morphed to an impressive shade of blue. But when he turned his eyes on my legs, goose bumps rose on my arms and I was sorry I'd ever suggested such a thing.

"Where is this vicious guy now?"

I could feel Kenner taking in every detail and suddenly had a strong aversion to giving him license to snoop through my house. Not that I had anything to hide, I just didn't like the guy or his attitude.

"I guess he left." I sounded like a feeble child who'd been lectured. *I guess he left?* That was the best I could do? "Thanks for coming."

In the kitchen, Natasha squealed. Kenner and I barged around the corner, expecting to see the intruder. But we only saw Natasha pulling dishwashing gloves off her perfectly manicured hands as she said, "Sorry, Sophie. I have to go. Right now."

She fled to the front door, and Kenner muttered, "Me, too. By the way, if I were you, I wouldn't bug Wolf with so many phone calls," said Kenner. "But you can call me any old time."

I was tempted to slam the door behind him, but as he walked away, I saw Natasha and Mars arguing on the sidewalk. Mars held a can of tennis balls and gestured angrily. When he strode toward my house, Natasha watched him, her hands on her hips.

Mars jogged up to my front door. "Daisy! Hermione!"

"What's going on?"

"Nothing." The dogs loped over to him. He hugged Daisy, taking longer than normal, and I wondered if he needed her affection.

"Before you go, someone was lurking in my basement. Would you mind looking around upstairs to be sure no one is here?"

"Sure. C'mon, girls." Mars and the dogs were halfway up the stairs when he stopped and said, "What do you mean someone was in the basement?"

I told him what happened and after assuring him I would be fine, he headed upstairs to check things out.

I turned the dead bolt on the front door and did a quick check of the downstairs to calm my nerves. Mochie buzzed through the dining room and sprang onto the living room sofa. He crouched like a little tiger, his tail twitching. I cut through the den to the sunroom, where the kneehole of the desk provided the only hiding place. Mochie leaped to the desk, skidded past the topiary, flew off the other side, and pranced into the sunroom. That left the small family room, but it was empty.

I intended to tackle the mound of dishes in the kitchen, but when I placed Hannah's ring on the windowsill over the sink, I saw Natasha waiting on the sidewalk. She glanced at her watch and, judging from her expression, was sorely irritated.

Breathless, Mars bounded into the kitchen. "All secure upstairs."

"Natasha appears to be waiting for you."

He peered out the window. "She can wait all day for all I care." He grabbed the leashes. "Are you okay alone?"

The dogs needed a good run, and Mars had made sure no one hid upstairs. I would not let one idiot cause me to be fearful in my own home. I straightened my shoulders and tried to appear confident. "I'll be fine."

"We'll be back in a couple of hours." Mars started for the sunroom. "I'll let myself out the back gate."

"You can't go through the backyard, it's still under police tape."

I heard the sunroom door close. My ankles were starting to bother me, but I limped back and locked the door to be on the safe side. Through the sunroom windows, I saw Mars and the dogs charging through the backyard despite my warning.

As the gate slammed, the jingle of Darby's phone came from the den. I hurried back on aching ankles, hoping it might be Darby calling to find out where she'd left her phone.

I punched a button and breathlessly said, "Hello?"

A woman responded. "Donata? That you, girl?"

THIRTY-SIX

From *"Ask Natasha"*:

Dear Natasha,

I bought my best friend a kitchen appliance that was listed on her wedding registry. I know she'll appreciate it, but it feels so cold. How can I make a toaster oven more personal?

—Maid of Honor in Mayesville

Dear Maid of Honor,

Create your own wrapping paper and special card. Use craft paper as a base. Cover with paint, then add her new monogram freehand, or cut a sponge in the shape of her monogram and use it all over the paper. Or make copies of photographs of the happy couple and paste them on the paper. Use a feather to swirl silver and gold paint around the photos and she'll know you put a lot of thought and love into her gift.

—Natasha

Donata again. I cleared my throat and asked, "Who are you calling, please?"

The voice apologized for reaching a wrong number and hung up. But I knew she didn't have a wrong number. Telling myself that Darby might have borrowed her friend's phone, I returned to the living room, where wedding gifts were heaped on a table.

Unless Hannah changed her mind about Craig again, all of the packages would be going back. Remembering what Darby had said about meeting Phoebe when she bought Hannah's wedding gift, I moved the packages to the floor, in search of the present from Phoebe.

I recognized her handwriting on the envelope of an attached card and tugged off the white satin ribbon that encircled wrapping paper with an elegant silver and gold print. It was almost too pretty to destroy but I tore it and easily found the store's return receipt. Exactly what I'd hoped for—a phone number. Back in the den, I called the store, wondering what I would say if Darby actually came to the phone. I didn't think she would work today right after her return, but it was a possibility.

When I asked for Darby Beacham, I was told no one by that name worked there. My heart sinking, I asked for Donata Franchini. Donata, the voice said, was off. I should call back tomorrow. That settled it. Darby Beacham had lied to us, and so had Craig. Why would she use a false name, and why would he go along with it?

I turned to the computer and searched Donata's name, but this time I added Lina's name. Nothing. And Lina's name alone brought up too many results to be worthwhile. Then I typed Lina's name along with the name Emily Beacham. An article from a Vancouver newspaper came up about a nurse named Emily Beacham who had participated in medical missions around the world, including a place called Santa Lina. Beacham was married to a doctor. A little searching in the Vancouver phone directory led to a number for Craig and Emily Beacham in Vancouver. I felt sick to my stomach. Surely it couldn't be the same Craig. I called the number and held my breath.

A pleasant woman's voice answered.

I told her my name and continued, "I'm so sorry to bother you, but I'm looking for an Emily Beacham who was married to a doctor in West Virginia."

A moment of silence passed. "That would be me."

"You're alive." A stupid thing to say.

She giggled. "Yes, the last time I checked."

I apologized again and explained my call. "My sister married a Craig Beacham who used to be an internist in West Virginia. He retired young due to a heart condition, and he was previously married to a woman named Emily."

I heard a sharp intake of breath on the other end. "Who are you again?"

"Sophie Winston. You can call Detective Wolf Fleishman at the Alexandria Police Department to confirm." It was a risk. Who knew what he might say about me these days.

"I will. I'm sorry, I'm at a bit of a loss. It sounds exactly like my husband and me."

Good heavens. Was Craig married to this woman? "You're divorced?" My heart pounded.

"No. We're quite happily married."

Could there be two doctors named Craig Beacham? "Your husband, is he there now?"

Another moment of silence. "He's on a fishing trip."

A fishing trip to marry Hannah. I thanked Emily and hung up the phone.

Reeling from the new information, I returned to the kitchen and put on the kettle for a much-deserved bracing cup of tea. With the steaming cup of Irish Breakfast tea in hand, I nestled on the window seat with my aching ankles up—and then it hit me. If Craig's other wife was alive and well, who was the woman in Natasha's pergola?

Craig had lied about the dead woman's identity. And so had Darby. All we knew about her was that she called herself Lina. And now it seemed the woman who called herself Darby was really Donata.

Why would Darby lie to us about her name? I tried to recall Craig when he saw her. I didn't remember him being surprised. Maybe her name really was Darby, and she called herself Donata now for some reason? To protect herself from the no-good husband who'd deserted her? Or maybe she had other troubles?

But the bigger picture disturbed me. In spite of the hot tea, I felt cold all over. I'd convinced myself that Emily had come to warn Hannah. But if Darby was afraid of Craig, why did she come? If I could reach her on the phone, would she tell me?

Which brought me to the question that had been nagging at me, but which I hadn't wanted to contemplate. Why had someone been hiding in my basement? Was he looking for Hannah's diamond ring and simply hadn't noticed it on the stairs? Or did he imagine I was Hannah?

Another thought chilled me to the bones. What if the intruder was the same person who had been looking for something in my drawers and cabinets all weekend? I didn't know if it was more frightening to imagine that he was a total stranger or someone I knew.

The sound of someone at the kitchen door startled me, but it was only Hannah unlocking the door and rushing in with Phoebe, laughing. Hannah hurried straight to the refrigerator, pulled out a pitcher of iced tea, and threw ice cubes into tall glasses.

"It's unbearable out there," Hannah said as she shook the neckline of her dress to cool off. "Phoebe and I are parched." She held out a glass to Phoebe while staring at my legs. "What happened to you?"

I peeked at my ankles. "Maybe I should ice them again."

I fetched two bags of peas from the freezer, which was not at all as unorganized as Natasha claimed. Then I returned to the window seat, put my legs up, and positioned the bags on my ankles. Phoebe and Hannah were shocked to hear about the intruder, but I cut them short when they asked questions because I wanted to know about Tucker.

Phoebe held the icy glass to her forehead. "Isn't he here?"

"They let him go," said Hannah. "Joel and Kevin split to see some historical thing, and we had fun poking through stores on King Street. We thought Tucker would be back by now."

"I'm glad they didn't arrest him. His fingerprints on the knife are fairly damning." Tucker was trouble, but I couldn't imagine him as a killer. I adjusted the bags of frozen peas that iced my ankles. At least the throbbing in my head had subsided.

I was just about to close my eyes when Hannah popped out of her chair like a jack-in-the-box. "Humphrey!" She ran to the door. "Humphrey, come inside! Can you believe he's been following us? He's so funny. I'm through with Craig and it looks like Phoebe and Joel are having a tough time, but Humphrey stuck to us like glue."

He glided in, his eyes fixed dreamily on Hannah. I snickered into my tea mug. Maybe Mom had told him I thought he was sexy, but now that Hannah had, for all practical purposes, dumped Craig, Humphrey appeared to be fixated on her again.

"Do we have any cake left?" Hannah opened the refrigerator and peered inside. "All that prewedding dieting has taken its toll on me. I need chocolate."

"I think there's some chocolate cheesecake. Now tell me what's going on."

Hannah cut the chunk of leftover cake into four pieces and handed me a slice on one of the pink dishes. I shouldn't have eaten any creamy chocolate cheesecake, but I'd had a bad weekend and I needed strength after my run-in with the stocking-wearing intruder.

"We're going to sleuth in your neighbor's yard. She's away, isn't she?" asked Hannah.

"For a good while," I murmured with a mouth full of cheesecake.

"We should go over there. After all, that's where they found the knife. Maybe the killer left other evidence there, too." Hannah scraped the last bit of cake off her plate and jumped to her feet. "Let's go. There's no yellow tape and I know your neighbor—she wouldn't mind us prowling around."

Phoebe joined Hannah at the door, but Humphrey remained seated. "Maybe I should stay to help Sophie."

My ankles improved immediately. I removed the frozen peas and swung my feet to the floor. "All better!"

"You know, we're going to be trespassing." Hanging his head, Humphrey dutifully followed Hannah.

Testing my weight on my feet, I stood slowly. They hurt, but I couldn't sit around all day. I made my way to the kitchen sink and turned on the faucet to tackle the dishes. I'd washed exactly two plates when Wolf's car slid into a parking spot in front of my house. After Kenner's charming visit, I figured Wolf was avoiding me.

I was wrong. He knocked on the kitchen door a minute later. I opened it and said, "Yes?"

As formally as if he didn't know me, Wolf said, "Does the name Franchini mean anything to you?"

I am not a good poker player. Although I wanted to appear calm and collected in front of Wolf, I felt like someone had poured ice-cold beer over my head.

"I gather you've heard the name?"

I wanted to know where he'd heard it, but how could I weasel it out of him?

I must have waited too long because he said, "This could be important, Sophie."

Why did I feel like I was ratting on Darby? "It's not definite that it's connected to anyone who was here, but I sort of found it on the Internet."

"For Pete's sake, I need to know. The gun that lay next to Stan's hand is registered to a Tony Franchini."

THIRTY-SEVEN

From *"Ask Natasha"*:

Dear Natasha,

My fiancé wants umbrellas in our signature drink. We're having a black-tie wedding, and I think that would be cheesy. How can we garnish our drinks without making them look like they came from a tiki bar?

—Going to the Chapel in Good Hope

Dear Going,

Dip the rims of the cocktail glasses in liquor to wet them, then dip them in edible silver or gold sugar. For that extra bit of bling, wrap the bottom of the stem with silver and clear beaded raindrop garland and fasten with a drop of hot glue. The result is lavish and elegant, and your guests will talk about your signature cocktail for years to come. Visit https:// www.easyleafproducts.com.

—Natasha

The news about the gun's owner hit me like a lead bucket. "I think Darby's name might be Donata Franchini. Did you ask Robert about it?"

"He doesn't know anyone named Franchini and thinks the gun must have been stolen."

There must be a lot of people named Franchini, but I wasn't buying a coincidence. "You're running a check, right?"

Wolf gave me a look that meant I ought to leave the investigating up to him. My teeth hurt from clenching them. I didn't know what more could possibly go wrong, but I suspected I ought to forget about Wolf. Or should I try one last time? "Look, about . . ."

"Don't even go there, Sophie. I didn't realize you were the obsessive type."

"Obsessive?" I sputtered. How could he possibly think that? Sure, I'd wanted to have a romantic weekend with him, maybe even dance under the lights in my backyard, but I hardly considered that obsessive.

Wolf stubbed the toe of his shoe against the ground. "You know I'm busy. Calling me six times and setting up that meeting at Bernie's restaurant and then pretending you were attacked—that's obsessive. And manipulative."

"I didn't set up the rendezvous at Bernie's. And I really was assaulted. I simply asked the 911 operator to give you the message. Except for one call this morning, I haven't called you all day."

"Soph?"

Not the best timing. Daisy trotted up with Hermione on her heels and Mars walked around the corner from the backyard. At least he had the decency to look guilty when he saw Wolf.

"I'm sure it's not easy to have your backyard roped off as a crime scene. We'll release it soon and just keep the shed off limits. Until then, I have to ask you not to pass the yellow tape."

Mars, usually cool and collected, stammered, "I . . . I was just cutting through. I wouldn't have come in here . . ."

Wolf interrupted him. "I'll be in touch."

When he strode away, Mars loosened up. "I'm beginning to think he doesn't like me." He handed me Daisy's leash, said good-bye, and crossed the street to return Hermione to Nina.

I hated that Wolf didn't believe me. Why couldn't he believe I hadn't called him? Maybe someone else was leaving messages for him in my name. Darby? But why? Did she want Wolf and me together? Or did she want to be sure that neither of us was at my house? Maybe my attacker hadn't meant to harm me. What if he'd intended to search the house while I was gone?

Trying to put Wolf out of my mind, I headed upstairs to search the house myself. Mochie explored the closet in the room where Hannah slept, reminding me that he'd been trapped there the day Emily died. Could someone have searched the house in my absence? Voices drifted to me from the front window and I peered out. Tourists ambled past, but more importantly, I realized that an intruder could have seen Emily and me speaking on the street.

I opened all the drawers and poked through closets, but I didn't find anything of note. Not that I knew what I was after.

We made our way to the second floor, where I found a drawer in the bathroom hanging open. It contained extra rolls of toilet paper. I slammed it shut, frustrated. Had the intruder been up here earlier? Had he searched the entire house as I was doing now, made his way to the basement, and been pinned there when I returned home?

Another drawer hung open in my room. Mochie jumped inside and pawed around. When he sprang out, I straightened the contents and shut it. The thought of anyone going through my things frightened me. What could the person want?

A chorus of voices drifted up the stairs. Mochie and Daisy raced to the foyer to see who had arrived while I creaked after them on ankles that felt like an elephant had sat on them.

Phoebe bent to stroke Mochie. "We ran into Joel and took a detour to buy brats and burgers to grill. I can't believe I'm saying this, but I'm starved."

Joel rubbed his hands in anticipation.

"Where's Kevin?" I asked.

"He headed home. I think he was glad to get on the road."

I shuffled into the kitchen, where Hannah and Humphrey unloaded groceries. To my surprise, Tucker was back. His elbows on the table, he pressed his mouth against interlaced fingers. His day with the police had destroyed the joyous spirit that normally sparkled in his eyes.

"Are you okay?"

He nodded but wouldn't look at me.

I'd never seen him like this. "Could I make you a drink?" He looked like he could use one.

"Iced tea, please."

The Tucker I knew had never turned down alcohol. I poured a glass and handed it to him. "What happened?"

"He doesn't want to talk about it. We found him sitting on a bench outside a church." Hannah frowned at the pile of dishes in the sink. "Shouldn't those have been washed hours ago?"

Phoebe took that as her cue to wash dishes, and Joel pitched in to dry.

Hannah pulled me into the family room and whispered, "Phoebe and Joel aren't getting along at all. I'd really like them to stay another couple of days so they can work on patching things up, but the hotel was getting expensive for them. Would you mind if they stayed here? They checked out of the hotel this morning . . ."

I assured her that was fine and sent her upstairs to change

the linens on the beds. Hannah promptly enlisted Humphrey's help, and the two of them disappeared upstairs.

I ventured into the sunroom and looked out at the backyard, thinking about the open drawers and Stan and Emily and the intruder. The sun was setting, and my yard was so tranquil I resented the fact that we couldn't use it. It would have been a perfect night to cook out and build a blazing fire in the fire pit.

I shook myself out of what couldn't be and stumbled to the kitchen. Determined not to let my ankles and other bruises spoil our fun, I whipped up a batch of frozen margaritas and poured them into heavy, bubbled glasses from Mexico.

Addressing Phoebe, I said, "You and Joel are more than welcome to stay here."

Phoebe thanked me but had hardly gotten the words out when Tucker said, "How about me?"

He looked so pathetic I could hardly say no. Besides, I thought we'd better keep an eye on him. He didn't seem well to me. "You, too, Tucker. Go upstairs and tell Hannah to make up a bed for you."

Obediently, he rose and trudged toward the foyer. He stopped midway, turned back, and hugged me. But instead of heading upstairs, he wandered to the sunroom.

"I'm worried about him." Phoebe handed a drink to Joel. "Have you seen him like this before?"

"Dad brought him home late at night a couple of times, but he was always peppy and arrogant," said Joel. "Nothing ever got to him."

"Something got to him today." I wished Wolf and I were in good standing so I could phone him and find out what had happened to Tucker.

"Tucker?" I called.

He reappeared, dragging his duffel bag.

"Did you check out of the hotel already?" I couldn't help thinking something wasn't quite right. Tucker, who never rose before noon, had been here when I showered but I couldn't recall him arriving. "You slept here last night, didn't you?"

"I meant to sleep on a chaise in the backyard. But who knew it could be so cold in the summer?"

"So that was you I saw leaving through the back gate?"

His shoulders sagged. "You'll find out sooner or later, I guess. I've been sleeping in the Spider. Not much legroom."

"So you sneaked inside and slept upstairs last night?"

He shrugged. "The kitchen door was unlocked. You, Hannah, and Jen were dead to the world and Daisy likes me, so I prowled about a bit until I found an empty bed. Like Goldilocks. I'm family. I didn't think you'd mind."

Actually, I didn't mind. But I found it alarming that he'd so easily spent the night in my house without any of us realizing it.

Hobbling like a broken old man, he dragged his duffel bag through the kitchen and disappeared into the foyer.

I threw a fresh tablecloth over the kitchen table and limped to the dining room to filch one of the gorgeous wedding centerpieces. I asked Phoebe if she would carry a couple upstairs to the bedrooms to brighten them up.

When she left the kitchen, Joel stood, clutching his margarita. "Should I bring the grill around here?"

I kept a lookout for Wolf while Joel ducked into the backyard to roll the grill into the service alley by the kitchen. I lifted the yellow tape so he could slide it underneath, fervently hoping Wolf wouldn't return at that moment.

He positioned it close to the door. "Do you grill a lot?" I asked.

He held tongs over his head like a warrior. "I am the Grill Meister!"

While he took charge of the grill, I plunked small potatoes into a pot to cook. I chopped onions and pickles and hard-boiled eggs and slid them into a big bowl. I added horseradish mustard and mayonnaise. All it needed now were the potatoes for a warm German potato salad. I found leftover cooked asparagus and made a quick tossed salad with fresh tomatoes and greens.

The others returned in time to finish setting the table. Tucker still seemed out of sorts, but I noticed that he sipped at a margarita and took that as a good sign.

I should have been full, but my mouth watered at the scent of the seasonings in the bratwurst. I drained the potatoes, sliced them, and tossed them in the bowl.

Due to Tucker's fragile state, we chose not to talk about the murders over dinner. A conversation about plays and favorite movies kept it lively, but Tucker barely spoke.

After we cleaned up, I begged off and went up to bed early to catch up on sleep. But when I woke in the middle of the night and walked down to the kitchen for a drink, I discovered Tucker in the sunroom. Instead of his usual slouch, Tucker sat on the settee with his knees drawn up to his chin. I plopped into the chair next to him. He didn't change the angle of his head, but even in the dim light, I could see his eyes rotate toward me.

"I've been called a lot of things in my life, but no one has ever accused me of murder before. This is a life experience I could have done without."

I glanced out at the backyard. "If you had been awake, you would have had a perfect view of the killer coming and going from the shed."

He shifted his head backward and sighed.

"Tucker Hensley! You did see something."

THIRTY-EIGHT

From *"Ask Natasha"*:

Dear Natasha,

I love your show and never miss it. I adored the centerpieces that light up underneath the flowers and make the vases glow. My florist thinks I'm nuts and says he's never heard of a light that can go underwater.

—Elegant Bride in Elon

Dear Elegant Bride,

Submersible LED cubes and Floralytes add an unexpected punch of light and color in unlikely places. Vase illuminator bases that provide an uplight through clear vases are also fantastic. Surprise your guests with lighted balloons scattered among helium balloons. They're a great way to flank an entrance or a buffet table. Visit http://www.save-on-crafts .com/partyideas.html.

—Natasha

Tucker closed his eyes, and his Adam's apple bobbed. I leaned back against the cushion. He had to be protecting someone. Tucker would be the first to rat on someone else if it would keep him out of trouble. Who would he protect? "Hannah?"

"Yes," he said drolly, "the bride was running through the house in her wedding gown slashing people."

Did he think he was helping Hannah by not mentioning that he saw Craig? "You know that Hannah saw Craig leave the shed."

"Like I care about Craig." He unwound his legs and set his bare feet on the floor. "I can't imagine what Hannah sees in him. The man is like a bowling pin—smooth, bald, and dull."

He stretched out and draped his arms across the back of the settee. "I don't know what to do but stand trial. They can't convict me because I didn't kill him."

Tucker had relaxed considerably since I found him. Nothing bothered him for long. He went his merry way in life, unconcerned about consequences. Which made it all the more extraordinary that he would be willing to take the rap for someone else. I ticked through the names of the bridesmaids in my mind. Had he taken up with one of them? Darby! No, she and Kevin clearly had a thing for each other. Phoebe? Now that Phoebe and Joel were arguing, was Tucker such a worm that he would move in on her? But I'd forgotten that Tucker knew Joel and had introduced them. I leaned forward, not three feet from his face. "Joel."

The Adam's apple bobbed again.

"You saw Joel go into the shed with Stan?"

"Honestly, Sophie, I really was asleep. I didn't see anything."

"Then I don't get it. You're protecting someone, but you hardly know anyone involved."

He licked his lips and chewed on the lower one.

"Spit it out. You know you're dying to tell someone."

He hunched forward, bracing his arms on his knees. "You know about Joel's family losing their business, right?"

"And his dad died."

"You're simplifying things. Joel's dad had a shipment of majorly expensive pink diamonds coming into the country. The kind of stuff they show to customers in private back rooms of the highest-end jewelry companies. Capiche? You know anything about jewelry couriers?"

"Yes, of course, I buy diamonds by the gross."

"Very funny. There are two ways to go. You can hire somebody with an armored van, but there are cats on the lookout for those. The other way is kind of like a spy—you hire someone who blends in and won't attract any attention, and that's what Joel's father did. He contracted with an independent guy he'd used before. The guy goes to Miami to pick up the shipment, but on his way back, when he stops for gas, somebody bashes him over the head—bad, real bad. The cops find his car abandoned, no jewelry inside. But now the courier is paralyzed—permanently disabled, and his family accuses Joel's dad of setting up the heist and sues him. Between the loss of the diamonds, the lawsuit, and the demise of the family business, his dad was under unbelievable stress and had a coronary."

He sat back, satisfied and clearly finished with his sad story.

I squinted at him. Hannah had lost her engagement ring with the pink diamond before Tucker showed up. Joel must have told him the stone was a pink diamond. "It's improbable that Hannah's diamond was one of the stolen ones and, supposing it was, why would Joel kill Stan over it? There must be lots of pink diamonds in the world. When did the robbery take place?"

"About five years ago."

"Oh, right, like the diamonds haven't changed hands a

few times since then? I hardly think they're sitting in a pot somewhere."

His mouth twisted upward on one side. "Rocks like that aren't easy to unload. You have to hire somebody to break them down into smaller stones if you want to sell them."

I couldn't follow his reasoning. "You think Joel killed Stan and Emily because Craig gave Hannah a pink diamond?" Had he lost his mind? That didn't make any sense at all.

"I've been following Joel."

"Is that why you came here? To spy on Joel?"

"Of course not. I've been a little down on my luck— barred from some casinos. Weddings are good hunting ground for poker games. Failing that, they're also great places to meet women—and their mothers eager to marry them off."

"Aren't you a little bit ashamed for being such a parasite?"

"Is that how you see me? I'm not a common thief who would kill for a lousy $5,000."

"You took the tiaras."

"That's different. I thought the stones belonged to Joel. Don't you see, Sophie? I make the women happy, and let's face it, the men would lose their poker money to someone else if not to me. I provide . . . entertainment and amusement. I bring joy into their lives."

"Like moonshine. They're happy for a short time, and the next day you're like a nightmarish hangover."

"My, but you've become cynical since your divorce from Mars."

"Me? You've lost all semblance of sanity, living off other people's hopes and thinking Joel killed Stan because of Hannah's ring."

"You don't know Joel like I do. I've seen how he looks at Craig and his family. And then when Craig showed up with those tiaras with pink stones in them, I thought Joel would blow a gasket. In fact, I think he did—that's when he murdered Stan. Joel must have thought he was avenging his dad and his family."

"Not a chance," I protested. "Joel knew the tiaras were fake. Did you tell the cops your pathetic theory?"

He rubbed both hands over his face. "I owe Joel's dad. He pulled me out of some bad messes. The least I can do is save his kid."

Joel's father must have been an impressive person to inspire such loyalty in Tucker. I never would have expected callous Tucker to put himself at risk for anyone else. Maybe he wasn't as shallow as I'd thought all these years.

With mixed feelings about Tucker, and wondering about Joel, I shoved off to bed.

In the morning, I was the first one downstairs. I wore a comfortable skort and a sleeveless top that my mother would have approved because the V-neck dipped a skosh lower than usual for me. My ankles, hideous blues and purples, felt much better than they looked. My shoulder had become stiff during the night, but I thought it would loosen up as I moved around.

I brewed a pot of Hannah's favorite Mystic Monk coffee, and the heavenly aroma floated through the kitchen immediately.

Joel emerged from the foyer in shorts and a T-shirt, yawning. "Thanks for putting us up. The hotel was great but a little pricey. Besides, it's so cool to stay in a house that was here during the Civil War. I can just imagine it. When you watch a movie, it's all a set. But this is the real thing— living history."

I smiled at his enthusiasm. "You're welcome to come for a visit any time." As soon as the invitation slipped out of my mouth, I wondered if I'd invited a killer. He was so sweet, I figured Tucker's theory was wrong, but you never know.

I eased into the topic, hoping I wouldn't put him on

guard. "Tucker told me about your dad and the family business. I'm so sorry."

"Thanks." The corners of Joel's mouth quivered and he seemed like a kid trying to gain control of his emotions. "That was an awful time for us. My mother's parents worked hard to make their corner jewelry store a success. Losing it was crushing, but when my dad died, that sent us all in a tailspin. My sister and I grew up in the store. We never imagined we would do anything else."

"What does your sister do now?"

"She works at a mall jewelry store." He shrugged. "It's a job."

"Tucker said the courier went to pick up pink diamonds." I tossed the line out there casually as I handed him a mug of coffee. "They never showed up anywhere? The jewelry world has to be pretty small when it comes to high-ticket items."

"That's the irony of it all. We would have heard if the stones started turning up anyplace. Those thugs ruined my family and got nothing out of it."

If I had been alone, I wouldn't have asked him the next question, but I had plenty of company in the house. I set sugar and milk on the table and chose my words carefully, so he wouldn't think I was accusing him of anything. "Do you think the stone in Hannah's ring came from the robbery?"

Joel dragged his hands down over his mouth. "I wondered if Craig was involved the minute I saw Hannah's engagement ring. It's the kind of stone movie stars and the ridiculously wealthy buy. It's remotely possible he bought it for her, but I don't think so."

Deep in my heart, I knew anyone could kill, but even though Joel had the strength, there was a softness about him. A gentleness. I could imagine him bouncing a copper-haired baby on his knee and hosting backyard cookouts.

"Tucker knew about the ring and the heist, too. If you

want my opinion, he killed Stan to get revenge for what happened to my father. Tucker and my dad were real close. He thinks Stan was one of the thieves."

"You really think Tucker could have killed Stan?"

"I don't want to believe it. But Tucker's always been a bit of an enigma, and it's hard to know what someone might be capable of. There is a lot that points to him. Motive, means, opportunity. And just between the two of us, I didn't see him sleeping in the sunroom."

THIRTY-NINE

I nearly dropped my mug of coffee as I listened. I'd thought Joel could give Tucker an alibi, but instead he was practically convicting him.

When Hannah bounced into the kitchen moments later, she was wearing a vivid turquoise top and white trousers that belonged to me but made my bottom look like a hot air balloon. "You don't mind, do you?" she asked as she swept by me.

Mind? She could have them. They were darling on her. She poured a cup of coffee and swung her long hair to the other shoulder, revealing that she wore my earrings as well.

"I'm so glad that I don't have to dress in pastels anymore. Don't get me wrong, I like pastels, but I'm not into being demure."

Daisy pawed at the door. I'd been so excited to have a chance to chat with Joel, I'd forgotten to let her out. I started to open the kitchen door for her and remembered that she wasn't supposed to run in the backyard. What a bother.

"Humphrey's not up yet?" asked Hannah.

"Humphrey?"

"He intended to sleep in his hearse out on the street, so I told him he could crash in the den. I knew you wouldn't mind. I should wake him."

"Hannah, be careful. Humphrey's liable to think you're in love with him." I took my coffee mug and opened the door for Daisy. "I'll be back in a few minutes. How do waffles sound for breakfast?"

I thought Joel might drool just thinking about it.

Even though I knew the backyard was off limits, I ducked under the yellow tape to look around. "Be very careful, Daisy, we're not supposed to be back here." She wagged her tail like I'd told her a joke and trotted off toward the rear of the yard. I sipped my coffee and gazed at the chaos. Shepherd's hooks full of bright gerbera daisies still lined the runner and the empty white chairs remained in formation like good little soldiers, but the flowers on Natasha's heart-shaped wreath had wilted, along with the blossoms on the wedding arch.

Wolf had allowed the ice bar to be broken down and removed, but the little carpet that I'd thrown over the spot where Natasha's sculpture broke remained. I'd forgotten all about the ill-fated cupid.

After a glance around, I ambled to the potting shed, stepped inside, and tried to imagine what had transpired.

Idly, I pulled up the top of the cooler that contained bits of the cupid. The chunks of ice had melted into water. I flipped open the other cooler. Floating on top with tiny melting pieces lay a boutonniere box. The white rose inside was as crisp and fresh as it must have been on Hannah's wedding day. The cops must have seen it, but it probably hadn't meant anything to them. It was just another piece of wedding froufrou on ice to keep cool. But what if the person distributing the boutonnieres had gotten into a fight with someone, wound up with an extra one, and had to hide the evidence? I knew who had taken charge of the boutonnieres. I knew who might have wanted to drop Stan's boutonniere into the cooler to hide it. I knew whose fingerprints would be on the box. Robert.

I slammed the cooler shut and rushed to the house. Daisy, sensing excitement, romped along. I flew through the kitchen to the telephone and called Wolf.

The woman who answered the phone said, "Look honey, somebody has got to tell you that Wolf just isn't the kind of guy you can pursue this way. I'm sorry to be so blunt, but you have to be more subtle."

Doing my best to control my temper, I said, "Tell him Robert killed Stan. I'm certain of it."

"Give it up, honey. That's not the way to win him over."

I hung up, not knowing if she would tell him or not. When I turned, I realized my houseguests were staring at me.

"What happened? How do you know that?" asked Humphrey, his white hair tousled from sleep.

I told them about the boutonniere box.

Tucker lifted his mug to me like a toast. "Bravo! But that's hardly evidence."

"Does the name Franchini mean anything to you?"

They gazed at one another.

I didn't wait. I dashed to the den for Darby's phone. It

didn't have much of a charge left. I pushed buttons until I managed to find the number of the last caller. I scurried back to the kitchen and surveyed my options. Hannah, Tucker, Humphrey, and I sounded like southerners. That left Joel and Phoebe.

Explaining that I wanted him to find out what he could about Donata or Tony Franchini, I pushed a button and the phone dialed the number of the last caller.

Like a champ, Joel said, "Hey. I'm looking for Donata. She there?"

He shook his head indicating no.

"I heard she's with Tony."

We all heard the shriek that spewed from the phone. A woman's voice screeched, "She's back with her ex? When did he show up?"

"Hey, you know how I can get in touch with Tony or Donata? I've got a delivery for them that I know they want."

He motioned for a pen and I handed him a pen and paper.

"Her mom?" He scribbled a number on the pad, along with the name *Mrs. Pietra*. He thanked her and hung up. Seeming to enjoy himself, he promptly dialed the new number.

"Mrs. Pietra? I'm a friend of Donata's. We were planning to go out tonight and I have to cancel, but I can't find her and I don't want to leave her standing out on the street waiting for me."

A silence followed. Joel grinned. "Yes, I promise I'll pick her up next time."

Another silence, but Joel began to scribble again. The rest of us hunched forward, hoping to hear what her mother was saying.

"Thank you. You have a nice day, Mrs. Pietra."

Joel hung up and tapped the paper. "It seems that Donata went to a wedding over the weekend with Constanzo and Roberto."

FORTY

From *"Ask Natasha"*:

Dear Natasha,

I hate wedding cakes. My fiancé and I adore malted milk balls, but we can't just serve those for dessert. Do I have to pay for an expensive cake that I don't want?

—Malted Milk Lover in Mount Airy

Dear Malted Milk,

Set up a candy bar for dessert. Use glass bowls and vases of different sizes and shapes and fill them with all your favorites. If you provide darling little bags, they can double as favors, too. And if you'd like a hint of cake, set cupcakes on a tiered display next to the malted milk balls.

—Natasha

"Constanzo and Roberto?" Hannah wrapped her arms over her abdomen like she was comforting herself. "You mean they weren't his relatives?"

Humphrey reached a tentative hand toward her shoulder but withdrew it before he made contact. "Do you think he asked friends to play the part of his family?"

"A charade? It was bad enough to imagine Craig might have killed Stan, but this would mean he deceived me . . . us." Hannah unwound her arms and drummed her coffee mug just like our mother did when she was thinking. "Isn't it possible that all this information is wrong? That the gun was stolen and that Joel just talked to the mother of someone named Donata whom we don't know? Maybe the phone doesn't belong to Darby. Maybe one of the other guests left it."

"Excuse me. Doesn't anyone else see the similarities in the names? Robert—Roberto, Stan—Constanzo?" I felt terrible for Hannah. There weren't many possible scenarios that would appeal to her. Either she was married to a murderer, or her husband and his buddies had deceived her, or, I shuddered to think it, both.

Hannah snatched up Darby's cell phone and punched buttons. "Rats. She doesn't have many numbers stored."

Humphrey peered over her shoulder. An excuse to get closer? "I think the charge died."

In disgust, Hannah set the phone on the table.

"We can buy a recharger for it." Obviously, Phoebe wanted to cheer up Hannah. "Let's go."

Humphrey said, "What about breakfast? I get woozy if I don't eat."

"I can start waffles while you buy a recharger, and then while we eat we'll see what else we can figure out from the phone."

Hannah practically pushed Humphrey out the door. I could hear him insisting he would faint if he didn't eat.

Trying to forget about the mess, I apologized to Daisy for ignoring her and took her for a quick walk.

We crossed the street and passed Natasha and Mars's house. I wondered if Natasha had erred in buying a place so close to mine. I didn't suffer from delusions that Mars pined for me, but we were friends and he clearly considered his aunt's house, now mine, a haven.

We crossed another street, and I focused on the murders and whatever odd game Craig's relatives, if they *were* his relatives, had been playing. It followed that Stan was Constanzo and Robert was Roberto, but then who was Tony? Stan had Tony's gun, and according to the woman on the phone, Tony was Darby's ex-husband. Was he the one who'd walked out on her?

We turned left and started walking back. I chuckled to myself about the problems we might have created for Donata/Darby when her mother asked her about the new boyfriend who'd called.

But my chuckles subsided when I glimpsed Wolf near Mordecai's house. I hoped Humphrey had told him our theories, but I wasn't in the mood for another unpleasant confrontation. Praying that Wolf hadn't seen us, I cut through the alley that passed behind Nina's and Natasha's houses.

A hand grabbed my shoulder and I jumped. Wolf had caught up to us.

"Humphrey called me." Wolf squatted to pet Daisy.

"Do you think Robert killed Stan?"

His nose wrinkled in a cute way, and I couldn't help thinking how attractive he was. "I don't think I can build a case based on a boutonniere box, but I'll keep it in mind."

I could understand why Wolf didn't think the boutonniere box was significant, but someone had bothered to hide it in the cooler.

Wolf's phone buzzed and he stood up. "At least I know it's not you calling. Excuse me." He used the earbud and listened. "It's a message from you." Speaking into the phone, he said, "What time did that call come in? From what number? Thanks." He removed the earpiece. "Looks like I owe you an apology."

That confirmed my suspicions. Someone had been calling him and saying it was me. "Why would anyone call and claim to be me?"

"You didn't arrange for us to meet at Bernie's restaurant yesterday?"

"Afraid not."

"Don't you think it was too coincidental that Mars happened to be there? Did you bring him with you?"

"Didn't do that, either."

Wolf sucked in air. "I don't get it. I'm supposed to meet you in the bar at Bernie's today at four o'clock."

"Should we go?"

"I'm pretty curious to see who else shows up. Sophie, I truly am sorry. I should have realized that you weren't the type to play games." He waved and started back to Mordecai's.

I didn't want to go in the same direction as though I were following him, so I continued through the alley and turned onto the sidewalk. We were almost to the corner when I thought I recognized someone in a parked car.

Poor Daisy probably thought I'd lost my mind. I spun and tugged her to the alley. Then I peered around the corner. The Mazda3 bore New Jersey license plates, and the person in the driver's seat leaned forward like she was watching the street. Darby was back.

I didn't want her to know that I'd seen her, so I swung open the gate to Natasha and Mars's garage. Daisy ran through and I closed it behind us. But when we entered the grassy part of the yard, we found Natasha turning in a circle, salt spilling from a container in her hand. She yelped when she saw us.

"What are you doing?"

"There's just no privacy in this town. Why are you here?"

"I'm avoiding someone. What's with the salt?"

"You won't tell anyone?" Natasha blushed. "You know how superstitious my mom is. She's convinced that Emily's spirit will haunt us because she was so brutally murdered."

"The salt?"

"To ward away evil spirits."

"Shouldn't Wanda be out here helping you?"

"She's inside, lighting incense. Please don't tell anyone. I couldn't stand for Mars to find out. That's why I couldn't tell the police my alibi for Emily's murder. I was at a fortune-teller's trying to get a love potion."

I tried not to giggle. "A love potion for Mars?"

Pain invaded her face. "I might as well come right out and ask you. Are you and Mars having an affair?"

I bit my lip so I wouldn't laugh, but I had to answer her. "No, Natasha, we're not."

"Then why can't I get him to propose to me? I was so certain that Hannah's romantic wedding would flame Mars's fire, but if anything, it seems like he's even less interested."

"Is that why you bought those silly glass diamonds for the single men?"

"I thought he should have a diamond available in case the mood struck him."

I finally began to understand. "That's why you hung all over Kevin."

"I thought it would make Mars jealous. But all he did was flee to you."

Her plan might have worked better if Kevin hadn't spent the weekend running away from her. "Mars hung around me complaining about your interest in Kevin."

"He was jealous? Maybe those things did work."

"What things?"

"I put chamomile in his wine. And the wedding cake—it was supposed to have aphrodisiac qualities, too. Sophie, how did Mars propose to you? I mean, did you discuss it first or did he surprise you?"

Mars's proposal brought back warm memories. We'd been so young. Barefoot, walking on the beach in the moonlight. But that wouldn't make Natasha feel any better. "You can't push Mars or he'll dig his heels in. Give him time." Daisy and I strolled toward the service passage.

"Oh, Sophie," said Natasha, "I'm sorry about the way things worked out with Wolf. I'd have been better off if he had been around for the wedding. Mars would have seen you two together and, well, I think I made a big mistake. I've been trying to get you back together, though."

Oh no! She wouldn't have! "Have you been calling Wolf to set up meetings with me?"

"Please don't tell me it backfired. Mom and I thought Mars should see you with Wolf. Then he'd realize he couldn't win you back."

I held out my hand. "My phone, please?"

Part of me wanted to lash out at her. She'd caused me a lot of heartache. "You know, you could be arrested for that."

She flicked a hand at me and laughed. "Don't be silly. It's not like I called 911. They were personal calls. There's no law against that. Besides, I did it with good intentions. You're my best friend. Do you need help organizing that freezer?"

I didn't answer. Instead I turned to leave, and Daisy and I ran through the service entrance to the street, before Wolf could come along and be angry with me anew for being behind the yellow line.

We walked toward Nina's house, and I wondered where she and Hermione were. Normally, she'd have shown up for breakfast at my place. I knocked on her front door, but no one answered.

At the opposite corner of the street, I hoped we were far enough away to be out of Darby's range of vision. I risked being caught by Wolf, walked to the alley, and slipped through the back way so Darby wouldn't see us.

Hannah was still out, but Mochie greeted us at the door. Daisy trailed to the water bowl, drank, and sprawled on the floor. Neither of them acted like anyone else was in the house.

I peered out the bay window. Darby had parked where she could observe my house. Kneeling on the floor so I wouldn't be too visible, I kept an eye on her, wondering why she was back. She'd been afraid when she left. What could be so important that she would risk returning?

A spot of light danced on the wall. It was a reflection from the sun glinting off Hannah's engagement ring, which rested on the windowsill.

The diamonds. Everything came back to the pink diamonds. I buried my head in my hands as the pieces began to fit together. Maybe Jen hadn't overheard Stan threatening to ice Craig. Maybe Stan wanted the ice—the diamonds. And that meant Craig had them. Joel could have been right that Craig didn't buy Hannah's engagement ring. And it probably wasn't a coincidence that none of Craig's relatives had been invited to the wedding. Then, when Darby saw the wedding Web page, they all descended on him to collect the diamonds. No wonder they'd searched my house. They all thought he'd stashed the loot here. But where was it?

I dialed the police, crushed that Darby was involved in the murders. I left a message for Wolf to call me as soon as possible but had my doubts about when he might receive the message.

Mochie sprang onto the window seat and rubbed against me, purring. I ran my hand over his silky fur and glanced out the window again. Darby had left her car. She crossed the street and disappeared from view.

FORTY-ONE

I waited for her to appear on the sidewalk. Seconds ticked by but they felt like an eternity. What if she wasn't coming to the front door?

If I waited for her in the sunroom and she came through the backyard, she might see me, and that would give her an advantage if she meant harm. I checked the front again. No sign of her. I sped through the kitchen and foyer and up the stairs. Hannah had a great view of the shed when she was getting dressed. I dashed up to the third floor, Daisy and Mochie running along, excited by my frenzy.

A breeze swept through the open windows, but reminders of the wedding lay everywhere. Hannah's wedding dress was still draped over a chair, blood caked on the hem. The tiara sparkled on the dresser. She must have hated coming up here last night to sleep.

The gate in my backyard creaked open. I sat down so I wouldn't be noticeable, a move Daisy identified as an opportunity to have her tummy scratched. Darby closed the gate and, watching my house carefully, tiptoed across the yard to the potting shed. She opened the door and I heard her stifle a shriek. She stepped back and Robert emerged.

Darby's rigid posture suggested she hadn't expected to find Robert in the shed. Had she meant to hide there? I had no idea why they were in my backyard, but I wasn't taking any chances. They might be meeting here for completely innocent reasons, but I didn't think so.

Hoping Wolf was still in the neighborhood, I called information, only to learn that Mordecai's number was unlisted. I knew Nina wasn't home, but Natasha was. I dialed her number and Wanda answered.

I didn't dare mention Robert, lest she come running over. Instead, speaking softly, I said, "Tell Natasha to fetch Wolf and bring him to my house. He's at Mordecai's."

"You girls! Always trying to set me up with Mordecai. Well, listen up. I am not interested in him . . ."

"Wanda. Wanda." I tried to interrupt with no success and finally hung up.

Leaning forward, I sought to hear what Darby and Robert were saying. They exchanged a few words I couldn't hear, and Robert led Darby to my patio. With a grandiose gesture, he invited her to take a seat on a chaise.

Their voices drifted up to me.

"Are you sure no one's home?"

"Doesn't matter. I'm the bereaved father-in-law, remember? My brother was murdered in their shed. They can hardly blame me if I sit here for a bit and mourn him. Good riddance, huh? It was all Stan's fault. Every last thing that happened was his fault. I should have killed him on the spot when he bashed the diamond courier."

I recoiled. Robert and Stan were the thugs who stole the diamonds in the first place.

Robert continued, "Tony knew he'd be dead as soon as he turned over the ice. Stan should have waited. It's not right to threaten a man on his wedding day. I couldn't let him shoot Tony; I already lost five years with my son, I couldn't lose him again."

His son? That meant Tony, the owner of the gun, Darby's ex-husband, was Craig!

"If you stabbed Stan, why did they find Tucker's finger-prints?"

"I saw him clowning around with the knife." He pulled a hankie from his pocket. "But a gentleman always carries a handkerchief. They're very useful for picking up things like guns or money clips without leaving prints. And I knew the prints and the money clip would make Tucker a suspect."

"Think Tony'll show this time?" asked Darby.

"He knows I saved him from Stan. Besides, Hannah played into our hands. He'll be back for her."

I shuddered at the thought. Maybe Humphrey had been right to fear that Craig/Tony would whisk Hannah away. Suddenly, I hoped her friends would keep her out of the house a bit longer. Where was Wolf? I dialed the police again. He should be here, hearing this.

Their backs were to me, but I could see Robert reach over and pat Darby's arm.

"Once Tony gets here, you better scram, kid. Lay low for a long time."

"Where you going?"

"Ahhh. I have a ticket to Roma." His arm flew up in the

air with more grace than I'd have expected of him. "*La dolce vita*. And you, Donata, would be wise to stay away from that young man you met. Look what love did to Tony."

At the sound of a creak on the stairs, Daisy flipped over. I looked back to see Craig/Tony in the doorway.

Daisy wagged her tail tentatively and when Craig said, "Treat, Daisy," she ran to him for the dog bone he held out. "I told everyone that you would be the problem but they didn't believe me."

I scrambled to my feet. "How did you get in?"

He held up a key. "When I saw Lina hanging in the pergola, I knew there would be trouble. I made a copy of Hannah's key, just in case."

I needed to stall for time. Someone had to arrive soon. I used my left hand to fuss with my hair, hoping to draw his eyes away from the fact that I was trying to press 911 on the cell phone in my pocket with my right hand. I tried to act nonchalant. "Hannah will be relieved to know you didn't kill anyone."

"Where is Hannah?"

"She ran out to the store." Trying not to be obvious, I searched in desperation for something, anything to defend myself. I swallowed hard. He might not be the killer, but he was desperate. "So were you the one who unscrewed the lightbulbs in the shed and left the knife out there?"

"Stan never would have let Hannah and me live in peace. When he had what he wanted, he would have killed me. But you probably can't understand that. You don't know what it's like to look over your shoulder every day, every minute, everywhere you go."

"You left the day before the wedding. You could have disappeared again."

"I tried." He no longer made an effort to hide his emotions. Haggard and wretched, he said, "I couldn't do it. All

I wanted was to live a quiet life with Hannah, but Stan would always have been one step behind me. There would be no peace as long as he was alive."

He blocked the doorway. If I could just wedge past him . . . I edged back, hoping it would prompt him to step inside the room and clear the doorway. It worked.

I moved to the right and sought something to say. "I heard your vitamin business did very well."

"Ironic, huh?"

If he wasn't a doctor, as I suspected, he could have killed someone with his vitamins. "Were they sugar pills?"

Proud of himself, he said, "They were real vitamins. I bought them in bulk and rebottled them under my label. Who knew people would pay so much for them?"

"So how many wives do you have?" Oops, probably not a clever question.

But he didn't seem angry. "Just the one, Donata— Darby."

"What? Wait, what about the Emily Beacham in Vancouver?"

"Well, well. You did find out quite a bit, didn't you? I was never married to her. I just assumed her husband's identity."

I judged the distance to the door. "Then who was the woman in the pergola?"

A shadow crossed his face. "Lina, an old friend from the neighborhood." He winced. "Constanzo's wife. I'm certain she wanted to warn me that everyone knew about the wedding and Stan would be on the way. She knew he would kill me as soon as he had the diamonds. She knew how vengeful Stan could be.

"You could leave now, you know. Stan's dead. You didn't kill anyone. You could take off and be gone."

His eyes fierce, he said, "Not without Hannah. I want her with me and, you see, there's one person standing in the way of our happiness." He bent his knees and extended his arms like a sumo wrestler. When he came closer, the dreadful clump of comb-over hair fell backward, revealing a wound near the top of his head. The kind of wound a glass diamond would inflict.

In one large bound he would be upon me. He outweighed me and stood at least a foot taller. It was now or never.

I yelled, "Mochie!" as I grabbed Hannah's wedding dress and launched it at his head. Mochie appeared on cue. Craig struggled with the unwieldy mass of wedding silk and tripped over Mochie and Daisy. Calling them, I ran for the stairs.

But Craig was on his feet too soon. He struck me with the back of his hand and knocked me down. "I should have finished you when I caught you in the basement."

When I stood again, he blocked my access to the stairs. Holding Hannah's dress in his hands, he wore a sick smile like he was enjoying himself.

A familiar clank came from the foyer downstairs. Distracted, he turned his head to listen. It was only my mail slot being opened and the mail shoved through. But I seized the moment and barreled into him as hard as I could. He fell backward, down the creaky stairs. I nearly tumbled on top of him but caught hold of the ancient banister. I could see his chest moving. Afraid he would hurt Mochie, I staggered down and swept him into my arms, called Daisy, and kept going. But I was moving too fast on the worn old steps. My foot missed a tread and I bounced to the bottom. I lay on the foyer floor gasping for breath as Craig's hulking shape bore down on me with vengeance.

I rolled to the side and stuck out my leg. He fell face-first and a split second later, Natasha's huge heart topiary smashed into bits on the back of his head.

When I looked up, Darby was wiping her hands. She

held them out to me. "Can you stand? Do you need a doctor?"

Fearful of another attack, I blurted, "Where's Robert?" I stumbled to my feet and opened the front door. Wolf and Natasha were running toward my house.

About time.

FORTY-TWO

From "THE GOOD LIFE":

Dear Sophie,

After three years of dating, my boyfriend popped the question. We're shopping for engagement rings, but I don't want a blood diamond that caused suffering and death in a country engaged in a civil war over diamonds. Is there another stone I can use?

—Taking the Plunge in Lake Wynonah

Dear Taking the Plunge,

Sapphires and rubies are excellent alternatives. Shy away from pearls, though, because they can't stand up to everyday wear and tear.

But if you have your heart set on a diamond, conflict-free diamonds are rapidly becoming available. Ask your local jeweler or check the Web. Visit http://www.brilli

antearth.com   and   http://www.leberjeweler.com/index.php3.

—Sophie

"My topiary!" shrieked Natasha.

Wolf handcuffed Craig, who appeared to be dazed. The heart shape of the topiary had landed on the back of his head intact, like a crown of ivy and orchids.

Natasha gripped my arm and allowed me to lean on her. "Robert killed Stan," I said to Wolf. "And he was in the backyard a few minutes ago."

Natasha helped me to a kitchen chair and brought me a bag of frozen corn for my throbbing head. "I think you're out of peas."

Mochie jumped into my lap and Daisy nuzzled my hand. When Natasha tried to shoo them away, I stopped her. I closed my eyes and tried to breathe normally. Sirens blared in the distance. I placed Mochie on the floor and hobbled to the foyer.

Behind me, Hannah and her friends burst into the kitchen. Hannah inched closer. "What happened? Is that Craig?"

Humphrey, Phoebe, Joel, and Tucker crowded around to peer at Craig. I didn't think he'd moved. Hannah kneeled next to him and lifted the heart off his head. The flap of hair he combed over his balding head stuck to it. She pried it off and clutched the heart.

I tried not to sound like an obnoxious big sister when I said, "His name is Tony Franchini. He stole the identity of a doctor."

"Is that true?" Hannah asked him.

"He's a diamond thief," I added. "The worst kind—he double-crossed his own father and uncle at the heist and stole the diamonds from them."

"But I didn't kill anyone," he croaked. "I was going to give them the diamonds. For you, Hannah. So we could be together."

His hand snaked out to Hannah but she recoiled. "How could I have been so blind?"

Emergency medical technicians barged into my foyer, and we shuffled out of their way.

Wolf put away his phone and stared down at Craig. "Don't be too hard on yourself, Hannah. The Franchinis were good, very good. Their identification was top notch. Fake, but excellent work. I'd bet they've had a lot of practice fooling people."

Craig pleaded, "I still love you, Hannah. It's not too late for us."

"Are you kidding? I don't even know you. And to think I was so upset when you told me you had been married before."

Hannah sniffled. She looked at an emergency medical technician who was preparing a head immobilizer. "Will he be okay?"

"He'll live."

Wolf touched my fingertips. "Do you need medical attention?"

"I'm just bruised and a little shaken. What about Robert?"

"We're looking for him right now."

To make room for the EMTs, we returned to the kitchen, where Natasha was pulling cookies from the oven and serving tea. "I hope you don't mind. I found the dough in the freezer. Sophie, sweetie, should I put some rum in your tea? I saved her life," she announced. "I knew something was wrong when she hung up on my mother. A nice southern girl would never hang up on someone's mother."

I was aiming my bruised behind at a chair when Humphrey threw his arms around me. "I should have been here to protect you."

Good heavens. I didn't want him thinking he had to hang around all the time. "I'm glad you were looking out for Hannah."

I winced when my bottom made contact with the chair seat, and then I realized everyone was staring at something behind me.

Darby hovered in the hallway leading to the family room. "Come join us," I said.

Scared as a baby bunny, she shuffled toward us. "Do you think they'll arrest me?"

I patted the chair beside me. "Sit down, Donata, you saved me from Craig. Or should I say Tony?"

She perched on the chair as though ready to flee. "You know I'm not really Darby? No wonder Tony was out to get you."

"Thank you for saving me. Why did you do that? You could have walked away and saved yourself."

"You didn't deserve to be killed. Neither did Lina— Emily. Besides, I had my own reasons for wanting to bash Tony over the head."

"Because he walked out on you?"

A whisper of a grin crossed her lips. "I've been looking for him for five long years."

"Then who killed Emily?" asked Humphrey. "What about the necklace with the silver C?"

Darby's mouth dropped open. "So I was right. C for Constanzo, whom you know as Stan. Robert told him not to wear that necklace!"

Joel sat next to Phoebe. "But why would he kill her?"

Humphrey and Hannah peppered her with questions. Darby held up her hands. "I'm sorry, Joel, but it was Robert, Stan, and Tony who intercepted your courier. They'd heard about the shipment and thought he was an easy target. But then Craig—er—Tony double-crossed everybody and disappeared with the diamonds. And that same day, Lina, who was Stan's wife, left him. Everybody thought she ran off with Craig—er—Tony." She stared at the table like her thoughts had transported her elsewhere. "Stan must have knocked Lina off to scare Tony into giving up the diamonds. When I found out somebody killed Lina, I knew it had to be one of us. Who else would kill a nice person like Lina? It scared me half to death. If they killed Lina, they might kill me, too. I was so glad when you offered to let me stay here because I figured I was safer here with your nice family."

Hannah leaned toward Darby. "So the dead woman wasn't Craig's ex-wife?"

"No. That was our friend, Lina." She looked at me. "This pretending to be somebody else is hard. I almost slipped up and told you the truth. Tony was never married to Lina. He's my husband. He's the bum that took off on me. Imagine my surprise at seeing the wedding Web site. I was nervous about coming, so I brought the gun he gave me for protection years ago. Stan must have found it when he was changing clothes in the den. When Stan turned up dead, I figured Craig killed him, and that he was gonna get us all. Every last one of us who knew about the diamond heist. Only his dad and me were left."

"I gather Stan used your gun to threaten Craig in the shed and that's why Robert killed him," I offered.

Hannah's hand crept to her throat. "So the diamond necklace Stan gave me really was Lina's like Sophie suspected? Ugh." She shuddered. "Darby, would you take it back to Lina's mother for me?"

"You know, Craig meant to give you a necklace like that," I said. "Jen has it."

"She can keep it. I never want to wear another diamond necklace in my life."

Joel sat back, his face a thundercloud. "Darby, if you were so scared, why did you come back?"

"Craig promised us diamonds on Monday. That's today. I wasn't part of the heist, but I figured I was due my fair share for all Craig put me through. Once I got home, I felt more scared. I didn't have the gun anymore and I was all alone. I figured loads of people would still be hanging out at Sophie's and that I could pressure Craig into giving me some of the diamonds. He owed me."

"If he was your husband, why did you let me marry him? Why didn't you say something?" asked Hannah.

"You think I wanted that creep back after he ran off with those diamonds and left me?"

"Then who was Kevin?" I asked.

Darby smiled. "A very hunky man who I plan to look up."

"He wasn't part of the heist?"

"Of course not. I'm through with scoundrels."

Hannah retrieved her engagement ring from the window over the sink and placed it on the table in front of Joel. "I think this belongs to you."

Humphrey perked up. He seemed happier than I'd ever seen him. "All this is great news for you, Hannah. If Craig already had a wife and fraudulently induced you to marry him by posing as someone else, then your marriage can be annulled."

Mars barged past Wolf into the kitchen. "I just heard. Is everyone okay?" He handed me a package and a bunch of magazines. "Your mail was on the floor."

"Thanks." I placed it on the table and turned back to Darby. "But why was everyone searching my house for diamonds?"

Darby grinned. "Loot-stashing 101. Hide it in plain sight or hide it with someone who doesn't know she has it."

Tucker nudged me. "They weren't the only ones looking for something." He pointed to the drawer where I had stashed Stan's necklace.

Claws extended, Mochie hooked the side of the drawer and pried it open. He sniffed inside, then wandered away, no doubt in search of more interesting scents.

"Uh, Soph," said Mars, "this package is from Craig." It rattled when he shook it.

Even Wolf, wearing an earbud, crowded in to see what it contained.

"He mailed it Saturday, the day he disappeared." I ripped it open. Inside were two dozen white vitamin bottles with Dr. Craig's label on them.

"At least he was polite enough to send you a thank-you gift," said Hannah.

After a moment of silence, we all grabbed bottles and broke the seals. In a heartbeat, a pile of pink diamonds rested in front of Joel.

"He gave them up for you," Darby said to Hannah. "That was his deal with Constanzo. If everyone would leave the two of you alone, he would hand over the diamonds."

I expected Hannah to cry, but she fought to maintain composure.

The kitchen door flew open and Nina dashed in carrying Hermione, who wore a fancy bow on her neck. "What's with the police? What happened? Are those diamonds?" She handed off Hermione to Joel and picked up a diamond.

Instead of explaining, Joel walked around the table to Phoebe. Holding Hermione, he dropped to one knee. "I wanted to do this earlier, but with all that happened, the time never seemed right. Phoebe, will you do me the honor of becoming my wife?"

Phoebe turned a shade of pink that clashed with her copper hair. "You suspected Craig all along. That's why you were against the marriage?" Bending forward, she kissed him.

"Need a diamond?" asked Tucker.

Joel smiled. "Those are blood diamonds through and through." He handed Hermione to Phoebe. "If we're going to build up a jewelry store, we'll need a guard dog."

Nina wiped a tear from her cheek.

Phoebe cuddled Hermione. She felt the bow around Hermione's neck and her eyes grew wide. Grinning, Joel removed a diamond ring from Hermione's collar and slid it onto Phoebe's finger.

"Nina," I chided, "you knew about this and you didn't say a word."

She flushed. "I can keep secrets when they're worth keeping."

Natasha ran to my refrigerator. "I knew there would be champagne, since we didn't get to drink it at the wedding. Mars, be a doll and open this while I find glasses."

Wolf rested a hand on my shoulder. "Good news, folks. They located Robert on his way to the airport." He caught my eye and motioned to the foyer.

I left the others congratulating the happy couple and followed him. Orchids and damp soil marred the floor where Darby had incapacitated Craig.

Wolf took one of my hands into his. "I don't think moonlight and champagne would have been more romantic than that." He ran a finger across my cheek to whisk a hair away. "I'm sorry, Sophie. I hope you can understand why I acted as I did. But I'd still like to find out who was leaving messages under your name."

"If the calls stop, does it matter anymore?"

He thought for a minute. "I guess not."

"And do you believe me when I say there's nothing romantic going on between Mars and me?"

He wrapped his arms around me and, ever so gently, kissed me. When I didn't push him away, he kissed me with such fervor that my toes tingled.

He released his hold and looked deep into my eyes. "I have a lot of work to do to wrap this up. Meet me at Bernie's for dinner?"

I would even wear eye makeup and something alluring. "One thing—what happens to Darby?"

"She used a fake ID and lied to us, but she did save you.

If she cooperates, I imagine she'll go back to her normal life."

He kissed me on the nose, and I watched him walk to the corner before I closed the door behind him.

When I returned to the kitchen, Natasha held a glass of champagne and was saying, "I see a Civil War theme for the wedding. Blue and gray, with pewter accents. Muskets and bayonets in vases." She gasped and held a hand below her throat. "The men in the bridal party can dress in uniforms and the women will wear hoopskirts . . ."

Over my dead body.

RECIPES &
COOKING TIPS

Sophie's Easy Pulled Pork

1 pork shoulder roast (the cut is important)
2 tablespoons paprika
2 tablespoons dark brown sugar
1 tablespoon salt
Pepper

If your grill comes with a smoking arrangement, then follow the instructions for your grill. If not, place wood chips or pellets for smoking in a small disposable tin pan and cover with water. Be sure to open vents. Preheat the grill to 300 degrees.

Mix the paprika, brown sugar, salt, and pepper to taste, and rub the mixture on the roast. Wrap in heavy-duty aluminum foil, but leave the top open so the meat is exposed. Close the foil after 3 hours.

Place the roast on the grill and the wood chip pan next

to it. Close the cover and roast slowly for 5 hours. Keep an eye on the wood chips so they don't dry out and burn. About an hour into the process, you may need to replace the wood chips with a fresh pan.

After 5 hours, remove the roast from the grill and let stand 30 minutes. Be careful when removing the foil because fabulous juices will be in the bottom. Serve with the juices and your favorite barbecue sauce.

Beer-Bottom Chicken

1 whole chicken, giblets removed
1 can beer (12 ounces)
Salt

Preheat the grill to 400 degrees. (Note: Cover the center burner with aluminum foil so the chicken juices won't clog it.) Drink or pour out half the can of beer. Rub the chicken with salt. Seat the chicken on the beer can and splay the legs so they help the chicken "sit up." It may lean forward a bit, which is okay as long as it doesn't topple. Place the chicken in the center of the grill (be sure the burner underneath is off; if using charcoal, spread it to the sides to avoid flame-ups under the chicken). Close the lid and roast for 45 to 50 minutes. The legs should move easily when done, and you shouldn't see any pink inside. Be careful when removing the beer can—it will be very hot.

Wedded Blitz Martinis

1 jigger vodka
¾ jigger peach schnapps
1 jigger cranberry juice
½ jigger mango nectar

Pour into a martini glass and enjoy!

Natasha's Aphrodisiac Cake

Natasha made this cake with Buttercream frosting, which can be piped into beautiful decorations. For those who prefer a less sweet icing, please visit divamysteries.com for an alternate.

6 eggs at room temperature
1 cup sugar
½ teaspoon finely ground pepper
½ teaspoon ginger
½ teaspoon cinnamon
¼ teaspoon cloves
1 cup flour

Preheat the oven to 350 degrees. Butter and flour two 9-inch cake pans or line with parchment paper.

Beat the eggs and sugar until thick and lemon-colored. In a separate bowl, mix the pepper, ginger, cinnamon, cloves, and flour and gently blend into the egg mixture. Pour into the prepared pans and bake 15 to 20 minutes.

Remove from the oven and cool completely. Turn the layers out of the pans.

RASPBERRY FILLING
10-ounce package frozen raspberries, thawed
1 envelope unflavored gelatin
1 cup heavy whipping cream
½ cup powdered sugar

Drain the thawed raspberries, reserving the liquid. Sprinkle the gelatin over the reserved liquid in a small saucepan. Let stand 10 minutes. Meanwhile, whip the cream and reserve ⅓ of the whipped cream. Place the gelatin mixture over low heat and stir constantly until dissolved. Mix the gelatin into the thawed raspberries. If the mixture is warm, refrigerate briefly until cool, but not set. Beat the raspberry mixture into the whipped cream and refrigerate while making the chocolate filling.

CHOCOLATE FILLING
2 squares semisweet chocolate
2 tablespoons butter
¼ cup raspberry liquor
Reserved whipped cream (set aside earlier)

Melt the chocolate and the butter and blend well. When it has cooled, stir in the raspberry liquor, then mix with the whipped cream.

To assemble the cake, cut each layer in half with a serrated knife, so you have four layers. Place the first layer on the cake plate and cover with half the raspberry filling.

Place the second layer on top, then spread with the chocolate filling.

Place the next cake layer on top. Spread with the remaining raspberry filling. Top with the final layer.

BUTTERCREAM FROSTING
   1 cup butter, softened
   3 cups powdered sugar
   1 tablespoon vanilla
   2 tablespoons heavy cream

Beat the butter with the sugar. Add the vanilla and cream. Frost the cake, reserving part of the frosting for decorative piping.